SOMETHING BENEATH

KENNETH PASSAN

SEVERED PRESS
HOBART TASMANIA

SOMETHING BENEATH

WWW.SEVEREDPRESS.COM

ISBN: 978-1-922323-87-3

PROLOGUE

For decades there has been an increase in the number of people who believed that global warming was neither made up nor someone's false belief. Evidence for it began to manifest itself in the forms of more frequent and severe storms over the planet, increases in the ocean's height and tides, decreases in some areas of coastlines, and warmer sea temperatures. Still, many others blamed these and other extraordinary weather phenomenon on a fluke of Mother Nature and their ideology of "it is what it is".

For the most part a lot of people, too many in fact, ignored or chose to brush off and be indifferent to the numerous warning signs of an insidious global event that would impact the entire world. Scientist today are continuing to warn societies and governments that what is continuing to impact our world in a negative way will not stop unless we do something about it starting now.

Some of the currents in the world's oceans are changing in ways that impact global weather. At the poles, the ice is taking longer to form during the winter months and quicker to melt during the spring and summer more than ever before. At the North Pole and the surrounding Arctic areas, the wildlife is finding it harder to survive and find food. The polar bear population is starting to dwindle. Many have died trying to find food from the ice they depended on so much. Although they are land mammals, they need the ice to hunt for their favorite food: seals. With no ice, they cannot catch seals which also depend on ice to lay for rest between times in the water, and often for breeding.

In the Antarctic, each year thousands of tons of ice are breaking off from the ice shelf in huge masses. Antarctica itself is a continent all its own but with the ice breakouts, it is shrinking while the oceans rise. Although the sea temperatures there are still ice cold by our standards, by *Antarctica's* standards they have warmed up considerably.

Still, the penguins that live there know no difference. They still do their thing for living, breeding, raising their young and walking miles from their inland habitat to the coastline and dive into the sea to hunt once again for food. They have no clue that the waters there are warming up. For thousands of years, they lived there and their only main two predators are leopard seals and orcas. Orcas appear only occasionally but the leopard seals stay there, waiting to ambush unsuspecting penguins--their primary food source--that happened to jump in the water near them. The penguins somehow know they are around and cautiously look around before taking their giant leap. As hungry as they are, they do not want to become a meal. Sometimes their caution pays off. Sometimes it doesn't.

It would soon become apparent that something else would take its place on the Antarctic's predator list. Deep on the ice-cold floor of the Southern Ocean, movement on the surface of the floor interrupted the quiet stillness that was a normal characteristic of sea bottoms. The movement was undetected by the many organisms of life that lived down there. As alien as the floor would appear to us, the movement which began in subtleness and gradually increased in frequency would seem even more alien than the floorscape itself. Meanwhile over in the Ross Sea, off the Antarctic coast, another similar movement at its bottom was unseen and unknown to everything.

Time meant nothing down there. Whatever it was did not seem to be slowing down or stopping. The length of the sandy movements continued to increase in size. If it could be measured, it would be about the length of a school bus. Even so, the length continued to increase beyond that of a bus. Gradually it slowed down, eventually stopping. If that were its true size, whatever it was, its measurement would be larger than a blue whale.

At its other end, the sand lifted up. Something round, dark, and the size of a silver dollar poked up from beneath the sand. For a few moments, the movement stopped. The black hole just laid there.

Then, about four to five away from it, another movement. More sand lifted. Something else poked up. This was also round but larger, about the size of a CD disc. About two feet to its left, another round object poked out, looking exactly the same as the first. Dark green, it had one long sliver of black running vertical along its center.

Above the sea's surface, numerous penguins dove into the water, seemingly oblivious to the fact that there was a sea leopard in the area. The surface was choppy and the wind, if measured, was blowing at fifteen knots. The skies were partly cloudy making it quite a beautiful day. The only real sounds that broke the air's silence were those of birds flying above in their search for vulnerable fish just beneath the surface. One spotted a fish, dove down and quickly plucked it out of the water. Meanwhile, the diving of hundreds of penguins into the water continued unabated.

Somewhere underwater, a lone sea leopard swam on its seemingly endless search for food. Down here, it was at the top of the food chain. Its only nemesis were orcas, but it had not seen any for quite a while. Consequently, it felt no concern and focused entirely on what it wanted to feed on. Every so often it would come across a lone fish and gulp it right up. But its favorite delicacy, by far, was the penguin.

As it swam, it thought it saw movement far below it. Its instinct made it want to check it out. If it were a penguin, it would have its first meal in at least a couple of days. It was hungry and was determined not to miss this opportunity.

It dove down deeper into the crystal cold clear water until it neared the sea floor. With its large black eyes, it saw something laying on the sea floor. Not knowing what it was it, however, it seemed to know it *was not* a penguin. There was some movement in it, although very subtle. Its size was monstrous. It had never seen anything like it before. There had never been anything that had predated it, so it knew no danger. The seal did not know that the thing was looking at it. Did not know it to be a living creature. But it did know that it was much larger than its own twelve-foot length.

In the clearness of the surrounding blue water, the seal noticed a movement out of the corner of its left eye. Turning its head quickly it saw the penguin. As the rest of it turned as quickly and started to propel itself upward toward the prey, it felt a sharp pain plunge all the way through its skull and then total blackness.

Silt from the ocean floor mixed with the large amount of blood that filled the water. A seemingly interminable amount of time passed before the brown and red murkiness dissipated. By that time, there was neither any sign of the seal, nor any signs whatsoever that it had ever been there: no tissue or fascia, no bones or skull. Nothing. The blood had dispensed and been carried away by the current. All the area showed was that *something* had been there. There was an elongated gulley in the sea floor that was at least ninety to one hundred feet long.

It was now on the way up. Ahead of it were the unwary penguins. Where they had been the hunters before, now they were the hunted. For most of them, their families back on shore would never see them again. Had they had a forced choice of predators they would have quickly chosen the leopard seal over this thing. For all of them, they would not even have the time to see what they were dealing with. What began for them would end quickly and decisively. For the world, it had not even started yet.

1

Wednesday, October 5, Kermit, Texas

"Mommy, Jamie's throwing Rice Crispees at me with his spoon!" yelled Sarah in her squealing seven-year-old voice.

"No, I'm not," he retorted in defiance. "She's always blaming me for stuff!"

Their mother turned around and saw some cereal strewed over the kitchen table. 'Knock it off you two. Next complaint you will both be grounded from the swimming pool today. Cabeesh?"

"What does that mean?" asked Jaime inquisitively, wanting to get the subject of grounding today off the table as soon as possible. "Caaarr…. beesh."

Rita put her hands on her hips. "It means, 'understand', she answered quietly with a slight smirk on her face. "And don't try to change the subject, young man." She knew he threw the cereal at his sister. She saw him do it once before and did not want to waste time arguing about it.

"Oh, Ok." He began eating again.

Often her kids got into a little scramble with each other. She figured it to be normal sibling rivalry. Not knowing for what, she decided that it was probably for attention. With Jaime being the older and bigger, it was necessary to keep an eye on him and not let his rambunctiousness toward Sarah get out of hand.

"Don't take too long, guys. Your school buses will be here shortly."

In a few minutes they were done. Rita always made sure they got up early enough to wash their faces and brush their teeth before getting dressed.

After they dressed themselves, she checked them to make sure their clothes were appropriate for school and matched in patterns or colors. Often, she would have to help Sarah with the matching part. Rita remembered she had that little bit of trouble when she was that young but eventually got over it. With Sarah taking after her mother for that, she figured she would get over that as well.

A few minutes later they kissed and hugged her goodbye and, with backpacks on and the usual kid eagerness of little ones looking forward to something, they scooted out the door. The timing was such that the bus arrived in front of their house at that moment. With waves of goodbyes to each other, the bus soon disappeared into the distance.

Back in the kitchen, she prepared herself a light breakfast and coffee before heading out to the university. Her husband John was a forty-five-year-old trauma surgeon who often worked long hours simply because of the nature of his work. He had already left for work early because of a 6am scheduled surgery in the OR at Austin General Hospital, which was about fifteen miles away.

She herself was an assistant professor at Bradwell University in Odessa where she taught paleontology and aspects of herpetology related to ancient fossils. Ever since she was a little girl, she had always been interested in the sciences, especially about dinosaurs. She loved reading and learning about them. In fact, it had almost been an obsession with her. Sometimes she would drive her parents crazy wanting to go to this museum and that one.

Born in 1972 near Houston, she had a sister who was born two years later. Her name was Susan, who would later show no interest in dinosaurs. Her interests differed from Rita's as much as they could be. For her, fashion was the thing and that is the world where her path would eventually lead her down. There were no other siblings. Although their career worlds separated them geographically with New York City becoming Sue's eventual home, they always kept in touch regularly.

When Jurassic Park came out in 1993, the twenty-one-year-old Rita just *had* to go see it. At the time, her undergraduate studies in paleobiology were nearing their end. But she wasn't ready to stop there. Studying for a masters in paleolithic ecology would eventually lead her to her PhD in paleontology and a career that would bring her to the top of her field.

She had been at the university for about ten years and was close to obtaining her tenure there after writing another book on the subjects she was a master in. There was also a lot of research she had done and had made trips through grants she obtained in search of particular fossils that had not been identified. With each trip she made, she hoped to discover something new that hadn't been studied yet. Her friend and a colleague, Samantha Brewster had sent her an interesting picture of a Paleolithic tooth from a large predator for her to examine and get her opinion what it could be.

She looked at it and decided to investigate it further when she got to her lab at the school. Samantha didn't often send her pictures being the expert in her own right. She sent it because she found it intriguing and thought that Rita might be interested.

As with John's work, hers also took her away from home for periods of time. Fortunately, that happened usually no more than once, sometimes twice a year. For those occasions, they had a stay over nanny to take care of the kids until she returned. She always made sure her children were well taken care of. Although John was a good father when he was home, his work absences sometimes took a toll on their relationship.

The Bloomsworths been married for ten years. At that time, she had gained her PhD. John was finishing his surgery training at the hospital in Austin and had already been accepted and planned to move to New York where he would fill a surgery fellowship position in trauma.

Rita happened to be a friend of his sister. June had always been a good friend to her. Although she lived over in New Mexico, they kept in touch and sometimes would take turns flying out and visiting each other. It was at a get together at June's house one summer evening when Rita was visiting from Texas that she met June's husband Paul.

'Clean cut and handsome' was what she instantly though at the first sight of him. He was tall, about six two, on the muscular side. His dark blonde hair contrasted nicely with his large green eyes and matched perfectly with his alluring but sincerely friendly smile. When he looked at her, she felt a slight lump in her throat and couldn't help but smile back at him. It was a look of no more than *'nice to meet you and welcome to our home.'*

She was no slouch either when it came to looks. She was tall also at five foot ten, slender and still shapely in her early forties. Her shoulder length, wavy brown hair seemed to accentuate her slightly upturned blue eyes and small, upturned nose very nicely. Because she was not one to dwell on her looks except to make herself to always look presentable, she was clueless to the fact that she would be quite a "catch" for the right man.

2

Unlike the day before, this day in Oxford, Mississippi was a gloomy one. It was late September and all of the elementary and secondary schools were well into their new school year by at least three weeks. The colleges in the state had recently begun their fall semester. For today, the forecast was for hot humid weather with a sixty percent chance of rain showers. Great for being indoors.

So, thought Sam. She didn't mind rain too much as long as it wasn't overkill to those below it. But she hated hot and humid as most other people. Here in her cool air-conditioned laboratory, she could be comfortable while performing her work and conducting her studies.

Samantha Julia Brewster was a young assistant professor, unmarried as yet, and had a few dates now and then when she had the time. Her slim shapely figure and long straight brown hair which curled up at the ends contributed to her attractiveness. With a smooth, fair complexion and girlishly plump cheeks, she looked considerably younger than she was. Although she knew that, there were never any thoughts in her mind of flaunting those assets. She was quite dedicated to her work in paleo archeology and even more so in her marine biological paleontology studies. She had earned her PhD in paleo-biology three years before and had expanded her studies to include prehistoric marine biology. After years of hard work, research, and field trips to particular areas all over the world, she had made her mark in the academic world and had published her first article about the evolution of prehistoric organisms and their connections to modern day marine mammals and reptiles. Her drive and scientific passions kept any idea of a love life well in check. After being well received by the academic community and well respected as a renowned expert in paleobiologic reptiles, including dinosaurs, others would come to her for related information and as a valuable resource. Soon other writings by her would be published in scientific journals and her name would eventually become synonymous with "world expert".

Born into a family of three, she was the fourth that would finalize their number. Her life began in Rehoboth, New Jersey, when her father was a millworker, her mother was a part time seamstress for a tailor shop, and her brother, her only sibling, would eventually join the Marines and then the police force after his three-year stint and discharge.

Her family was devout in their Christianity, and that included her. She believed in God and still did. She was glad, though, that they didn't become the holy rollers type-so strict in beliefs that none of them would have been allowed to do anything that might be fun. Even so, there were some rules that had to be followed. Eventually, when she was old enough to leave the nest, she attended college and that's when her interests and passions within the academic community began to soar.

In her lab, she turned around from her counter filled with discovered artifacts and saw the pounding rain outside the window. She quickly turned back to her work. There was nothing out there that she hadn't seen before.

Although she taught a couple of classes during the semester at the University of Mississippi, most of her work involved research and studies on fossils and various types of discovered artifacts. Her assistant, Martha, had taken the day off and wouldn't be back until tomorrow. Normally she helped with the studies and research and sometimes picked up equipment that the lab needed repairs on or replacements for.

Currently Sam was studying a fossil tooth that had been recently found in the Gulf of Mexico. It was an unusual find because even if you knew that something was down there in a certain area of the sea or, in this case the Gulf, something like this would still be difficult to locate. The fact that it was huge, almost six inches long, made it quite the exceptional find. She suddenly heard the door open to the lab. It was Susie, her professorial colleague and friend.

"Hey," she called out. "Anybody home? Oh, there you are," she noted as her eyes focused on Sam at the other end of the long lab counter.

Susan McGrath was five years older than Sam but had been friends with her for much longer than that. She was shorter in stature and slightly on the heavy side, but her bubbly personality always seemed to overshadow those characteristics. Making friends easily was a natural part of her nature.

"Hey stranger," replied Sam. "What's happening out there? Anything exciting?"

She approached Sam as she responded with a "Naw. Nothing special. On my way out, Thought I'd check in and see what's up. Hadn't seen you in a while. Want to come over for dinner tonight? Bruce is away on one of his sales trips and won't be back for a couple of days at least."

"Where'd he go?"

"Down to Gulfport. Has to see some hospital bigwig about a large piece of equipment his company is on the verge of selling to them. He basically has to close up the decision gap and make the deal and sell. Anyway, could use some company tonight. Making nothing fancy, just meatloaf, potatoes, and a veggie."

"Ok, sounds good. Love meatloaf. What time?"

"Six, I think but come before that if you want." Her eyes looked down at what Sam was holding in her hand. "Say, that's a good-sized tooth you have there. Holy Moly! Species?"

Sam looked at the tooth and turned it in her hand."Not sure yet. I suspect possibly marine. Was found in the waters of the Gulf. But then it could be land mammal, depending on its approximate age. Don't know that yet, either. Could have been land where the water is now. That is yet TBD.

"TBD?" asked Susie curiously.

"To be determined. You done for the day?"

"Yep. Finished my last class for the week, about half hour ago. Thank God it's Friday," she said loudly, with a smile and stretched out arms. "Well, I'm heading on home. Gotta prepare for supper. Come over now or whenever you're ready to."

"Ok. I'll just finish up on this thing and I should be leaving in about a half hour. Probably go right to your place from here."

After saying their "see ya laters", Sam looked back down at the huge tooth. She didn't think it was from a Smilodon. Something about it didn't fit the characteristics. A little too narrow. Dinosaur maybe? Marine predator?

Putting it down, she rubbed her eyes. It was nearly four thirty. She'd been here since eight this morning. It had been a long day. After examining other artifacts and classifying them, this one was taking a little longer. But there was no way she would finish this today. It was now the weekend and although she was bound and determined to find out what the original owner of this was, that could wait until Monday, she decided.

She stood up, removed her lab coat, and left the specimen on her desk in the corner of the room, where she would continue her study of it when she returned. As she turned out the lights and locked up the lab, she felt the hunger pangs and was now really looking forward to that meatloaf and potatoes, glad she had accepted the invitation.

3

"Mm. That was good, Sue." Sam said, wiping her mouth clean.

"Want more?"

"Oh no way." replied Sam. "I am absolutely full."

"Me, too. Room for dessert?"

Sam declined. "But I will have coffee if you have any."

Sue got up and started to empty the table, with Sam following suit. While Sue made the coffee, Sam rinsed off and put the dishes and utensils in the dishwasher.

"Why thank you, girlfriend. That helps a lot. My back has been hurting me today. I hadn't looked forward to bending over like that. Probably would have washed them by hand."

"Hey, not a problem. I do this all the time at home. Besides, you made the dinner. And what are girlfriends for anyway?"

They both laughed. After finishing up in the kitchen, the brewing coffee was ready and they were soon back at the table, sipping and chatting, mostly small talk. Then Sue brought the talk back around to the tooth Sam had been holding back at the lab.

"That was some size tooth you had there today. That the only one you found?"

Sam swallowed her sip of coffee then put the cup down. "One that size, yes. We found some other smaller specimens further away, but they looked different from the type I was holding. They were definitely not the same species of animal."

Sue was thinking for a moment, taking her eyes off of Sam's. Sam could tell the gears were turning in her head. Likely trying to think of a prehistoric land animal that could have a tooth that size. She agreed with her colleague that the water there now could have been land millions of years ago.

"Have you come close to identifying it yet?"

"Nope. Working on it. Not knowing if it's marine or land might take me a little time. But I'm beginning to rule out some species."

Sue made a suggestion. "Let me take a pic of it tomorrow and while you're trying to dig up something on the marine side, let me figure out the possibilities of it being from land. I've got a little free time so I can check it out. Will let you know if I come up with anything."

"Ok, sounds great. Thanks hon. As long as it doesn't interfere with any of your research."

"If it did, I'd still find a little free time. Besides, it's got my curiosity going. I have some ideas, but also ruled out some also already. One thing I *am* sure of: it's not from a T-rex."

"I didn't think it was," Sam said. "It's too thick and wide. If it was a bit slender, then maybe from a baby rex. But there's no way it could be from an adult. It's much too short in length anyway as well as too wide."

With both women agreeing on those points, they lingered in a few moments of silence, then Sam finally prepared to leave. This get-together dinner was nice and lasted longer than she had expected. Tiredness had crept up on both of them.

At the door, they quickly hugged.

"See ya tomorrow?" asked Sue.

Sam nodded. "I'll be in at eight. My first class is not till ten but I want to research that spec, and a few other things I'm checking on also. I'll leave the tooth in the combination drawer of my file cabinet. Combo is two forty-seven. You know the directions. I'll be gone for about an hour and a half if you want to take a pic of it."

Sue watched her until she disappeared down the street in her car. She closed the door and prepared for bed. 11:30 had come awful fast tonight.

4

Tellmore Research Station, Antarctica

Antarctica is the only true ice continent on the planet having no soil. All of the winter ice covers the landscape. The landscape, unlike every other continent on earth, is comprised not of dirt but of volcanic matter which has been solidified as much as any regular ground you could find. Over thousands and even millions of years this volcanic ground, originating from Antarctica's active volcano Mount Erebus, accumulated into hundreds and even thousands of feet of volcanic material. In the spring and summer, you can walk on and move tons of very heavy equipment on it. Even in the summer areas of ice and snow still cover and dresses the landscape. The pure whiteness of it is awe-inspiring for most people.

The continent has six months of daylight during the summer and six months of darkness during the winter months. It's coldness and extreme subzero temperatures in the winter, frequent blustery winds, and severe storms are rivaled by nowhere else on earth. Among the various other things that makes the region unique from everywhere else is the lack of air, land, and noise pollution. It is as pristine as if man never set foot on it. It is a wilderness ruled by immaculate surroundings and the sounds of absolute silence that is as golden to many as the sun is in perfectly clear skies.

Yet at the same time, it can be as strange and eerie as if all sounds disappeared suddenly on a traffic-clogged street. With no birds to fill the skies or insects to buzz the air, it is a condition in which a person can either embrace the silence or be unnerved by it. For those who go down there, it's usually the former.

Respect is a word that one should never forget when the job takes a person down there. This includes abiding by and maintaining the rules of complete non-contamination by anything humans produce. This includes prevention of all wastes and littering outside the confines of the station buildings. Everyone stationed at all of the numerous international stations planted on and around the continent is responsible for all this in addition to their assigned scientific duties. This is so required of all and nearly always adhered to. If all the stations were to suddenly pick up and move out, only the permanent buildings would be the sole evidence that humans had ever been there.

December of this year was typical of most summers down here. For the researchers and scientists, as at all other stations on the continent, it was a brief respite from the bitter cold of winter which could dip as low as minus fifty degrees or even lower. Now it was a balmy twenty-five above zero. For this place, it would be the rough equivalent of ninety degrees Fahrenheit in the US or the UK during their peak summer season.

Even so, no one there could let down their guard when it came to the weather. Storms could hit them at any time with hardly any warning, with winds that could gust or sustain up to or more than a hundred miles an hour and plenty of horizontal blowing snow. It would not be a situation one would want to be exposed to, even for a minute. Each of the five buildings there would have to be strong enough to withstand sustained winds twice that velocity. And they were, which is why they had lasted for more than fifty years.

Deep inside the main compound building marked as building 24, Beth Ann Trenton, was checking her computer on the latest finds they were studying. The previous day she, and some of the other scientists on her team, had done their respective studies on the coastline a couple miles from the station. She was a graduate of the University of Manchester and had done her postgraduate studies at Oxford, eventually earning her doctorate.

She picked up her walkie talkie. "Hey George, can you come to CR for a minute?"

She waited a moment for the climatologist to answer, then his gruff voice came over loud and clear. "What's oop dahlin?" He had a fairly distinct British cockney taint to his accent. If you didn't know him personally and heard only his voice, you would have thought he was one of those who scrounged around the street corners of London looking for handouts. Despite his gruffness, knowing him proved beyond a doubt that even sounds could be deceiving. His smartness and intelligence was certainly echoed by his PhD and full professorship status at Oxford. His specialty: marine ecology.

"Got something here you might want to take a look at. I don't know if it's anything but thought you might want to have a look anyway."

"Ok. Cooming right now."

A couple of minutes later, George Kenore stepped through the door into the CR, or computer room. In his mid-fifties, he was brawny and on the muscular side. At six foot one, he was certainly not one you'd want to mess with. With his somewhat longish, graying hair and short beard, he could have been a fairly good portrayal of an aging Paul Bunyan. Despite his tough exterior, he was a pussycat most of the time. If provoked to the extreme, he could be a serious threat to the provoker. Fortunately, they never had to worry about any provocations down here in the coldest regions on earth. They couldn't afford any kind of behavior like that here. Everyone had to rely on each other because of the ever-present danger related to the nature of this environment and climate.

He walked over to Beth Ann sitting at the computer on the other side of the nondescript room. It wasn't often that he was called to look at something. He hated computers because of their what he called-*stupid glitches*-and other annoying things which tended to interfere with operations from time to time. But at the same time, he knew that they were a necessity, without which they couldn't do much of their work.

"What cha got?"

Beth pointed to an area on the screen showing a lot of little dots. "See these?"

"Yep. Sure do. What are they, besides dots?"

"These are penguins. You can't see it when you look at it quickly, but after a while you would see they are moving. I think they are the Adele penguins moving slowly toward the coast."

He followed her finger as it pointed at the group and then traced across the monitor in the direction of the coast. "Ok," he said. "They are going that way. So why do you think I should see this?"

"For the past week, I've been monitoring this group. They're about twenty-five miles from here, close to their nesting area northwest of us. Almost always at this time of year, the adults that were hunting for food in the sea return before now. They haven't returned. That's what's got me stumped. I've never seen this before."

He could only grunt in response, unsure of what to say. But he was thinking, which was another reason why he was grunting. "Well maybe the hunters are having trouble finding food. Or the leopard seals got to them."

She turned around and looked up at him. "I don't think so. For one thing, there are hundreds of those penguins hunting right now. There wouldn't be enough leopard seals to decimate even a quarter of them."

Leopard seals live only in the Antarctic waters. They are the top predators down there most of the year. Their main prey are penguins and they wait for them to jump into the water from the ice mass cliffs. Occasionally there will be Orcas that make their predatory appearances.

"What about their food? Maybe you should check with Tom and see if he's discovered any anomalies in the fish population down there."

Beth wasn't sure what to make of this, if anything. Was there something going on? She didn't know. It was nothing to be alarmed about. At least not yet. But she figured it was worth checking out, if for no reason other than to gain some peace of mind.

"So, you don't think it's anything we should worry about?" she asked.

He stood up straight. “I don’t think so, luv. At least not right now. Might want to keep an eye on them, see if there’s any more changes in their numbers. Might want to check with Tom also to see if he’s noticed anything on his end “

Tom, or Thomas Billington, was the team’s ichthyologist. If there was a change in the fish population in the area which could affect those who preyed on it, he would know. Beth decided first to see if results he had might be on his latest findings and maybe see if there was any linkage to the seemingly decreased Adele penguin population.

“Yea, I’ll check with him later. Thanks George.”

He turned and headed toward the door. “Keep me posted. If you discover anything else significant, let me know.”

After saying she would, she was again alone in the lab to contemplate the situation as she looked at the small dots, now in a slightly different area than before, ever closer to the sea.

Antarctica, the Southern Ocean

The leopard seal, another one that inhabited the area, has always been on the hunt, always looking for its next meal. Although it will eat krill and other species of seals, it loves penguins. With an insatiable appetite, it has always found its home waters here prolific in the penguin population. There was little to no competition down here for food, even with other leopard seals around.

It’s been swimming around for a long time now without running into one. Often, it can take quite a while before it runs into one, or one runs into it.

After a hunt, the hunting female penguins return to the ice mass and waddle back to their home nesting area to their mates and babies. For them, this could be a journey up to twenty miles. This could be happening now.

Once they arrive and feed their chicks, the hunting mother penguins now take over as babysitting penguins as they relieve their mates of the duty, which then allow those penguin fathers to take their turn to feed and bring back food to their chicks. Now it’s *they* who have to make the long journey to the ocean.

So, the seal is not overly concerned at the time with no sight of the birds. Besides, it can also feed on fish and other seals while it bides its time, which is usually on its side. Orcas are its only predators and because they are here only infrequently, the seals show no fear. For them it’s always been pretty safe.

Oddly enough, it’s been awhile since it has seen any fish. Usually there is an abundance of them around. It had swum around continuously for unknown empty miles without seeing any. Its hunger pangs are beginning to increase because it's been longer than usually since its last meal. As it continues to swim, not even other seals have appeared in its sights. Except for occasional krill spotted near the surface, it has seen no sign of life anywhere so far. If there are any other leopard seals around, they have yet to be seen.

Approximately two miles behind it is an exceptionally large patch of red on the water. Surrounding the patch float a large number of pieces of blubber and flesh. The entire region is devoid of all vessels and although whaling vessels in the past have been known to leave bits and pieces of blubber and flesh after capturing a whale and slaughtering it, there have been no vessels in this area anytime recently. No one is around to witness the sight. No predators have homed into the area on what would have been a free meal for them. In fact, the entire region and surrounding areas are devoid of all life, including birds in the area. This leaves the area also devoid of all sounds that are normally present.

On the outskirts of the patch, a large fin--likely from a whale-- floats around and drifts with the waves and the current. Then another fin appears a short distance away. Humpbacks and pilot whales sometimes swim in these waters, as well as the gray whale. Because of the latter's size and grayish appearance, a scientist discovering it might classify it as being from a humpback.

What happened here and whatever it was that tore apart the whale was enough to make the entire food chain of the ecosystem here disappear mysteriously.

A few miles northwest along the Antarctica coastline, more bits and pieces of blubber and flesh washed up against the icy edges. A huge black fin drifted up on the small shore and part of a head with the eye still in its socket, looking out without seeing. It was the remains of an orca which seemed to have met the same fate as the humpback miles away. The penguins looked down at it from the ice cliff above wondering what it was while sensing a level of danger in the air. That sense made them hold back from jumping in for their hunt. When enough time passed, their level of hunger would become so great that it would overcome any resistance to the danger of the waters, and they would go ahead with the jump.

When it came time and they saw nothing out there, one took the plunge and soon the others followed suit. Hundreds of penguins took their turns coming to the edge and then jumping and diving in. The hunt was on once again for this group. They had no way of knowing this would be their last. Most of them would never see their families again. Only the sounds of their contact with the water broke the unusually dead silence of the air.

For them, this hunt would be unlike they had ever experienced before. Swimming around with the swiftness of birds in their air with the grace of ballet dancers, they were a sight to behold if one were to witness what they were doing.

This went on for hours without any of them showing anything for their efforts. Their usual prey was nowhere to be found. Their main food, lantern fish, had mysteriously disappeared along with some other types which included sardines and smelt. Even cephalopods, such as squid and octopi, were not around. Desperately, they started swimming further away from their usual hunting grounds as their search for food continued. As their hunger increased, any thoughts of their primary predator, the leopard seal, were extinguished. They were totally oblivious to the approaching danger.

***

It neared them slowly and nonchalantly. It was in no hurry. There was more to eat, and it looked forward to it. Its black and green eyes were the sauce of saucers above its five-foot jaw. Its mouth was huge enough to swallow a man whole.

The swimming penguins came into its view. Not knowing what they were made no difference to it. They were alive, which meant only that they could be eaten. As it approached the perimeter of the penguin area, its huge size blocked out a substantial portion of the area around it. Some of the birds saw it, sensed danger, and started swimming toward the surface quickly. The huge maw opened as it instantly picked up speed and started swallowing up mouthfuls of penguins. All the penguins were now accelerating at maximum speeds toward the surface. More mouthfuls of the birds were taken by the black maw as they desperately tried to escape. In their panic, some of the birds crashed into each other. Not a normal thing for penguins to do, even when leopard seals were hunting them, these events could be construed as a cause leading to catastrophic consequences. In essence, this would be a first for them and for the entire ecosystem of Antarctica.

By the time survivors reached the land mass and were able to skirt back onto the ice shelf, their numbers were significantly reduced from the originals. Some of them looked back to see if any more were arriving. After a time seeing no more jump out of the water, they turned and headed back to their nesting grounds. Fearful and traumatized, they waddled as quickly as they could back to their families, hungry and without any food in the water to bring back to their chicks. For many of them, if not all, it would be a death sentence. Going in the water was not an option anymore. They didn't know what it was that had eaten most of their numbers, but they knew it was no leopard seal. It was far worse. They would die if they went back in and would likely die here on the ice mass for not having eaten. And their families would die from the lack of food that's normally brought back to them.

The sea meant life to them. It provided their only sustenance. But suddenly without knowing why, its meaning had changed to its polar opposite. As they continued their long journey back, tired and weaker than before, they couldn't have known that their group was being satellite monitored by human scientists. But what these scientists saw would be disturbing enough for the news to be quickly circulated throughout, not only the scientific world but that of the public as well.

5

Odessa, Texas

"Rita, phone call for you," Joan announced over the phone intercom. She was the educational assistant who worked in the department office across the hall. Some of her work involved patching phone calls to various staff.

"Hello, this is Professor Bloomsworth, how can I help you?"

It was Roger Cornish, a professor at the University of Mississippi, and a friend of many years. He was an anthropologist who specialized in forensic anthropology, but also had a special interest in paleo as well. She had scanned him a picture of the tooth along with its measurements. She had anticipated that he'd call soon after she sent him the photo, and her expectation not surprisingly came to fruition. He was as efficient as much as he was thorough.

"Oh, hi Rog. How are you?" After their usual cordial greetings and small talk banter, Roger decided to cut right to the chase because he knew that's what Rita was waiting for.

"I took a look at that picture you sent me. Interesting, I should say the least."

"That's what I thought, too. Jurassic you think?"

He was silent for a moment. Rita knew him enough to know that meant he was in a thinking mode.

"I don't think so, Rita. I've done some research on this specimen. So far, I've come up with finds similar to comparing apples with oranges, regarding what kind of animal this came from. Fortunately, the measurements of it on the pic helped me eliminate many of the prehistoric animals that would not have this kind of tooth. Based on the tooth type, it is a canine because of its size."

"You mean it's too large *not* to be a canine."

"Exactly."

"This has to be prehistoric. *Smilodon* maybe?"

"Hmm, I don't think so. Too large for the tusks of a sabretooth. Too thick. I think it's something else. I mean, you're correct when you say it's prehistoric. Adult tigers of today have canines that are two and a half to three inches long. We're talking prehistoric here. Think about what I'm saying here. Most large animals back then were larger than their surviving descendants today. Much larger. That means larger teeth."

Rita picked up the specimen, looking at it in her hand as if it were an alien object. "I wonder what kind of adult creature this came from. Dinosaur? Marine reptile, maybe?"

Roger looked at it and then his eyes went up to her. "I don't think it's from an adult."

Her eyes moved to meet his. "What? You think this is from a baby--whatever it was? Roger, this is three inches long. I don't know of any prehistoric reptile or mammal that had babies with teeth this long. This thing, when fully grown, would have to be absolutely gargantuan, almost beyond our comprehension."

She heard him manipulate the paper in front of him, picturing him in her mind trying to get a better view of it. Both knew it was not nearly as good as seeing and handling it in person.

"I'm really not sure but I have a good feeling. And my gut feelings are often on the money. But it looks like…maybe, the Cretaceous or Paleogene. However, don't take my word for it. I have some ideas though. And I believe without a doubt that it's from a predator. An exceptionally large one. But I'd need to thoroughly inspect the tooth itself to get a better idea of that."

"Well we know it was from a pretty large creature, agreed?" she asked.

He acknowledged her statement. "Yep. You know it. In fact, from what this came from, well. I strongly suspect it was from something far from fully grown. If it *is* from a baby of whatever creature it was. Question is, marine or terra firma?"

She looked at it. "Oh my. A three-inch-long canine. From a baby. Good Lord, can you imagine how big that thing as an adult would have been? I got an idea. If you have some time, maybe we can split up the research or if you can check on one thing for me at least."

"Rita, you only have to ask. And I've known you long enough to know what you want. My answer is yes."

"Hey, I didn't even ask you yet."

"Yes, you did," he retorted. "And I will take terra firma. I never did learn how to swim anyway. You can dig into the marine. We can keep in touch now and then via emails as well as calls to mutually update. How's that for a brilliant idea?

Rita laughed. "Ok, you got a deal. This will eliminate a lot of research time. You can come over when you get time and see it for yourself. He agreed but told her he'd do the research first to come up with the most promising preliminary ideas before he made the trip.

After saying their goodbyes for now, she looked at her specimen again and went into her computer to start the search. Actually, her search would take far less time than before the appearance of computers. She might just find the answer today. If her tooth was from a marine creature. Maybe Sam also would come up with something more about it.

Oxford, Mississippi

Unknown to Sam was the fact that she had possession of an artifact that someone else had as well. Of course, she didn't know who that someone was. It was just a feeling. She therefore had no reason to connect it with anything at this point. Like all scientists, she wanted a lot of answers but always seemed to have a lot more questions than answers. It didn't frustrate her, though. In fact, just the opposite. She was more determined than ever to answer some of those questions.

She started examining the tooth under a microscope, looking for fine orsmall clues to determine its possible origin. The fact that it was from a predator was a no-brainer. The end was pointy, indicating a predator tooth, rather than a flatter end of a herbivore. Slight curves on the top and bottom of it also indicated it was almost certainly a carnivore and a huge one at that.

Although the entire piece was nearly ten inches, it appeared that some of the artifact was probably bone that the tooth was attached to. The tooth itself was about six inches long from where it had attached to the jawbone to the pointed tip. It certainly appeared large enough to be from an adult, whatever it was. But she had to find out.

Odessa, Texas

She had been on the phone with her husband. Apparently, John got caught in a major trauma case that had been whisked to the hospital in Austin by the Life flight helicopter from a major traffic accident. It happened just before he was to leave to come home. It wouldn't have mattered if he had left anyway because he happened to be on call anyway. He wouldn't be home until late in the evening and he wanted to let her know. An unfortunate happening because she had been ready to cook him a nice dinner. Such is the life of a surgeon's wife. Sighing, she picked up her purse and looked around ready to leave the office.

Just as she started to turn off the lights, her phone rang. "Well for heaven's sake, who could be calling me now?" she said out loud. "Hello, this is Dr. Bloomsworth."

"Rita, it's me. Sorry to bother you so late." It was Roger Cornish.

"Roger, hi. You caught me just as I was to leave. Must be important. What's up?"

"Oh, sorry. Won't keep you. Just heard something on the news that I found a bit disturbing. Wondering if you heard anything. Something's happening down in Antarctica."

"Oh? What do you mean something's happening down there? What's going on?"

Rarely was anything from there on the news unless it was pretty significant, such as a new discovery or a large chunk of land mass breaking off.

"Well they didn't go into great details. What they mentioned was that the area's wildlife seems to have disappeared from the area or significantly and suddenly reduced in numbers. That's what the scientists down there have reported, and they don't have a clue as to why, so far."

She frowned. Although it didn't seem to have anything to do with her or her work, still, she was concerned because of the many different ways any changes in Antarctica could impact the planet. Most people might not know this. But the well-learned amateurs and scientists would. What Roger heard could certainly impact the planet in some way, but she wasn't sure how.

"Think it might have something to do with global warming?" she asked.

"Hmm, possibly. Maybe most of the wildlife migrated further south or north because of the warming waters."

Rita shook her head. "That's really strange, Roger. How many millions of years has it been the way it's been and now something like this happens? I mean, how bizarre is that? Did the report say how long the population decrease has been going on?"

"Well, not exactly. They believe it's been a few months. They recently happened to notice on their satellite computers that keep track of the penguin movements; that the numbers have been consistently decreasing from the previous norm. That's all that was said."

Rita looked at her watch. "Well, I better get home. Got to get supper ready and get to the kids. Thanks for the update and keep me posted, will ya?"

"Ok, will do. Sorry I delayed you from leaving but thought you might want to know this."

"I'm glad you called. Thanks again and have a great night."

"You too."

In her car, she couldn't help thinking about what she'd been told. It was disturbing, yet what could she do about it? Even though it wasn't really her field, as a scientist she did have connections. Maybe tomorrow she'd get a hold of someone she knew who might have some ideas about what's happening down at the southern tip of the world. For now, she had to get home and prepare for the usual evening rituals.

6

Gulf of Mexico, one hundred miles east of Tampico, Texas

No one seemed to be aware of it but the waters were a bit warmer than the previous year. Although global warming was apparently common knowledge everywhere, there were effects that were so subtle that no one noticed; effects that would eventually have serious impacts on not only the global marine ecosystems, but also on people's lives as well.

One of those nearly imperceptible effects was happening on the Gulf floor. Down there the currents weren't as strong as they were further up. A sudden ripple on the sandy floor was followed by a few more ripples. The sandy bottom started filling the surrounding area with its silty murkiness which grew larger in size by the minute. The few fish that swam there quickly scurried away, and any bottom dwelling creatures that were there sensed a danger that they didn't know and also quickly left. The huge murky brownish colored area of water continued to grow in size and started spreading upward.

A shark that sensed the vibrations in the water from a distance away approached the murky area of water out of a naturally instinctive curiosity. It entered the murkiness letting its incredible sense of smell and vibratory organs lead it to potential prey. It swam around aimlessly but never understanding what it was looking for or the very real danger *it* was in.

After a while, the murky area became lighter as it dissipated. A large tail about half the length of a bus moved quickly upward as the creature sought what it was immediately hungry for. Anything that might be directly in its path was swallowed up without the creature slowing down.

It followed the light, knowing somehow that it was going to get there soon. Although it had fed, it was still hungry. It had no sense of time. There was no way for it to know that it had lain dormant for at least a million years rather than being dead. It was a far different world now than the one it had known. It would not know any difference.

The shark, a twenty-foot Great White, sensed an unusually large number of vibrations in the water that it felt was moving its way. It instinctively changed direction, sensing something that might mean danger to most prey fish but not to itself. But then, because it was inherently programmed to investigate anything unknown, it turned back toward it.

Tellmore Research Station, Antarctica

The winds had picked up as if a gigantic fan had just been turned on, making the snow fly horizontally and almost impossible to distinguish the cloudy white skies from that of the snow and ice-covered ground. It was another typical stormy day which, no matter how long you were there or how acclimated you were to the weather and climate, was still quite a challenge. Even for the veterans down there, it was always prudent to not go out into it for any reason, unless you absolutely had to. It wasn't just the near hurricane force winds that could blow you away: it was also the absolute whiteout that could get you lost from even a few feet away from the shelter as well as the 80 below zero temperatures that could kill you very quickly. Down there, Mother Nature was devoid of all remorse.

Deep inside the warm research facility, the scientists were doing whatever inside work they were supposed to do. However conditions were outside, they always had important work to do. Inside research was just as important as out in the field. When the weather was good, which meant no high winds or blowing snow, they would take advantage of what they needed to do outside. In a very real sense, it was Mother Nature who decided where they would work.

While some were on their computers, others were studying the newest Antarctic ecological patterns and population shifts of the local wildlife. Barbara Cornwall was studying the current track of the storm outside and the predicted upcoming weather patterns on her computer. Because the computers ran on generator power, they didn't have to worry about power outages.

In another area of the main facility building, Beth Ann Trenton and George Kenmore were trying to figure out the reason for the penguin population decrease that appeared so suddenly. Initially they wondered if there was a sudden increase in the leopard seal population but quickly squashed that idea. That kind of increase would have to be quicker than was possible. Besides, their latest sonar findings when out in the boat the previous week indicated no such occurrence.

"George, look here," Beth pointed her finger at a spot on the screen. "See this area?" Her finger showed a narrow area where the penguin dots appeared to converge into one. It was right at the edge of the cliff or land mass. George focused his eyes on that spot.

"Yes, I see that" he responded with a frown of concern. "That's certainly odd."

Both of them as experts knew what that could mean. The question was, were the penguins sensing danger in other areas of the edge and saw only this one spot as *less* dangerous? Dangerous from what, though? They knew they were vulnerable to leopard seals but had to take their chances anyway. They really had no choice since the sea was their only source of food. Sure, they would hesitate before jumping in because their natural precautious instincts kicked in. They wanted food, not to *be* food. Even when one or two were picked off by a seal or two, there had never been any visible dent in their population on their return to the land mass and there would likely never be. Until now.

"Have you noticed them moving forward or back?"

"Well for the last few minutes they seemed to be not moving either direction. As if they're standing still, waiting," Beth replied. She picked up her mug of coffee and took a sip.

"Since yesterday they seemed to be moving back. That's pretty strange because they always move forward and jump in after taking their usual wary inspection. A few did jump in initially but that was about an hour ago. Since then, nothing more. Oh, look—the spots seem to be retreating back."

The two scientists stared at the screen and the penguin dots. Sure enough, the dots were indeed retreating back in the direction of their nesting grounds.

"Holy Moses, Beth, what's going on over there?"

This time the dots continued to move. Very slowly. This was certainly not normal behavior. In fact, it was out of character for them to do this. It seemed that something was not only spooking them but causing their retreat. Although orcas, whenever they appeared, could certainly spook them for a while until they moved on thereby causing a delay in their jumping in, their appearance never made them retreat back in the direction of their nesting grounds. The same thing with the leopard seals except that they were always around, and the birds knew that. Because of that and their ever-increasing hunger, they always eventually made the decision to jump in. They had to. Consequently, one or two out of the hundreds were fallen victims to the seals. Such was the normal lives of these aquatic birds.

But this was different. Something, perhaps in the water, was causing the risk of jumping in to overwhelm their driving hunger to the point where they seemed to consider starvation less risky. This was something totally unnatural which bewildered the scientists to the point of shock. She couldn't imagine what could scare them more than starvation.

"George, what do you think of this? Ever seen this before?"

"Hell no!"

Although his facial expression didn't register too much regarding surprise, she knew he was. He never answered like that, with those words and in that low tone of voice unless he believed something was seriously wrong. It was an ominous sign. Of what, they had no clue.

Beth picked up the phone and dialed an extension. Before calling Jessica, she wanted Tom to see this and get his take on this penguin behavior. Although it wasn't always necessary, she was one that never wanted to leave any stone unturned before notifying the chief scientist.

"Tom here."

"Tom, Beth. Can you come to the lab right away? I need you to see something which is a little disturbing and I'm not sure what to make of it. Need your bird expertise."

"Hm. Well well. Ok, be right there. Nothing catastrophic I hope?"

"I, uh, don't think so," she replied while continuing to stare at the moving dots on the screen. "I hope not," she muttered softly as she hung up.

Five minutes later, Tom Billington was staring at the screen along with the other two scientists. "What am I supposed to see besides those penguin dots?"

"Their movements," Beth replied. "Watch."

As the three continued to screen stare, the movements continued in the direction of the bottom of the screen toward their nesting grounds. Tom's eyebrows raised. Never an alarmist, he rarely exhibited any surprise at anything. This was his way of showing considerable surprise, which he did his best at always keeping in check. Then he straightened up.

Beth and George turned their faces up toward Tom's. "Well, Kemosabe, what do you think?" asked George.

Tom adjusted his glasses. "I think we all know that is a bit unnatural. What to make of it, I'm not sure. Have to say I have never seen that before. For the instinctual drive to feed being overcome by something else, something unbelievably bad had to be that something else. What that could be is anybody's guess. How long has this been going on?"

Beth sighed. "I'm not sure. But I've been in here for about an hour.

When I first came on here, I noticed the birds stopped near the edge of the precipice. No dots were disappearing which meant none of the birds were jumping into the water. For a while I thought it was either Orcas or leopards that were delaying their jumping. But they were still far longer than usual. After a few more minutes I noticed them started to retreat, then stop, then retreat again. Surprised the hell out of me. In fact, it just about blew me away. I wondered what the hell is going on out there."

George immediately jumped on it. "Know what I think? I think we should go out there and find out."

Beth and Tom looked at George. "You're right, ole buddy," Tom replied. "We need to do that. Looking at a computer screen provides us with only superficial information."

Beth took the initiative. "Ok. I'll check in with Jess and get her into the loop. She'll need to know this and gather up a team." Picking up the phone, she immediately contacted their chief and explained what happened. After hanging up, the told the men that Jess was getting on it right now.

"How far away are the birds? We are getting the chopper?" asked George.

"Yes," she told Tom. "According to my calculations, they are about fifteen miles to the northwest of us. I'll figure out the coordinates and give them to the chopper pilot. You two want to go along?"

"Of course," they both answered simultaneously.

Beth turned and looked up at them. "Well aren't we the zealous ones?" The men looked at each other while she smiled, almost breaking out into a laugh. "Go one, guys. Get your gear. I'm getting mine. Departure I figure is in about thirty minutes."

After they left, she looked at the screen momentarily and noticed the cluster of dots closer to the center of the screen and significantly more concentrated than before. That suggested to her that they were closer to a large huddle. What the hell? She felt a cold chill run up and down her spine and suddenly realized that whatever was happening out there was not good. Not good at all.

She got up quickly and left the lab. Time to find out what it was.

Gulf of Mexico, east of Tampico, Texas

Contrary to what most people believe, Great White sharks are not devoid of intelligence. In fact, they are more intelligent than previously thought. Despite their elongated brains which are smaller than a human's, they still allow some complex processing within their simpler structures for the shark to determine if a potential meal can be had or not. Their instinct to investigate for deciding to bite or not is s sign of thought processing and intelligence.

For this twenty-foot Great White, it was intelligent enough to sense something not right well ahead of it. Its skin felt huge amounts of vibrations in the water. It smelled something ahead which was completely unfamiliar to it. With its large black eyes and excellent vision, it saw something far ahead of it which was large and appeared to be growing larger. Whatever it was appeared to be growing larger very quickly. Somehow it sensed real danger. The shark was smart enough to know that *it* was more likely to be the thing's prey rather than the other way around. Without much hesitation, it turned to swim away from it. It had decided that whatever it was, it didn't want to be its dinner.

As it swam in the opposite direction, it felt vibrations becoming stronger behind it. The shark swam faster, which didn't seem to make much difference. Was it being chased? It dove deeper and swam upward, but those vibrations seem to always stay with it and still become stronger. By now it sensed that it was in trouble. Up to this time, it had always been the top predator in these waters. Now it sensed it was being pursued as prey for the first time.

The attack was swift and unavoidable. The huge black maw overtook and engulfed the shark. Huge teeth penetrated through its entire body and was soon no more as it became a pulpy mash.

Tellmore Research Station, Antarctica

The Bell 407 was always kept inside its hanger when not in use. The large station had a mechanical engineer, a mechanic, and two pilots to maintain and operate the invaluable flight transport vehicle. Sheltering it inside was a part of maintaining it due to the high velocity winds and blizzard conditions that can suddenly assault the area with little to no warning. Their extreme location prevented easy access or transport for chopper parts if it broke down, not to mention fuel for it. It was vital for all concerned to make sure it was always in top, flyable condition.

The engineer opened the hangar door with the hatch-protected button on the outside. The main pilot then entered, putting his bag inside the chopper, and did his outside inspection of the entire chopper as required. When he was satisfied, he did his inspection of everything in the chopper, checking his fuel gauges to ensure the tanks were full. They were always to be filled on return from a flight.

He got out and he and two other men pushed the chopper to outside the hangar. It had wheels on its skids which made it possible for them to do this. Once in place, the pilot reentered it, started the engine and rotors going. Once warmed up, he took off for the other side of the large spread out station. There, the scientists were waiting for their ride to near the other side of the continent. Their destination was to the northwest corner. It actually was a twenty-minute direct route to the location where they saw the penguins on the computer.

Beth Ann and George rode in the large passenger section behind the cockpit. As they flew toward the location, they had to wear headphones so they could hear themselves talk over the loud chopper engine. They chose not to talk until they got there. Not knowing what they would find or discover, each of them seemed to be involved in their own thoughts, wondering about the strange behavior of the birds, intensely interested in finding out what the problem was.

Twenty minutes later, the pilot voiced his news.

"The coast is coming up ahead, folks. Straight ahead toward the eleven o'clock position."

Both scientists looked slightly to the left out the front windows and could see the surrounding Southern Ocean in the distance.

"Take us near the coastline and let's see what those birds are now doing down there, will ya?" said Beth Ann.

"Roger, you got it."

The chopper turned in the anticipated direction to where the birds were seen on the computer. The pilot brought the chopper down a bit to see below better. Flying over the area, they initially didn't see them.

"C'mon, where the hell are you, little birdies?" said George softly. From their height, the vastness of the white continent could never be understated. The whiteness seemed to go on forever in all directions. Cold, forbidding, and inhospitable to all but the most stubborn and hearty of people who were willing to endure the deadly bone-freezing cold that only Antarctica could offer, the icy land supported those penguins as a refuge, if you could call it that, from the equally deadly aquatic environment of the ocean.

But there was something else in the water. Something that was making these birds not go in. Not even out of hunger. Beth Ann was disturbed that something was scaring them so much it overpowered even their primal natural urge to feed. That was bad. She had to know what that something was.

"There, over there," shouted Beth Ann as she pointed to her right. The others' heads turned as they spotted the moving lines of black figures on the ice shelf.

"Get you get it down a little more?" asked Beth Ann to the pilot.

"Ok, going down to seven hundred feet."

Approaching the decided elevation above the ground, the two scientists and the flight crew observed a closer view of the penguins. All seemed to be walking fast in the assumed direction of their nesting area. Yet why? They hadn't fed. How were they supposed to feed their chicks, let along themselves? And why the waddling so quickly?

"Something in the water must have scared them a lot for them to do this. Even this far from the water, they still seem to be frightened." George said out loud what they all observed.

Beth Ann agreed without answering. "Jim, can you fly over the water a bit? Maybe we can see something that might clue us in."

"Ok, not a problem," the pilot replied. The chopper then turned slightly to the left and headed directly toward the coastline. Near the water, the ice cliff slanted toward the water's surface. She didn't know for sure how the birds could get up that steep embankment but somehow, they did. The spot which now should be normally filled by penguins ready to dive into the water below was now eerily devoid of life.

Heading out over the water, the scientists looked down to see if they could spot anything. So far all seemed normal. The surface was undisturbed by anything. There was nothing they could see that would suggest anything out of the ordinary. The answer to what could have scared the penguins off so intensely eluded them.

"How far out do you want to go, Beth?" asked the pilot.

"Just another mile, then turn around. I'd like to land on the area where the penguins would be, near the cliff edge. Maybe we could spot something from that angle."

After reaching the invisible mile border, the chopper turned around and headed back toward the ice shelf. Beth Ann and George didn't spot anything with their binoculars. They hoped to see some kind of clue after they landed but weren't overly optimistic. One thing for sure was that they wouldn't give up. If something wasn't done about this, the penguins would likely starve to death with their chicks the first to go: or they would die trying to obtain food. That meant that either something was in the water which was not their natural predator but a threat anyway, or there was a lack of fish. She decided it was the former because it was scaring them into starvation. She would like to know what that something was.

7

Oxford, Mississippi

Even at home, Sam couldn't help wondering about that tooth. She figured it was always in her nature to always wonder about what she didn't have the answers to. Ever since as far back as she could remember, her curiosity for things unknown to her never left her. In fact, it would always grow, and her need to discover what made things what they were and how they ticked was intense enough to spurn her into follow-up actions. She was far from the type to just let sleeping dogs lie.

This fossil was not something she had seen before. The fact that it was prehistoric excited her and her need to find out just kept intensifying. It became almost an ecstatic intensity.

She got up from her lounge chair and went to the table where her laptop was and wasted no time hitting the internet. She googled everything she could that was related to prehistorical teeth, focusing more on reptiles. This was no mammalian tooth, not even a sabretooth.

She went through several web sites and hundreds of photographs of found reptile tooth fossils. Her focus remained on the largest reptiles on land. Even with all the websites available, she did not find one that matched what she held in her hand right now. Having brought it home for safekeeping, she wanted to make sure this thing never left her sight.

Time flew right past her. It was already past midnight, but she had no idea when she started, but believed it was hours. Her desire to find the identity of the creature this tooth had come from drove her into almost obsessional determination.

It was about 2am when she found something that caused her to pause in her search. Although it was hard to tell just from a picture and comparing it to one she actually had, it was the closest to a match she had seen so far. Carefully and methodically she compared the two, taking her time so as to not overlook any fine details.

She read the printed details of the tooth on the screen. The fact that "prehistoric" was mentioned only intensified her interest. It was a picture of an item from the New York Museum of Natural History and Paleontology circa 2003. It stated the name of the creature it came from. That told her the period and era.

The creature had been a marine reptile. It's not commonly known among non-experts and has been considered extinct for millions of years. If this is what she had, it could be a real find and she was determined to find out for sure. But in the middle of the night, no one would appreciate her contacting them. Her decision to wait until a decent time would be much better. Picking herself up, she headed to bed.

***

At 9am she called her friend Rita over in Texas to tell her about it. She was lucky. Rita picked up and after their cordial greetings and a little small talk, Sam finally got into the reason for her call.

She was lucky. Rita picked up and after their cordial greetings and a little small talk, Sam finally got into the reason for her call. After hanging up, she took a picture of it with her phone and sent it to her. If Rita affirmed the possibility of it being what Sam believed, she might call the local museum and request a further analysis by the experts there. First things first, though.

Sam called her back after it was sent to check on it.

"I don't know, let me see,' Rita replied to her friend's question of whether or not she received the picture.

Within seconds, she got back on the phone. "Yes, I got it. Looks interesting. You say it was found in the Gulf?"

"Yes. Someone found it buried in the sand on the shore of Mississippi. I have an idea what it could be from, but I wanted to get your take on it. See what you think."

"What do you think it's from?" Rita asked.

"I can't be sure. I believe it might be from a marine creature. Looks too big to be from a land creature, even from T-rex."

"Hmm, I think so too. I've got some charts and lots of images of all kinds of fossils. Hundreds, if not thousands of these things. Maybe I can give you a hand and do some comparing."

"That would be great, Rita. Right now I'm thinking sometime during the Cretaceous period or Jurassic."

"What makes you think those periods?"

"I don't know. Just a hunch, I guess. Have to start somewhere so that's where I'm going to start. I'll do those two if you want to start on one of the others. When you have time, that is. I know you're busy so don't try to break a leg on this."

"Don't worry sweetie. I'll do what I can. I'm sure I'm not busier than you. Anywhere, gotta go. Class in thirty minutes."

After Sam thanked her and they said their goodbyes, she looked at the tooth and wondered. There were a lot of geological time periods in earth's history. Was she starting in the right place? Right now it's anyone's guess but she had to start somewhere, like she told Rita. On her laptop, she went into the school computer program on prehistorical sea creatures and began her research into solving the tooth mystery. She knew it wouldn't be as easy as it sounded. But then not much was. She had no classes today so there was no time like the present to begin.

The Southern Ocean, fifty miles northwest of Antarctica

It could not know where it came from and never would. Time was unknown to it. The world it was swimming in was almost all that it knew. The only other thing it knew was that it always had to feed. Its hunger was literally insatiable and its appetite unfathomable. The creatures it had already eaten had been unfamiliar to it from the prehistoric world it had originated in. Why it was still alive was not something it could even think about because it could not think.

As it continued to swim, it moved smoothly through the deep ocean in undulating patterns from shallower to deeper waters. The periodic creatures it would confront along the way would be taken into its five-foot-wide open jaw with its rows of nine-inch bone-pulverizing teeth. Its path took it slightly more in a northern direction than western, which headed it a bit more toward the bottom of the South American continent. It had no fear of the unknown and never had. Back in its time it would have occasionally run into other large sea creatures which competed with it for food. Now, so far it hadn't run into anything of significant size. At least none that came close to be a threat to it.

Ahead of it, it sensed other creatures that were large but still much smaller than it. The two creatures that were bigger than most of the others it had seen were not predators. The humpbacks included a large and smaller one. A mother and her calf. They were swimming away at a somewhat faster speed as it approached them. Although they were intelligent enough to realize the extreme danger fast approaching them from behind, it would not be enough to save them. Their speed was far too slow for the quick swimming creature behind them.

The mother quickened her speed, hoping her calf would be able to keep up. It tried but started slowly getting behind. About three hundred yards behind them, the large tooth-filled maw started opening up. Soon it was a hundred yards. When it reached 50 yards, its jaw was wide open as the whale calf came closer and closer.

The calf started calling out to its mother with its sonar sounds. The mother slowly turned around and saw her calf being sucked into the gargantuan mouth. Its mouth quickly closed, crushing the calf, and causing its internal organs to violently explode outward. Soon even they disappeared into the deadly cavern until no sign of it was left, except the huge area of blood-filled water. Whatever the creature was had disappeared into the depths. The mother humpback cried out in a combination of what could be described as "grief" then terror as the thing it never had seen before kept swimming toward her underwater.

The humpback turned around and headed away as fast as it could. Knowing now that it had easily taken her calf, she had no choice but to try and escape the area. Its brain processed the fact that as big as she was, the thing was even bigger. That alone made *her* a target. If she ran into any Orcas, which were equally her enemy as this thing was, chances are they would turn and run as well, quickly forgetting about her.

Heading more northerly, she hoped to hit warmer waters in time. Perhaps this thing could tolerate only colder waters which the Southern offered plenty of. But though she was swimming as fast as she could despite her huge bulk, it turned out to be no match for her stalker.

She felt more pain than she ever felt before as the huge unknown predator's nearly foot long teeth sank deeply into her flesh. The rear half of her body was sucked into the maw as the jaw clamped down, biting her in half. Blood and entrails gushed out of the now dead humpback as the thing started eating her. It didn't take long for the rest of her to go down its gullet. Within a matter of minutes, all that was left of the whale was lots of blood and bits of entrails floating around. The thing had made short work of her.

It then continued to swim on as if business as usual. If it could easily kill and eat whales, what else could it do? There would be more confrontations. But for now, it kept moving ready to obliterate and engulf anything and everything in its path.

Antarctica

Rather than have the chopper continue flying around wasting fuel, Beth had the pilot land on the shelf. They needed to get a closer look at the water and shoreline to see if there were any clues that could be found. Whatever the penguins saw or sensed Beth hoped they would be able to also.

Although the skies were clear with only puffy fair-weather clouds scattered about, the sun did not provide any warmth. It was a bitter minus twenty degrees Fahrenheit and that was with the sun at its peak. One by one they exited the chopper with some small, light portable equipment including their sunglasses, and wearing their heavily furred arctic coats and hoods. The pilot stayed in the chopper keeping it running to prevent the oil and fuel from freezing in the exposed bitter cold. They all agreed that this wouldn't take long. The last thing they wanted was for the chopper to run too low on fuel for their return trip. So, they had to time this carefully after finding out the maximum time they had before the chopper had to take off.

George led the way with Beth close behind. With the always-important binoculars hanging around their necks, they slowly plodded their way to the cliff edge about two hundred yards away. Along the way they noticed the thousands of penguin foot prints, with mixtures of those coming toward and coming away from the edge.

The trek wasn't easy but after about fifteen minutes they arrived at the edge. Looking down, they saw the icy slanted slope where they knew the penguins jumped onto before sliding quickly into the water. A little further down, the embankment near the water was less steep and provided a few precarious footholds where Beth suspected the birds climbed back up. Even penguins knew enough not to jump from a place where there was no way to get back up.

Scanning slowly with their binoculars, they searched for what, they didn't know. Hoping to find some kind of clue as to what spooked the entire flock, they looked for signs of leopard seals, the penguins' main predator. Of course there were none. In the sky, the lack of any birds indicated a lack of fish underneath the ocean surface. Usually there were hundreds of hungry birds in this area. But for some reason it was eerily quiet and devoid of any signs of life. There was basically nothing for them to see here, which was bad. Whatever the birds had seen or sensed, it seemed to be gone.

Still, Beth knew something was very wrong. She couldn't put her finger on it, but it needed to be investigated. She was afraid there was a real danger that the penguins would starve to death if they didn't go hunting in the water soon.

"George, we need to get back to base. We should high-tail back here with the *Arga* and find out what's going on here."

The Arga was their one hundred-thirty-foot research vessel which they used for oceanographic and marine biology studies on the open water. On it, they had state of the art equipment which included radio communications, sonar, fathometers, current speed indicators, water temperature indicators, weather equipment, and countless other items used as backups for emergencies or research reasons. The government had provided them well with everything they would or might need. Their distance from home, as well as the horrible weather conditions that often prevented deliveries, made that necessary. All their supplies, including food, were generously provided to the point of overabundance.

Whatever they needed to do on the vessel, they would more than likely have what they needed.

"Yea, I agree. Let's get the hell out of here so we can get back here."

Once in the helicopter, they were back at base within thirty minutes. They didn't waste any time letting the others know about the mission. It was planned for them to get underway in two hours. The *Arga*'s captain was notified as well as the first mate and the rest of the crew. Soon the base camp was abuzz with movement and talking as preparations were being made quickly.

The Southern Ocean

The medium size Japanese whaling vessel, *Yakura Maru,* was underway at ten knots, heading south-southeast. Although they were in international waters. certain anti-whaling factions were known to patrol these waters to run these vessels out of here. To most anti-whaling supporters, these whalers were criminals running whales into extinction. To the Japanese, it was this group of anti-whaler ships that were the criminals. The Yakura captain knew about these ships. Yet he hadn't run into any yet. Besides, he had protectors in the form of harpoon ships which were his security as well as the mother ship's.

For now, all his concern was to find whales, kill them, and get them to the mother ship for processing. Although it was easier said than done, it *was* done and all too often they succeeded without a hitch.

The skies were cloudy and there were no storms in the area, fortunately for them. The wind had picked up a bit, blowing at fifteen knots, according to their anemometer. The ship was headed into the wind and the three-foot waves.

Communications were ongoing in the radio room and on the bridge. Some of them were between the Yakura and the mother ship, *Suzaki.* So far the Yakura hadn't spotted any whales. They had been sailing for six days and not one was seen anywhere. Because of this, as well other ships reporting the same from other areas, whale harvesting had come to a virtual halt. Consequently, the fleet commanders were starting to worry. They knew this was the time when the animals would be spotted, and they had always been able to get a few by this time.

Because the area directly to the south of the Yakura was not yet covered, its captain decided to head on down there, hoping his luck would change for the better. Ordering increased speed to fifteen knots and turning to starboard to a heading of 150 degrees, the helmsman instantly put the order into action and soon the ship was headed south.

For the next several hours, its journey was unremarkable. Its crew was always on alert in case a whale was spotted. There were no signs of anything in the vast waters, but that was to be expected. The Southern Ocean was large and seemingly endless, encircling Antarctica from below sixty degrees South latitude. Whales, especially humpbacks, were known to migrate there at certain times of the year. Other sea creatures would migrate there also to feed on krill which lived in the cold waters around the Antarctic continent. It was common for these whalers to find whales along the way.

However, the Yakura captain was rightly concerned. Still nothing. He wondered why. What was so different about this year that none of them appeared? They *had* to come up for air. No blowholes were spotted. Yet many of the crew continued their vigilant watch for signs of one in all directions around the ship.

Another couple of hours went by and it was now mid-afternoon. It would be dark in another three hours and they'd have to call it a night.

Suddenly a shout from one of the crew on the stern. He yelled out a whale spotted about two miles to the west-northwest. The captain barked orders to immediately turn the ship toward the heading of the whale. They couldn't lose it. They might not see another one again.

After they turned, the captain ordered their speed increased to twenty knots. The engines roared louder as they worked to speed the ship up to the required velocity. Everyone was excited and laughing, confident that they were finally going to get their first whale after all this time.

The captain ordered the preparation of the bow harpoon as they neared the distant blowhole spouts with every second. The crew down below prepared the slide on the back of the ship to pull the harpooned whale up its incline into the hold below decks where it would remain as they continued to look for other whales. Those along the side on deck would handle spear like instruments to prod the dead whale along until it reached the ship's stern and inclined open slide. There they would manipulate it until the harpoon line caught on a special hook which would pull it up.

That was how they usually did it and that's what they planned for. For them it was considered routine. For animal activists, it was barbaric. As they neared the whale everyone manned their assigned posts on the ship. The captain started barking orders as they approached the three thousand-yard distance. The harpoonist quickly removed the cover off the huge, deadly spear and became ready at the bow, with his finger on the trigger. All hands on the bridge and on deck were staring at the unsuspecting whale, just swimming along, and blowing spouts of water and air from its blowhole. Alongside it was a calf which the ship's crew either didn't see or didn't care if it was there.

The captain ordered increased speed to twenty-two knots and to come about to starboard another twenty degrees. The helmsman complied and the ship responded, which led it on an interception course to spear the whale at just the right moment.

Just before the captain ordered the harpoonist to fire, something happened which caused some confusion and delayed the firing order. The whale suddenly and snappily turned to its left side and then seemed to be in some kind of distress. The captain brought his binoculars down to try and see with his naked eyes what he hoped he wasn't really seeing.

The calf which was seen beside its mother suddenly disappeared below the water line and a huge spray of gushing blood blew high into the air as if from a water cannon. Then the mother lifted her head high above the water and was then engulfed in a huge black maw with what looked like the largest teeth the captain and crew had ever seen. It dwarfed the humpback and as the maw closed the whale disappeared down it and the thing disappeared quickly below the water's surface. A thirty-foot spray of blood geysered into the air with pieces of flesh rising violently within it. The captain did not see what had destroyed the whale. Even if he did, his brain might be at a loss to process what would be envisioned. It would be like nothing on earth he'd ever seen. Identifying it would be impossible. A sea monster perhaps? If he told his superiors that back in Tokyo or the ship's owner, he'd be laughed right out of his captainship and perhaps the business for good.

Maintaining control of himself, after some moments of silent disbelief, he ordered the helmsman to decrease speed to ten knots so he could survey the bloody area where the whales had been shortly before. As he scanned the ocean surface, he noticed no chunks of flesh or blubber. This suggested to him that what happened was as they saw. The whales, both of them had been devoured by something, but not before being crushed first by the huge teeth of something far bigger than the mother whale itself.

Unfortunately, there was no proof of what happened that they could collect. No one on board had the presence of mind to take pictures or videos because it happened so quickly and unexpectedly.

As soon as the captain overcame the initial shock, the realization that they could very well be in immediate danger themselves hit him like a brick wall. He didn't know what that thing was, but if it could take down a huge humpback whale like that with hardly an effort, what else could it do? Even to his ship? There was no question what he had to do next.

8

After ordering the ship to come about, they started heading in the opposite direction from the incident. He then ordered the ship's speed increased to full. As the ship sped up to its full twenty-seven knots, he called down below and ordered the full manning of the sonar It wasn't as sophisticated as their navy's but was ordinarily used just to locate whales and it worked just fine. It wasn't manned constantly but only at the captain's discretion. This was one of those times.

On the bridge, the first mate stayed on top of what was happening and advised the captain he would check with the sonar man for anything on the scope. When he checked, the sonar operator advised him that there was nothing showing on the screen so far. All seemed to be quiet. Not only were there no whales to be seen anywhere, but there were not even any fish.

As the miles increased between them and the site, the captain soon decided to decrease their speed to ten knots. No sense using up precious fuel on what seemed to be a wild goose chase. He wasn't sure what their next move would be. Their frequent monitoring of the sonar resulted in no sightings of anything. The skipper then contacted the mother ship far to the southeast in the Southern Ocean to update their status. There was a lot of crackling and static on the radio. He heard faint voices and then a screech which nearly pierced eardrums of all who were on the bridge. The skipper cursed under his breath in the only Japanese cuss word he normally used.

Trying again, another voice came over from another harpoon ship, the *Sakuru.* According to what the skipper knew, the Sakuru was much closer to the mother ship and about seventy-five miles southeast of the *Yakura.* The voices were considerably clearer but higher pitched as if in a panic. When the skipper identified himself and his vessel, he asked the Sakuru if they had caught or at least spotted any whales down in their area. Their response was no. They quickly advised the skipper to turn his vessel around and head back to Japan because they were doing that themselves.

The skipper's jaw dropped. This was unprecedented. Could that be related to what they had seen-the killing of the mother and baby humpbackfrom something below? If it was, it suggested the oceans had become hunting grounds for something dangerous to everything: including ships!

But what it could possibly be was anyone's guess.

Quickly the *Sakuru* radio operator informed the skipper that the Suzaki had been attacked by something in the water and had sustained some damage on the port side amidships. It was taking on some water but was not serious enough to sink it. Its large size made that difficult. Damage control was on it. It had informed the rest of the fleet that it had turned around and was heading back to Japan. The *Yakura* hadn't heard the transmission. He advised the Yakura to do the same and said he had to get off the radio now because all hands were now called to their emergency stations. Something was happening to them. Then the radio went dead.

The Yakura captain tried to call the Sakuru back but no one answered. Now he was even more concerned. Quickly, he barked the order to the helmsman to increased speed to twenty-five knots and gave the order for the general heading back to their homeland. He had the navigator plot the course for them to get back home.

A voice suddenly erupted on the internal comms radio addressing the captain. Sonar had detected a huge blip on the radar that appeared from the southwest. It seemed to come out of nowhere. In fact, the blip was so large it took up nearly half the screen. The operator knew this was no whale, not even a Blue.

From his cabin, the skipper told his first mate to take over the bridge until he returned, then headed as fast as he could down to the sonar compartment. When he arrived he looked at the screen and his eyes widened in disbelief. Nanite kotoda! *Oh my God!*

He noted its bearing and immediately ordered his first mate to turn to in the opposite direction at full speed. There was no room for error here and the ship could only speed up as quickly as the engines' capabilities.

Then he got on the loudspeaker and announced to his crew the news. He hoped to outrun whatever thing was stalking them. But he also addressed the crew to brace themselves for a possible impact with something unknown. Before he could finish on the mike, the Yakura was suddenly forced to the side by something incomprehensibly violent and unexpected.

Things were knocked over and crew members, including the captain and the helmsman, were knocked off their feet. The shipped tilted far to the starboard side before righting itself back up. It had begun.

Antarctica

Captain Paul Gibson was a sailor with decades of experience on the water. When he was a boy, he always loved to sail with his father on their small but versatile twenty-foot sailboat back on the Chesapeake Bay in Virginia. It was a pleasure he just couldn't seem to get enough of.

He had always loved the water anything to do with it, including water sports. As a teenager, he had become an avid boater, although he didn't get his boating license until he was sixteen. The following year, his skiing skills had improved enough to where he could water ski on one ski. He just couldn't get enough of it at the time.

Once he obtained his license, he was able to take the boat out by himself and became rather good at it. When he turned 18, he enlisted in the US Coast Guard to gain professional sailing experience and learn new skills that he might otherwise not learn on a small boat. That included all phases of seamanship, deck and navigational skills, and leadership skills as well.

Although he liked the military, it was not something he wanted for a career. When he left the service four years later, he decided to continue his sailing experience by studying for his master's certificate. He wanted to become a civilian ship captain, and eventually he did. By certain connections and good fortune he was eventually able to connect with sailing a scientific research ship, the Arga.

The ship was making preparations for getting underway within the next two hours, and Captain Gibson was staying on top of it. He wanted to make sure that all went as planned and that their time to depart would be as close to being on time as possible. Sometimes little things got in the way of leaving exactly when planned, so he allowed a certain amount of flexibility in that regard, within reason of course.

The aft deck, where the gangplank was located, was an area of hustle and bustle activity as scientists brought some of their portable equipment on board to supplement the ship's permanent research equipment. They might not have to use all of it. But considering the distance they were going from the base, which was about six hundred miles, it was better to bring a little too much than not enough. One never knew when it came to confronting the icy wilderness. Add other unknowns to that and it became a near necessity.

The deck crew, not scientists themselves, were hired for their important roles when they were needed. Often, they were utilized to provide certain kinds of assistance to the scientists when the ship was not underway. Currently, they were preparing the lines for casting off as the scientists brought their equipment inside to their perspective spaces. Time to get underway was forty-five minutes away. If all went well, that time was 0600. The long daylight period of Antarctica often created havoc with people's internal body clocks. However, the issue at hand appeared to nullify that in everyone. For some, apprehensiveness for what they might find at their destination made them a bit less relaxed than some of the others.

The captain was making his last checks with the navigators for the various courses they would take to get to the northwestern part of the continent. He had already checked the weather and it was looking good for departure time. For now. He, like everyone else there, knew all too well how quickly and drastically the weather can change down there. In addition to the weather conditions, icebergs were also a frequent hazard to shipping there, so he made sure all his navigation and electronic equipment were working, including his sonar and radar (both navigational and weather). Everything that was needed to work while the ship was out at sea would already have been checked and certified for full underway utilization.Fuel tanks were filled, and the engines would be started in about fifteen minutes. Everything was a go at this point.

Beth Ann and George had come aboard earlier to set up the equipment they anticipated they would need. To the untrained eye it seemed like an awful lot of work for what they had to do. Where they were going, however made all that an absolute necessity. Besides, for them it was routine.

Fortunately, the weather was good, with partly cloudy skies, a cold thirty below zero breeze, and three-foot sea swells. It was a good day to be out on the water. That is, if you didn't mind the frigid temperatures. They were all used to it in a sense because they'd all been there for a while.

Beth Ann went to the science lab to ready the equipment. George, with his expertise also in meteorology, went to the bridge to check the route of navigation to their destination, and then went below to the weather room to check on the weather radar there. They had one on the bridge also, but his room below made it better for him to decide on any alternate course of action should the weather suddenly turn on him. He could concentrate more on what was going on in the atmosphere above and see if there was anything that could delay their departure.

As he looked carefully, he saw nothing that would do that. Although there were no guarantees, unless there was something immediately evident of that, there was no reason to delay. Wind and sea conditions were amicable for sailing and there were no storms in sight. At least for now.

He checked with Captain Paul, as he was unofficially called with his permission and relayed his determination that weather-wise the trip was ago.

Gibson called down to the science lab to check on her progressin readiness for getting underway.

"I'm almost finished here, Cap," Sam replied into the wall intercom. "Couple more checks and should be good to go."

"Ok. Let me know when you're good."

Sam clicked twice, which was also unofficially a way of acknowledging without more verbalizations. Sometimes it saved a few seconds time.

The time expected away was unknown but not expected to last more than a week or two. The two weeks out there could mean there was a problem. But when one travels to the unknown in or around Antarctica, anything could happen. So it was not considered a safe journey by any means

As soon as Sam had completed her checks, she notified Captain Gibson.

“Paul, I’m done. We’re all set and ready down here.”

“Roger, Sam,” he acknowledged. “All hands, ready to get underway. Lines one and three, cast off.” As the crew complied, the captain continued to bark the orders until the ship was free and clear of the dock. It was now on its way and soon sped up to the cruising speed of fifteen knots.

For the most part it was uneventful in regard to the weather. The only thing that seemed to be a little off from the norm was the lack of any seabirds. Often, they would be seen flying around looking for fish below. The fact that none were seen in the area didn’t escape the attention of the scientists. In fact, no seabirds would be seen anywhere along the entire route.

Odessa, TX

At the lab Rita had come across some interesting prospects on the computer program of Paleolithic creatures, including those in oceanic categories. So far, she had seen nothing that caught her attention for similarities to the tooth she had. But she was not one to ever give up. Confident she would eventually find the proper comparison, she decided to call it a day and head on home. Her search would continue the next morning.

John had gotten home early that morning from his exhausting sixteen hours of surgeries at the hospital. After sleeping for a bit, he got up in time for the kids returning from school. He was off for the next two days after being on duty for five days and having on-call for two nights. His mood was good because he loved the time that he could enjoy his home life uninterrupted.

Fortunately, their house is where the school bus stopped. Most families with kids weren’t that fortunate. But he was still vigilant at the open front door watching them get off the bus and run up to him.

“Hey guys, what’s up? How was school,”? he asked as Jaime and Sarah came scooting up to the door.

"Daddy, look! cried Sarah as she showed him the drawing she had done for the teacher. "I drew a picture of my teacher," she said excitedly.

"Oh wow, that is beautiful!" he said with his happy glad-to-see-you voice as he looked at it in amusement. "Oh my, that looks like her doesn't it?" he asked, with a laugh.

Of course, it didn't. The skinny stick figure of a woman with a triangular dress, overblown blouse and two dots for a nose as well as the red bushy hair which complimented the top of her was all too typical of a little child's drawing but one he would always treasure anyway, if it could survive the ongoing years of her growing up. She gave him a big hug.

Jaime was glad to be home too, talking about his soccer game at school and how he had scored a goal. John congratulated him on that and gave him a big hug. He then told them to change their clothes because 'mommy would be home soon.'

After the kids were upstairs, he went to sit down and look at the morning paper. A few minutes later, Rita came through the door.

"Well hi stranger," she said. She went up and kissed him. "How was work?"

"Tiring as usual. Sixteen hours of surgery. After all these days, I'm ready for a couple days off. Anybody calls me from work, tell them I'm not available."

"I hear ya, honey."

"How was *yours?"*

She smoothed her hair back and sat down to unwind for a few minutes. It was 4pm and soon it would be time to start preparing supper. For now she had a little time to relax.

"Interesting day, I think. Saw a picture of an ancient monster tooth that a colleague sent to me. Largest tooth I have ever seen."

"Really!?

"Yea. Thinking about going over to her lab and seeing it in person."

"When would you do that?"

She rested her head on her hand. "Don't know. Haven't made up my mind yet. Anyway, how are the kids?"

He told her, which made her smile. She got up and went to the bottom of the stairs. "Hey, my little grumpkins, mommy's home!"

Soon the pounding of little feet sounded on the floors above and in a few seconds, they yelled out hi's to Rita. They were already changed into their play clothes."

Telling them they could go play until supper, they bounded back up the stairs to their rooms. "Well, guess I'll prepare to prepare for supper."

John was into the paper again. "Ok hon. Want some help?

"Sure. If you could just cut up the carrots, I could do the rest."

He jumped up and said, "Consider them done."

Now how many husbands would say something nice like that? she thought. But then again, he had the day off. Yet, that was John. He would have said that even with a lack of sleep. Then she wouldn't have asked him for help. Decreased sleep could cause increased chances of injury. But today was her lucky day.

9

The Southern Ocean, on board the Sakuru

Loose items flew everywhere. Anyone in the way would have gotten smacked without warning. Those crew members not already holding onto something were thrown around like loose sacks of potatoes.

Up on the bridge the captain yelled orders to come about to ninety degrees starboard and increase to full speed. He also yelled down over the bridge intercom to the engineers and asked for a report on any damage down there in the engine room.

So far there was no damage but that didn't guarantee anything. *Bang!* The entire ship shook, and this time a huge five-foot dent caved inward in the engine room. The crew down there were terrified and yelled back up on the intercom to report the serious damage. Still no leaks but they reported that another hit like that and a huge hole would replace the dent. Yet they tried with whatever ideas they could come up with to prevent any further damage.

No one on board had a clue as to what was hitting them. The ship's first mate had reported that there were no iceberg sightings in the area. The sonar had detected something huge underwater, but it couldn't be identified. But it was moving and moving quickly. Icebergs don't move like that.

Bang! The entire ship shook and was pushed to its port as it struggled to maintain headway to its starboard side. It was being thrown off course by something below the surface and it seemed to be pursuing them. Suddenly the hunters had now become the hunted. Could it be a huge whale? That ran through the captain's mind, but he thought that was farfetched. Whales don't do that to ships.

Despite the Moby Dick tale that he was familiar with, the force that the ship was being pummeled with seemed to be far more powerful than from even the largest humpback. Blue whales were not in the area. So he ruled out whales. But if this thing wasn't a whale, what the hell was it?

BANG! This time they were in trouble. The skipper knew for sure when the report came from the engine room. Ominous noises advertised the various overwhelming stresses that the ship's bulkheads and frameworks were undergoing. One pipe among hundreds sprung a leak. It was in an area of the engine room where no one was. It was small but still a harbinger of what could likely come if it wasn't taken care of soon.

The Southern Ocean, one hundred miles east of the Yakura

On board the *Suzaki*, the crew members were frustrated that they hadn't gotten a single whale delivered to them by their three harpoon ships. They couldn't understand it because every year this was the time of year when the whales were on the move and they normally could easily catch them. Their quota was set each year by their government, although this was not a quota that was condoned by the international community and animal activists worldwide. They were even surprised that there hadn't been any reports of the Sea Shepard activists that were in past years always trying to stop their whaling missions dead in their tracks. No sightings, no reports.

This was what the mother ship's captain was thinking. He had the radio operator contact the *Yakura* to find out what was going on with them. Sure, he was glad that no Shepherds were in the area. On the other hand, he didn't know if that was good or not. He sensed something amiss but couldn't put his finger on it.

After about three minutes, the captain started becoming impatient and asked the radio operator what was going on with the transmission. The operator reported so far, no response, even after numerous attempts.

"Keep trying," he ordered the man. "And try different frequencies that they might use."

As the communication attempts continued, the captain ordered a decrease in speed to just five knots. He had a gut feeling about something but didn't like it at all. He might have to make a move he didn't really want to make. *Chikusho! Damn it!*

He asked the first mate where the last position of the *Yakura* is known to be. The man checked and reported it to his boss. The captain then ordered him to plot a course for that position. Once he did and recommended it, the skipper ordered the ship to come to that course and heading and increase speed to twenty-five knots.

"Any word yet from the *Yakura*?" he asked the radioman.

"Negative, sir. Still no response."

There was no way of them knowing if that was where the harpoon ship was. Chances were low that it was still there, but they had to start from somewhere.

For now, the mission to catch whales was on hold. The captain of the Suzaki liked neither surprises nor mysteries. Out in the middle of a huge ocean, those kinds of challenges were never welcome.

Just as the engines were quickly revving up and the ship started picking up speed, something hit the port side of the ship close to the stern causing the ship's stern to jolt to starboard and tilting the ship precariously toward that side. It shocked the hell out of everyone and a few of the crew ended up on their backsides.

"What the hell was that?" yelled someone on the bridge.

The captain, thinking quickly, knew he couldn't waste time thinking about what it was. He needed to move more quickly now and ask questions later.

"Lookouts, get out there and find out what you can see. Helm, increase to twenty-eight knots. Steer to port, bearing 275. Now! Sonar, what have you got?"

The helmsman moved the controls. The whine of the engines, now increased to their maximum capabilities, grew louder. They couldn't go any faster. The skipper hoped it would be enough to get them away from here.

"Bridge, sonar. I have a large blip, our location. It does not show the echo returns of any whale. It is not identifiable."

The captain muttered an expletive under his breath. *What the hell could that be,* he thought. "Very well", he responded.

"Bridge, engine room." The skipper looked over at the intercom. *Now what?* Someone on the bridge answered the intercom.

"We can't sustain maximum speed for too long. It will put a big strain on the engines. We could lose one or both. And we just found a leak down here in one of the pipes."

The bridge crewman relayed that to the captain, who then went to the intercom.

"Engine room, this is the captain. What pipe and how big a leak?"

"Sir, it's one of the hydraulics pipes. It's um, well sir, it's to the rudder and it's relatively large.

"Can you fix it before we lose helm control?"

"I don't know, sir, but we will do our best."

"Make sure your best is successful or we will all be in big trouble. Our lives depend on you right now, son. Get on it.!"

The skipper switched his attention the helm.

"Maintain this speed for the next ten minutes. Wait for my order to decrease."

"Yes, captain" the helmsman replied.

The captain then pressed another button."Sonar, report."

At first there was no response. "Sonar, report!" he repeated at the intercom after waiting for what seemed like minutes.

"Sir, I uh I see the same huge target now right behind us. I still don't know what it is. Seems to be following us."

The skipper looked up for a minute. Following us?

"*Behind* us? Are you sure it's not a large whale?" He knew that some whales can be quite curious, especially orcas or humpbacks.

The sonarman below looked with cringing eyes at the huge blip, seeing the sound waves pulsing outward.

"No, sir. I don't think so. Appears too big to be a whale. Plus, it's not sending out any sonar of its own."

That sent a chill down the captain's spine. Not only was that not good news, it was ominous. He didn't like it and he didn't know what to do about it. In his twenty-four years in this career, he'd never experienced anything like this before.

Everyone on board knew that whales communicated by way of sounds it made. For a sonar target to not make any sounds would either have to be a submarine which had gone silent, or something not a whale or dolphin.

What the hell?"How long have you been eyeing it?" asked the captain.

"Just a few minutes. Plenty of time for it to make sounds. But there were none."

"A submarine?"

"No, sir. Definitely not a sub. The echoing sound does not indicate anything metal. Plus, its shape is irregular and fluctuates. Not consistent with anything man-made or any whale."

That told him they had a real problem. It was not manmade but something alive. But it was not any of the largest known living creatures in the sea: the whale. Yet it seemed to be larger than any of the above.

Suddenly they felt a thump on the ship's port stern. It was mild but enough for all on board to feel it.

"Kamashu, any response from the *Yakura* yet?" he intercomed the radioman.

"No, Captain. Nothing from them."

"Then get in touch with the *Koyibayashu.* Let me know when you get a hold of them. I want to speak to their captain." That was their other harpoon ship.

"Yes sir." He immediately turned a knob and spoke through the mike.

He looked out ahead through the bridge windows at the calm seas as another mild thump hit their back end. He was dumbfounded at what was happening in the water. Never in all his years of sailing and whaling had he ever encountered anything like this. He wasn't sure what to do about it. Before he radioed back to their home base in Japan, he needed to get as many facts as he could. If they needed a rescue in the upcoming hours, preparation ahead of time was imperative. In actuality, their chances of any rescue from home were slim to none. They were caught between a rock and a hard place, with both sides putting the squeeze on them tighter and tighter.

The Southern Ocean, somewhere west of the Suzaki

The *Yakura* was listing dangerously to the starboard side and starting to sink. Already the lower half was underwater. Two large holes had resulted from the continuous blows from outside of the ship banging relentlessly countless of times against the hull. Pipes had burst, and the engine was severely flooded. Oil and fuel leaked profusely from the broken tanks, darkening the surrounding water with their toxic mixtures. The captain did his best to maintain calm and order, but he might as well have tried to stop a tsunami with his bare hands.

The moment he realized there was no way to stop the ship from sinking, he ordered "abandon ship" several times. The order was echoed from the bridge all the way below to the engine room. Unfortunately, several hands there were killed by the rushing water and the boiling hot steam which burst from some of the pipes. It was filled with the chaotic noises of steam, rushing water, engine breakdowns, and death screams. There was nothing anyone can do for the doomed men.

A number of ship's crew members, both with and without lifejackets, jumped overboard. In the water a number of them were shocked at the sight of the ship's severe tilt to its starboard side and the bow starting to raise upward out of the water.

Inside, the radio operator had tried desperately to call for help but water from somewhere had gotten into the radio and it started sparking. Once he heard the abandon ship order and also saw the death of the radio, he jumped up and headed out to get off the ship. Other crew members were scrambling for their lives in a panic that was not unlike those unfortunates on the *Titanic*. One or two fell and got trampled.

Only a few minutes later was the once proud and hardworking *Yakura* looking straight up into the sky as it vertically sank into the depths of the abyss below. There was no one around to see the disturbing sight; for all those in the water had suddenly and instantly vanished below the waves, swallowed up by something unseen. Davey Jones would be deprived of welcoming these prospective guests.

10

Odessa, TX

Rita called Sam over in Oxford and as they finished their usual friendly small talk Rita brought up the subject of the tooth. She seemed to be obsessed about this particular artifact, more so than all the others that were under her studies. Usually ancient or prehistoric specimens are rarely complete or intact. It's not usual for something millions of years old to endure the ravages of time. Even if well stored and protected.

This one, however, didn't appear to show time's destructive influences. It was not just well preserved, from the pictures she saw, but was nearly completely patent. She felt she couldn't consider it *completely* intact until she saw it for herself, in person. Which is one reason she brought up the subject to her friend and colleague.

"So, what do you think? Any theories or conclusions right now?" Rita asked.

"Well, I have a theory which I have been working on," said Sam. "This is after I have comparing the specimen with hundreds of photos. I consulted with a professor friend of mine at UMISS who seemed to think it is plausible, although even he is not sure. But right now it's a good start. First of all, we think it's marine in nature."

"Really? Ok."

"And we believe it's reptilian."

"Interesting," replied Rita. "I was having a gut feeling about that. You base that on homodont dentition?"

"Yes. It seems to be the case."

"I have researched through all the various known marine sauruses from the late Cretaceous period and into early Jurassic. I first checked on toothmorphology of phytosaurs and amphicocoelias. Although there are a few similarities, this tooth appears to be larger than the largest of either of those two."

That's it. Rita knew she had to go there and see it for herself. The temptation was too great not to.

"Sam, listen I have another class in a few minutes here. I have none tomorrow. Then there's the weekend. Are you going to be there tomorrow?"

"Yea, I will be here. Have a couple classes tomorrow in the morning. My afternoon is free. Sure, come over."

By 'coming over', she meant Skype the visit. Both women chose that shorthand communications with their laptops.

"Will be glad to see you again anyway. Rather fascinating. Especially since the tooth, for an ancient fossil, is oddly in pristine condition. I never saw that before."

After they said their goodbyes, Rita gathered her things and headed out to the classroom. Her trip might take three or four hours, so she planned on leaving early tomorrow, sometime in the morning. She'd let her husband know later. Somehow she managed to keep her excitement for the trip in check as she headed down the hall. What she didn't know she couldn't have anticipated. For tomorrow, she would find out something that she might not be so excited about.

The Southern Ocean, the Suzaki, twenty-five miles southeast of the Yakura

Still running at twenty-eight knots, the skipper checked the engineers for their fuel situation. By leaving the hunting area, they were risking running low on that precious necessity. Luckily, they had been refueled by their area's fuel tanker two days previously, so they were still good at three

quarters full. They had felt no further bumping against their stern. Apparently outrunning whatever it was that kept hitting them, the skipper checked his sonar operator for any blips. The report came back with no large blips anymore. Just a few fish bogies. With that, he ordered the ship to decrease speed back to twenty knots. Even just by a seven-knot decrease, they could save a significant amount of fuel. Out here, there were no gas stations to refuel, so prudence was always the rule.

The radioman had the presence of mind and the intelligence to know he should keep trying to raise the Yakura. The sinking feeling in the pit of his stomach never left him as he continued to get no responses from their partnership. No news was not always good news and he believed this was one of those times.

When the captain asked him about it, he told him. Then he was commanded to contact the Koyibayashu and, after giving him the latitude and longitude of their current position and their course, the Suzaki radio operator passed on the command for them to proceed post haste to follow the mother ship. They couldn't have one ship hanging around where the mother ship wasn't.

Although things seemed to become overwhelming, the captain of the Suzaki didn't forget to check with engineering to see if there had been any damage from the earlier bumping. The answer was no, which was always a good thing when it involved any possible damage control.

As they got closer to the Yakura's last known position, the first mate ordered a couple of the deckhands to be on the lookout for sighting of the harpoon ship. They were still twenty miles out, so binoculars were needed. At the same time, a couple of the bridge hands peered through binocs as well, expecting to soon see some dot or large on the horizon.

According to what the Suzaki knew to be the Yakura's last known position, they should be heading straight for it. However, despite their correct course heading, there were never any guarantees out here. Anything could happen which could throw a ship off its desired position or course.

A couple of reports came in that there were no sightings of anything. Time seemed to stand still for the crew, especially the skipper. He felt the tension rise in him as he hoped nothing had happened to their primary harpoon ship and its crew.

There had been no distress call so at this point it was a little too soon to conclude anything. They could still be ok and out there, which was all the more reason to keep a constant, close lookout for them.

Another hour went by with no reports. Then suddenly, a crewman from the outside aft deck shouted he spotted something. It looked like a blinking light which was possibly in the water itself, but he wasn't sure. Slowly scanning the horizon, the bridge crew saw something at their one o'clock position and approximately ten to twelve miles away. There was no sign of anything else.

The light was seen sporadically blinking, possibly due to the distance and the rolling waves. When the ship's navigator heard the report, he informed the captain that where it was coming from seemed to be from the area of the Yakura. Seeing a beacon light blinking in the water could mean only one thing. They had to get there fast.

"Increase speed to twenty-five knots."

"Twenty-five knots, aye captain," repeated the helmsman as he shifted the indicator to his right to signal the engine room. Soon the engines whined a bit louder and the ship picked up speed.

As they closed in on the target area, they saw no sign of the Yakura. There it was, the beacon light, floating in the water. It was from the air-filled lifeboat that had likely opened up, automatically setting it off. No one was in it.

From the bridge, the captain looked around in shock at those things plus the large oil slick that was more than half the size of his ship. All hands on board were looking down at the water, on the starboard side. Because the seas were relatively calm, there was no reason to think that it had capsized

from bad weather or rough seas. Even so, weather and seas out here could be quite unpredictable and could change very quickly. The questions likely everyone was thinking would include: did the Yakura sink and if so, was it from bad seas or a fatalistic malfunction or fire on board? There was no way to tell for sure.

But one think was clear: after whatever happened to it, the whalers had lost the Yakura and its crew. All radio comms to the ship were now fruitless. The captain picked up the radio mike on the bridge, turned a knob and radioed to the Koyibayashu regarding their present position and advised them to rendezvous with them there.

ETA for the harpoon ship would be in three hours. After their acknowledging response, the Suzaki maintained its patrol around the tight area with a decreased speed of seven knots until the other ship arrived. Once they did, the two captains would confide with each other and the mother ship's captain-the one in charge of their mission-would decide on what to do next.

He then had his radio operator contact their home port back in Sukura, Japan. Although he was very much concerned about the fate of his harpoon ship, he was wise enough to know that with the evidence in the water, the absence of the ship here, the complete lack of communications, and no sighting of the vessel anywhere on the horizon for 360 degrees relative, it was pointless to search for them. Where would he have his ship go? Which direction? That was impossible to determine. And they did not have an infinite amount of fuel. It seems the ship had gone down.

He picked up the Mike again and called for the fuel tanker, which patrolled the area between where the Suzaki had been and the other harpoon ship. Static was his response. That was pretty much common out here. As with most other vessels in the open seas, one sometimes had to wait a few seconds for a response on the radio. For the most part, ship to ship radio communications was pretty reliable.

After a few seconds with no response, the captain once again called the tanker. Waited for a few seconds with the static. Still no response. He called for a third time, then a fourth. There was no response. Maybe they were too far away for the ship to hear them. So he called the Koyibayashu and requested their position.

Once they reported it, the skipper of the *Suzak*i knew that the harpoon ship should still be close enough for radio comms to the tanker, according to where they were supposed to be. He requested them to try to make contact with them and tell them to standby for a relay message from the Suzaki. It looked like the Koyibayashu would have to be the go-between.

While the captain waited for the harpoon ship to make contact and get back to him, he walked outside onto one of the bridge wings and looked down at the water and around up to the horizon. Empty featureless sea for hundreds and even thousands of miles.

To their northeast, about two thousand miles away was the tip of South America. To their northwest, about five thousand miles away was mainland Australia. Japan was about nine thousand miles away. If something happened to them out here, there was no quick rescue, except from other ships that might or might not be in the area.

He'd always loved the sea ever since he was a kid. Samuru Namayto was a sailor at heart. After spending a few years in the Japanese Navy, he decided he enjoyed staying out at sea as a career without being in the military. So after six years, he discharged from the navy and entered the career of commercial fishing, starting at the bottom at what Americans called a "greenhorn," but which the Japanese referred to as a "*gurinhon*".

After several years working his way up through the ranks, he finally earned his way to taking the written and practical tests to become a Master or captain of his own ship. His experience, love of seamanship, and excellent working skills as well as his high scores got him the license. Captain Namayto turned out to be one of the best captains in the country's whaling fleet. Although he was quite strict and mostly by the book in his sailing leadership and fleet protocol, he wasn't so rigid that he couldn't bend a minor rule now and then when there was no better option. He ruled rigidly yet cared enough for his crew members to always place their safety above money. In the simplest terms, he was a good captain to work for, as long as you stuck to the necessary protocol and safety rules.

Reentering the bridge, Namayto asked his first mate, "Anything from the *Koyibayashu* yet?"

"No sir," he replied. It had been at least several minutes, perhaps longer. The captain hadn't monitored the time as he was deep in thought outside. He picked up the mike and called the harpoon ship. Their response was surprising to Namayto. They were, so far, unable to make contact with the tanker. In addition, when they checked their radar, they saw no blips within its 20-mile range. That meant that the tanker was outside its radar range. It didn't necessarily mean they disappeared. But at the same time, the radio range would be significantly farther than twenty miles.

"Keep trying, at least for another twenty minutes," he told them. "We have to get a hold of them. Let me know after that if you've made contact or not."

"Ei, Kyaputen."

"Kuso yaro," he mumbled to himself. *Son of a bitch.* This mission was already turning out to be a nightmare and it seemed to be getting worse. Not only had they *not* caught any whales, now they were missing a ship, perhaps lost it permanently. And worse, there was a possibility of another missing ship. Their fuel tanker of all things. The one they needed the most. He waited anxiously and with a lot of internal tension. If he was anything at all, he was not one to advertise his overwhelming concerns. Perhaps it was not always good to keep everything internalized. But like his father, he needed to be outwardly strong not only for his crew, but for himself as well. And so he waited with great outward patience.

Despite his inner tension, he didn't fully realize that everyone on the bridge was also feeling it.

Research vessel Arga, southwest Antarctica

The ship starting sailing around the south westernmost point of the continent. Its destination point was closer to the northwestern point, so it still had some way to go yet. Perhaps another sixteen to twenty-four hours. After Paul Gibson confirmed the course and speed of the vessel, he handed the bridge over to his first mate Wilson so he could go below and check on things. It was something he didn't really need to do. He did it to give himself a bit of a break from the bridge and to keep his mind alert to at least some of the ship activities hidden from the bridge.

Although the skies had clouded over, their weather people did not forecast any inclement weather. The seas had three to four-foot waves, so there was some pitching and rolling. Otherwise it was pretty uneventful so far. Just the way he liked it.

On the way to the mess deck where he would grab a coffee, he stopped in to the science lab.

"How's it going so far folks?" he asked Beth Ann and George. They had been looking at some equipment and screens.

"Hey, there," said George. "Our illustrious skipper. Ok, cap. Doing some calibrating and underwater evals. Funny thing. We haven't seen any fish. Didn't even detect any krill at all. Usually there's millions around here. But we've seen none."

"That's odd, isn't it?"

"Yea. Although not enough to be alarmed, at least not yet. Never seen this before though. And the sonar screen has echoed back no blips. No dolphins or whales of any kind. It's like everything has disappeared."

Gibson wasn't a scientist but even he knew that for this area this was a little off kilter. He rubbed his chin. "So what do you think this could be from? Any ideas? "

"Nada. It's frustrating but we're working on it. Trying to come up with some theories. Maybe a current or other underwater passing anomaly that we haven't seen yet. Right Beth?"

She was finishing up recording something down in her logbook. "Yep. Probably that, although not conclusive yet. Too soon to tell. We have the sonar volume up a bit and the alarm set so if a significant blip appears it will let us know right away."

She closed her logbook. “If we can at least detect a penguin or even a leopard seal, that will be great because then we can rest assured that life still exists around here. But since we left base, there’s been nothing in the water.”

Not knowing what to say, concerned himself, he decided to continue on toward the galley.

“Ok, I’ll leave you two to solve the mystery. Gotta get some coffee. But please keep me posted. I’d like to know if you find something.”

“Sure thing, See ya later.”

After he was gone, the two fervently continued their search, rather than research. The tenseness of their facial expressions was a result of their belief that something was up down here in these waters, but they weren’t sure what. What they *were* sure of was that something wasn’t right, and things weren’t normal. No fish, no whales, not even the ever-present leopard seals which patrolled around the continent to feed on penguins, as well as fish.

Even with no fish around, these species of seals still had their penguins which had to go in the water to feed themselves and their offspring. But even the penguins weren’t going in. That in itself was not just strange: it was downright bizarre. That, with no fish, could plausibly explain the absence of the seals. *Could*, but they didn’t believe *did.*

Beth Ann checked the sonar. Still nothing.

“George, can do you me a favor?”

“Sure.”

“Keep an eye here for me. I’m going to talk with Tom for a minute. Need to find out something. Then I’m going to see if I can contact any other ships that might be in the area a hundred or so miles north and northwest in the meantime.”

“Ok. I’ll see if I can come up with any ideas or brilliant revelations.”

She went to find out from Tom about the fish in this area.

Topside, she found him in his office and presented him with her questions.

“Well you have the *toothfish*, the *silverfish*, and the *bald notothen*, to name a few,” he told her. They can be found around here; or they can be found anywhere in the Southern Ocean. They don’t have to stick around *here.* They migrate but generally don’t swim outside of this ocean. They are strictly cold-water fish only.”

“But isn’t it unusual for every species of all these area fish to be absent from here at the same time? I’m talking about not one of any of these swimming in this area. Is that naturally possible?” Beth asked

Tom gave him a slightly concerned look, briefly looked away and rubbed his face. Clearing his throat, he sensed something from the question.

"No, can't say I've never heard that before. There is always at least one or a few of the species present in the area. It's just a normal part of the ecology here. Are you telling me you haven't spotted *any* fish in the water?"

George nodded. "I'm afraid, my friend, that's what we are telling you. Not one. Not even a small one. Ever since we left port. I was going to say that maybe they all got tired of the cold and decided to pack up and move to Florida. But I won't say it."

That had Tom stumped, and he immediately went into action.

"Ok, listen, let me do some investigating on this. Might take me a while but I will get back to you when I find out something. Meanwhile, do what you can for whatever you guys can find out and keep me posted as well. We have to get to the bottom of this."

Beth nodded. "You got it." She turned and headed back below to check the sonar for signs of anything. She first wanted to get on their radio and call out to any ships she hoped might be around. Finding out if anyone else had seen any signs of whales, fish or other marine life around would be invaluable and would either squash any suspicions they currently had of something amiss that was very unnatural; or it would only strengthen their fears that the unnatural was happening-whatever that was.

Patiently, she waited for a response. Sometimes it took a few seconds up to almost a minute to get one, if someone was around. After a full minute and just static, she tried again as she checked the frequency to make sure it was the right one for ship to ship communications. It was.

Despite getting no responses so far, she kept trying for another five minutes. The likelihood of another ship being around, whether a tourist cruise ship or another, wasn't very high. So she wasn't surprised that no answers came her way.

"Shit".

The fact that there were no krill around certainly could explain the absence of whales because many species of whales ate the tiny creatures, which was their primary and only diet. Question is, why the absence of these creatures? They normally surrounded the entire Antarctic continent. Yet none were seen ever since they left.

Sure, they were found all over the planet and there were different species of them. For the most part, Antarctic krill usually stayed around this ice mass where they could hide around in avoiding predators; but they also fed on the algae which dotted areas of the underwater pack ice.

Meanwhile, Tom had called a couple of the other ice stations on the satellite phone they had. What he was told validated their own observations and seemed to only intensify the mystery which affected all their research.

The only stations he did not call were the two that were more inland and rarely had their crews venture to the coast.

With a third team member in this group of scientific mystery sleuths, perhaps they could better and more quickly figure out the solution to this.

But what they would find out soon enough would catch them all off guard and not only shock and terrify them but would leave them with more questions than answers. In the meantime, …

11

Oxford, Mississippi

The two women sat at either end of the lab counter with their laptops. Sam was on hers with Rita on the other end sipping her coffee. After exchanging some small talk pleasantries, the two discussed the subjects at hand. They exchanged their findings, thoughts, and ideas.

On one of the counters, there was Sam's research log and a number of pictures next to it. Sam picked up a couple of them and showed Rita what she had been studying. After Rita looked at the pictures, Sam went to her desk, unlocked a drawer with a key, and took something out.

Bringing it to her laptop, she was excited at showing it to her friend. "Here's what you've wanted to see, girlfriend. My prize possession."

Rita looked at it in wonder with a "wow" expression. "Oh my goodness. That is huge! If I weren't a scientist, I would have guessed from a T-rex or maybe a carnosaur."

It seemed larger in life than what any picture can depict. She held it in her hands. In length, it was about one and a half times the size of each of her hands. Only a hippo or elephant tusk would be larger, and it was smooth as porcelain. She estimated its weight to be about a half a pound.

"I see you smoothed it down a bit," observed Rita.

"Surprisingly, not very much. Just a little but not enough to change its normal appearance. Done very gently and cleaned with as much care. I keep this baby locked up. When I leave for the day, I put it into a safe only I have the combination to."

Rita looked at her in surprise. "Really? You that afraid of someone stealing it?"

Sam leaned over the counter. "Honey, you never know these days. For all I know, this may be one of a kind. Keeping it hush hush for now until I decide to advertise my conclusion."

"Are you saying that…?"

Sam nodded. "Yes, I am saying that I have come to a scientific conclusion about the origin of this tooth."

Rita stared at it then picked it up, turning it to examine every fine detail of it. She believed it was from a large predator, but not terrestrial. Her belief led her to the conclusion that not only was this NOT from a T-rex, but it was from something much larger. At least two to three times larger. Size-wise a brontosaurus or brachiosaurus would have fit the bill but were definitely out of the question. Those were herbivores and terrestrial. Even back then, they had no need for canine teeth. This was definitely carnivorous and marine.

There were maybe one or two carnivorous land reptiles back then that were a little larger than the T-rex. But she knew of none that would have been this size. So that left only one conclusion.

"So you think this is marine?"

Sam nodded. "I do. I also believe, although I can't be sure, that this tooth is not from an adult."

Rita looked at her with slightly widened eyes, then back down at it. She was trying to form her own conclusion in her mind. But it wasn't easy because there was nothing to compare it with other than pictures and it just may be the only one in existence.

Before she asked the really big question, she wanted to find out one thing more. "So, um, Sam, what makes you think this is from a juvenile or younger?"

"C'mere. Look at this," she told Rita.

Sam went over with her laptop to show what she had on her screen.

What Rita saw were various teeth artifacts from large prehistoric marine creatures. Bringing one of the creatures more into focus and making it larger on the screen, Sam zoomed in on the head and then the jaws of one particular creature. It had a long slender snout with multiple large teeth that made a crocodile look like it was toothless. Sam had moved the cursor too quickly for Rita to read the name.

But she knew. "You think the tooth is from this, the Mosasaur?"

"Yep. I believe most definitely that it is. And calculating the ratio of the tooth size on the picture with the size of the body and making further calculations, the results showed that the adult teeth are just a bit larger than this one. I've concluded that this is from a subadult."

Rita was awestruck. "So, this is what I've been wondering about all along. I suspected marine and got to believe it but didn't have enough time to determine the origin. Good heavens, Sam, you've got quite a find here."

"Yea, I do. Although not one that would make any professionals like you and me fall off their seats. A tooth yes, and not too common a one either. However, it has resolved our wonder and when the time comes, I will announce it. For now, I want to study it more, as much as I can before I lose the time to do it. But I'm glad I got to show it to you. I know you'll keep this under wraps for now, right?"

Rita nodded. "Oh, absolutely. I would do the same until the time was right."

Sam smiled and looked at her watch. It was about 3:45 pm

"Listen, I gotta go but let's keep in touch," Samantha suggested.

"Sounds like a plan. Talk to ya soon again. Bye." She signed off with a wave.

Picking up her cell phone, Rita dialed John's knowing that he wasn't on call tonight with the hospital. Luckily, he picked up and after relaying to him her plans for takeout, he said great. Pizza it was decided, and the kids would love it. He'd see her when she returned and was adamant about her trip back being a safe one.

After Sam wrapped up the tooth well in the lab and placed it into the safe, she put a few things away and then was out the door. Tomorrow she would think about it and then move forward with other projects and her classes.

Gulf of Mexico, ten miles off the coast of Louisiana

The oil rig platform, Gulf King, was about a hundred feet above the surface of the water. It had been there for about ten years. For hundreds of workers, this was their livelihood, albeit a dangerous one. But the money was excellent.

Its main drawback was that it was dangerous, subject to the weather, sea conditions, mechanical issues, and full of flammable material. It was certainly not a job for everyone and not for just anyone either.

For one thing, they had to spend two weeks on the rig 24/7. So, they were away from their families for that time. After that, they would alternate with a land rig crew for the same amount of time. That's when they could go home every day after their shift. So naturally they looked forward to that land job despite the money being less.

The ultimate danger on it was, as on board any ship or boat, a fire. But it was even more so on an oil rig for obvious reasons.

Whoever worked on it had to be tough and strong, as well as willing to get dirty and work hard. They had to have certain necessary firefighting skills because it was a well-known fact that their lives were on the line every minute they were on board. They had to be able to think fast and know where all the emergency equipment was on each of the different levels, especially the living quarters. And they all had to respond quickly. The latter being mostly common sense.

With the shift foreman going around checking on things and barking an order on occasion, things were pretty the norm and going smoothly. It's when things didn't go smoothly that sometimes you had to worry. Even the smallest glitch, mechanical or otherwise, could quickly develop into something major and potentially catastrophic.

Bud, the motorman, was checking all the gauges and equipment to spot any faults or malfunctioning on any of the platform's machinery. So far, he found nothing significant. Only one of the oil feeding gauges was a little off. He had just checked the elevator, a hinged mechanism that closes around the drill pipe. It appeared in good working order.

Everything that he'd checked seemed to be fine and he documented his findings on a special board he carried around. Every week he did this check during drill operation. If he spotted something, he'd make note of it and notify the rig supervisor who assign the rig's floor hand to take care of the problem. It was the floor hand who was responsible for overall maintenance of the rig.

As the men worked and the drill worked its way through the seabed floor toward what was believed the oil source, the toolpusher came out to check on the overall operation.

"Hey Jack!" he yelled over to his driller. "How's that plug-hitch doing?"

The man called Jack; the shift commander of the rig, gave his boss a thumbs up. "Working ok," he yelled back. On the platform, it wasn't easy to hear talking when the drill was running. Jack continued to walk around checking on things and the pipe turning within the hole. Every so often the pipe would stop, a drill mechanism would lift up, and another length of pipe would be attached. The pipe would very slowly and gradually descend, which meant the drill bit down within the seabed would be going a little deeper.

It was a little after four pm, not too long after the second shift started, that the minor shaking reverberated through the outside frames of the rig. Most of the workers were on the center of the platform itself and hadn't felt it. Work continued as usual.

One of the men was turning some kind of pipe with a large pipe wrench, likely trying to tighten it. Another man was pouring some kind of tar-looing liquid into a huge container. On the derrick, the derrickman was finishing tightening a bolt toward the top, to ensure the stability of the structure. He was the worker to made sure of its stability and ability to stay up as the drill was working its way ever so slowly downward.

As he got ready to descend, something beneath seemed to hit the rig with unbelievable incredible force. The entire platform shook this time. The man turning the pipe with the wrench was violently forced forward, hitting his helmeted head on the pipe. But for the helmet, he would have been far more injured. As it was, he was knocked out.

The derrickman wasn't so lucky. He fell off the derrick and plunged thirty feet down to the deck, breaking his neck. The platform was forced to a thirty-degree lean before it righted itself back.

Then the platform got hit again, this time with greater force. Things started becoming loose and falling to the deck where they slid to the leaning side. Some of the workers grabbed onto whatever they could.

Up in the office, the toolpusher grabbed the two-way radio and called for help, using the Mayday call sign. The rig had never used that before. After he yelled his call for help several times and received unintelligible static in response, he put the mike down and quickly looked out the window before running outside to the outside porch deck. He didn't like what he saw.

"Tom" he yelled to his driller. "Shut 'er down. Shut 'er down now!"

He didn't know if the driller heard him but then he saw him run toward the controls. He looked to his left and was shocked to see a man's body sprawled on the deck. The driller?

"There's a man down over there. Get him inside somebody."

The toolpusher started running down the stairs to see what he could do to help. After he and another man checked the fallen man and discovered it was Joe the derrickman, the toolpusher yelled, "Aw, son of a bitch. I think he's dead! They checked his pulse and found none. After seeing the strange angle of his neck and saw he wasn't breathing, the toolpusher realized the man was beyond help.

Bam! Another hit, even harder this time. "What the hell is that?" some men yelled out at the same time.

Answering no one in particular, the toolpusher yelled he had called for help and prayed somebody heard him. Then he smelled something foul, like burning rubber. The other workers noticed the smell too.

Before addressing that problem, the toolpusher needed to take care of this immediately.

"Let's get him inside somewhere now before we get hit again."

After getting him inside to the nearest cover, they noticed the foul smell getting stronger.

The smell was soon followed by the sight of smoke appearing at one of the rig's ends. It was black and gray smoke, which sent the fear of God in every worker, including the toolpusher.

"Fire!" yelled one of the workers. Immediately they rushed to the nearest firefighting equipment and supplies and started to break it out as quickly as they could. The toolpusher took command of the situation immediately. Joe would have to wait until they got this fire under control first. They would have to focus on the now.

12

Western Antarctica, the Arga

As the ship gradually made its way along the coast, the tension and complete absence of normality in and above the water was palpable. While those outside on deck were visually making their observations, those below on the sonar saw nothing on the screen. Usually there would be small pings and blips of fish and sometimes a larger blip of the sonar sounds bouncing off the objects and returning quickly to the sonar receptors.

But now the sonar screen was just as eerily devoid of anything as the visual observations outside. Was it an omen of something terrible about to happen? Or was it happening already? Or, was it an omen at all? At this point, there was nothing but questions without answers.

Paul stood on the bridge and looked out over the water with his binoculars. Off in the far distance to starboard was the Antarctica ice shelf. He chose to keep at least ten miles between them and the shelf to avoid any possible groundings with shallows. If they got too close, they could run aground on a shallow ice floor. It was easy to avoid that.

The fact that there were no birds meant there were no fish, at least not near the surface.

He went to the intercom and called down to sonar.

"Sonar, bridge."

Moments later. "Bridge, sonar."

"Is there anything yet that you see on there?"

"No, Paul, there isn't. This is really strange. I've never seen nothing for so long."

"Same up here. The second you see something, let me know, will ya?"

"Roger that."

There was not much else he could do. "John, what's our ETA to the site?" he asked the navigator.

John looked down at the chart. "Based on our speed, in three hours we should be there."

"Ok," acknowledged Paul.

***

Below deck, Beth was on her laptop, trying to figure out some things that had her puzzled. In fact, there were quite a few things now that had everyone puzzled. It seemed to be all part of a "game" called *"What's Going On?"* No one knew anything. At least not yet. She was determined to try and find out something.

She knew that George and Tom were doing whatever they could to try and find out something. They knew that there was an absence of a normal ecology system here now. A complete absence. It was if there had been an apocalypse and all life, except humans, had been wiped out.

But she also knew that wasn't quite true. Maybe for this area for right now. But was it happening elsewhere? And was it permanent?

Over in his office, Tom checked with sonar for any signs of fish. He got the same reply from them as Paul had.

"Shit! That's what I thought," he mumbled out loud to himself. Then he got an idea. "Brilliant, why didn't I think of this before?" Getting up quickly, he left his office and headed to where he needed to go. He hoped his idea would work. But he'd find out soon enough.

Southern Ocean, north, the Suzaki

The captain was now genuinely concerned because he hadn't heard back from the *Koyibayashu.* In fact, Captain Namayto hadn't heard from the *Yakura* either. What the hell was happening here? He decided to contact any ships in the area and see if they could help in some way. Perhaps his radio signals weren't reaching either of his other ship's but maybe the helper ship's might. He ordered his radioman to send out a call for radio help.

While his operator was doing that, he decided to go down to his cabin for a while. It was time to do some thinking about this and this was the quiet time he needed to take advantage of that. Telling his first mate that he had the bridge and to contact him if anything was reported by the radio operator.

In his cabin, Namayto fully realized his whaling season was finished for this year. There were no whales caught and he'd have some explaining to do to the powers that be. Although he wasn't in charge of the two harpoon ships or the tanker, he'd been in the same ocean with them when they all seemed to disappear. They will figure he must know *something.* How could he not?

But the ocean is an incredibly huge area which can easily hide even the largest ship. He knew it wasn't so far-fetched for a ship or two to get lost on an ocean. The question was, were his ships truly lost? If so, why weren't they answering? Maybe one ship could have their communications systems down. But two? Or three? This was nuts!

Suddenly a voice from his intercom broke the silence and his thought. "Captain, bridge."

He answered quickly. His radioman had received a reply from a tanker ship about thirty miles northeast of the Suzaki. Telling his radioman to have them standby, he wanted to talk to that ship himself to prevent any misunderstandings. His door wasn't fully closed by the time he exited the cabin.

The tanker was a Norwegian headed to South America. Namayto asked if they would try to contact the Koyibayashu and Yakura to see if they could get through because he couldn't. They agreed and asked him to standby for a few minutes. They needed to give it enough time for at least several tries.

After fifteen minutes, Namayto was practically biting his nails off. He did his best to hide his anxiety and if one saw him without really knowing him, he looked and seemed as cool as a cucumber.

Several minutes later, the Norwegian came back, but the news wasn't good. The ship had tried several times to contact each of the harpoon ships but received no response from either. Namato thanked them and turned back to the front of the bridge. Now what?

"Navigator, do you recall the approximate positions of the Yakura and Koyibayashu when we last heard from them and which was closer to our position at the time?"

Hito nodded. "That would be the Yakura, sir. They were about thirty-five miles from us, 045 relative."

Namayto nodded his acknowledgement. He turned to his first mate. "Toshu, find out from the engine room how much fuel we have. Hito, plot a course for that last known position of the Yakura. Helmsman, standby for orders to change course."

A couple of minutes later, the first mate informed the captain that their fuel tanks were three quarters full. Great!

"Very well. Hito, what have you come up with?"

Hito told the captain of the course plot at a suggested speed of twenty knots. That would get them there in about two to two and a half hours. Namayto then ordered the course change at the suggested speed and they were soon on their way. But to what?

Southern Ocean, the Arga

Tom went to where they kept what he called "junk fish". They were not for consumption but rather used as part of their research for baiting certain types of fish for them to study. It wasn't bait for catching fish for dinner. Nevertheless, he figured it might work. After all, even fish have to eat.

After putting some in a bucket, he went topside and threw some overboard. Watching carefully, he searched the cold waters for signs of anything that could attract a predator. Even an Orca would be a welcome sight to all this seemingly lifeless ocean. Or a leopard seal.

Some of the bait floated while other pieces sank down into the dark depths. There were no signs of anything coming for them.

Tom was patient, though. If any fish or seal was any distance away, he had to give them time to get here. Whatever came would be able to smell the bait and be lured right to here. He hoped. That's the way it usually worked.

Desperate times called for desperate measures and this was appearing to be one of them. Nothing came for the bait. After about thirty minutes, he realized that there really was nothing living in these waters. He felt knots in his stomach. The situation here seemed to be a terrible harbinger of what may yet come. He didn't know what that was but decided to pass this confirmation of no life here to his colleagues.

13

Gulf King Oil rig, Gulf of Mexico

There was nothing worse on any ship, boat, or oil rig platform than a fire. A fire on any of those would be far worse than any on land because there was nowhere for anyone to run, except jump in the water: provided your escape route to that water wasn't blocked by the fire.

Here the fire was spreading rapidly. Workers grabbed whatever fire extinguishers they could and water hoses to try to control and contain the flames. The smoke was getting thicker and blacker. The air was becoming more toxic. Soon it became necessary to don masks. Unfortunately, not all the workers in this situation had easy access to them. As a result, a few of the workers collapsed and began to succumb to the toxic fumes and smoke inhalation.

Another bang against the structure tilted it dangerously in the other direction. Deep below the surface, the part of the legs which were buried in the seabed began to falter and bend. As something continued to bang against them, the platform leaned further and further toward the water.

On the platform, the toolpusher was nowhere to be seen. Men desperately tried to help other fallen men and the slamming continued. Fires now raged throughout the entire platform. Men began to jump into the water. As the structure began to collapse, the last of the men took their final journey. The open pitch-black maw was ready for them as they each jumped off the 100-foot high platform, never to be seen again. They couldn't have seen the nearly foot-long teeth they passed as they were swallowed. Soon, the Gulf King was no more. What was once a prolifically productive worksite was now no more than a huge black oil slick and thousands of pieces of debris.

The noises of the bending and collapsing metal structure were those of a power structure that once provided careers and the necessity of something the world needed. As one leg sunk into the sea, it was quickly followed by another. When the last two legs collapsed, both upper and lower platforms were soon swallowed by the sea. There was nothing left but oil and debris-the only remnants of what once was.

Aboard the US Coast Guard helicopter

"Coast Guard Air Station Five, this is Airbird One."

"Airbird One, Air Station Five. Go."

"Uh, Air Station Five, Airbird One. We have arrived at the coordinates given to us for the platform Gulf King. There is no sign of the rig. We do see a huge black oil slick and what appears to be thousands of debris pieces floating around. We are checking coordinates now and will check sea grid in surrounding seas. No signs of survivors in the water so far."

"Airbird One, we copy that. Ok, continue for sea grid check. We will contact the parent company. There is a 378 on the way there within the next hour from base New Orleans."

"Roger, Station five. Airbird out."

The 378 was one of a number of cutters that were that size in feet and is one of the second largest ships the Coast Guard has. They each have a helipad just above their aft deck and could accommodate a full -size chopper. Although a ship this size was not necessary for this operation, it was the closest vessel to the site at the moment.

While the chopper was checking the surrounding area in an ever-expanding search, Coast Guard staff at the air station sent out an alert to the cutter for this S&A mission. Within the hour they would be underway.

In the meantime, word spread quickly, especially in the media.

On television, special report broadcasts in the gulf states were breaking into scheduled programs to report the incident of the vanished oil platform. So far no one knew what caused its collapse but there were plenty of armchair psychics who came out with their versions of the event.

While some believed it was sabotage and terrorism, others thought the same except it to be an inside job. Still others thought a fire by itself brought it down, along with an explosion it caused. The only problem with that last one was that an explosion would have been heard and seen.

While word was out about the rig collapse, scientists in various parts of the world were getting the word about the ecological anomaly down near Antarctica. Their concern was evident when they started making calls to other scientist groups and organizations. Some were in the process of calling the Tellmore Research Station, especially those in Great Britain.

Someone unknown had leaked this information to the press, despite everyone being told this was to be kept under wraps until the reported data was confirmed. They were not happy campers when they found out about the leak and the way they found out: by television of course.

Regarding the Japanese, they were doing well so far in keeping the missing ships a secret from the rest of the world. Captain Namota didn't want to start a panicky stampede of reporters bugging the hell out of him if he reported it to his government. He had enough to worry about as it was. So he decided to keep it under wraps as well. At least for now. He needed to find out more.,

There was no evidence that the two harpoon ships had also gone down after the *Sakuru.* But he did suspect, or rather *knew,* the ship had sunk. Why, remained a mystery. When two or more vanished under similar circumstances and with no apparent reason, that was no coincidence. There were no Sea Shepherds down here now and he knew, despite their past confrontations, that they would never have done anything to cause a sinking. Not intentionally anyway. He wondered about something else, which sent chills down his spine.

From whatever had caused first one sinking, then another, would *his* ship be next? He had to consider the possibility.

Oxford, Mississippi

"Sam, did you hear the latest word?" asked Susan the second she came barreling through the lab door.

Sam jumped, startled as all get up.

"Sue, what the hell? You scared the shit out of me!" Her hands were suddenly on her chest as if she was trying to feel her faster-beating heart.

"You're not going to believe this," continued her friend, still keeping her in suspense.

Sam looked at her, not having seen her this uppity up in who knows how long. "What, we at war with somebody?"

Sue ignored that remark and proceeded to tell her friend with the faster beating heartbeat about what was happening in Antarctica and then the mysterious disappearance of the oil rig in the Gulf.

"Do they know what caused these things?"

"So far, no. The vanishing of the oil rig could have a rational explanation once it's determined. But there seems to be no explanation, so far, for the disappearance of all the sea life down in Antarctica. Not even krill were found. No leopard seals, no whales, nothing."

"How long has that been going on?"

Sue shrugged. "Not sure. But they think at least a couple of weeks now."

The two women were silent for a few moments. Sam was thinking. Then Sue interrupted that silence.

"No bodies were found around where the rig disappeared. Shouldn't there have been some at least?"

"I supposed, although bodies can sink."

"But they don't stay sunk. They have to come up because of the decomp gases, right?"

"Yea, that's true," Sam agreed. "Unless they were eaten by something down there. Sharks maybe."

Sue was the one thinking now. "Problem is, there is nothing to show they were even there. No pieces of flesh or even blood. Sharks aren't that clean of eaters, are they? And there were no items of clothing found. Not one shred of anything! Don't you find that strange?"

Sam looked at her and did think that strange. She didn't know enough to come up with any plausible theory. But one thing was for sure. It had to be checked out. But who would she go to and what would be checked for? Although she liked a good mystery now and then, this was one she wasn't very happy about.

She started digging into the science realms of her computer. She had a special program installed for deeper research into specifics of her specialty. Using that she began her investigation.

Gulf of Mexico

The fishing yacht, *Sea Angel,* had been out on the water for several hours, with its five paying clients fishing for whatever they could catch, hopefully bluefish. They were not real fishing veterans or professionals in any way. Rather, they were a bunch of combination businessmen and blue-collar workers who decided one day to get together and enjoy a day out in the Gulf to see what they could catch.

"Hey Harry, great to get away from the old lady for a day, eh buddy?" said a chump named Louis who believed getting away from home was a paradisiacal thing. Divorced twice, he had enough of the home with the old lady crap and considered that the single life again was the best thing that ever happened to him. He turned back to his line when he thought he felt a tug. But it was so slight that it had to be due to the movement of the waves and water.

"Aw, don't know 'bout that, Lou. You're probably right. To a certain extent. But don't tell Marge I said that."

Harry Simpson loved his wife dearly and vice versa. But sometimes she could be a pain in the petunia with her tunnel vision beliefs of some things. And a day away for reasons like today was not always a bad thing, he had to admit.

As the two men fished and drank their beers, some of the others were relaxing, talking, and also drinking. The yacht skipper, Tony, stayed at the helm keeping a watch on it, although he would have none of the drinking. He was responsible for his clients, his boat, and himself. He didn't believe in drinking and driving. Lucky for all of them.

Although the boat wasn't noticeably big, it was large enough to be called a yacht but not enough to be considered one of luxury. With all of twenty-eight feet, for him it was big enough.

When he first bought it five years earlier, he hadn't figured on turning it into one for fishing excursions. He was going to use it for him and his now ex-wife for short trips and mini vacations to anywhere. After the divorce, he decided to use the boat for something financially more self-beneficial. So far it worked out very well.

Suddenly Louis felt a strong tug on his line. "Hey, looks like I got something here!" he yelled.

The line became taut and the pole started bending down. "Holy crap, something big is on the end here."

The line started bending down even sharper and Louis started getting up.

"No no no!," yelled Harry. "Don't get up, man. You'll be pulled overboard. Sit down and anchor your feet against the backboard."

Louis tried to hold the line and pole, but the line was now bending over, and the pole was almost bent over itself. Harry let go of his line and went to hold on to the other man to keep him from going over the side. The pole was now being pulled forward as both men struggled to keep the pole on the boat.

One of the other men came over to try and give them a hand but there wasn't much room for him to give help. He could only hold onto Harry. If the situation wasn't so serious, it would almost look funny.

The yacht captain suddenly yelled out. "Hey guys, you want me to pull forward? Maybe it'll help you get that son-of-a-bitch on board!"

The man on the rear yelled no. "No, Tony, don't do that. Louis and Harry might be pulled overboard."

"Hey! If you can't get that thing on board, just let it go. Better that than end up in the drink. You don't know *what's* down there. Could be a large shark."

Just the mention of the word shark got their attention. Just as Louis was about to let go, he got suddenly and violently pulled overboard and flew through the air with Harry attached to him. They both landed in the water hard and fast.

"Men overboard. Men overboard." The shouts quickly turned into action. While some went for life rings, Tony got on the helm and started to turn it around, bringing it up to speed for getting to the men in the water as quickly and as safely as he could.

After the boat was turned, they headed back to where they saw two heads bobbing in the water. As the boat approached them, they looked to be dazed but alive. Then something beyond comprehension happened so fast that their brains had a hard time processing it.

Something came out of the water. That is, a part of something. It looked like a gargantuan maw with the largest looking teeth they'd ever seen. It instantly took both men in-what appeared to be-its mouth and they disappeared down into darkness. Just before *it* disappeared into the depths, the men with their jaws wide open and their eyes bulging out in terror, saw something round and large enough to be the size of a dinner plate. It was facing in their direction and had a huge vertical black slit in the middle. Then it quickly slid below the surface.

In seconds, that area of water was calm again as if nothing had happened.

Tony ran back to the helm, accelerated as fast as he could while turning in the opposite direction. The other men on the deck were hard pressed for words. What would they tell people? Would anybody believe them? They don't know what they saw, but it was not something that could be discussed at anyone's dinner table. In fact, it would be difficult to discuss with anyone because who would believe them? But it had to be reported because their families, not to mention the authorities would, of course, want to know.

It would be up to the skipper to get them back. *Who* would they report this to first? The men's families would have to be notified. They didn't look forward to this. The media would be all over them.

Their terror couldn't be more complete. Despite the fact that seamen don't leave their sea buddies behind and their natural instinct was to look for them, they had seen what they'd seen and could not deny it.

Tony turned the boat in the opposite direction and revved up the engines as much as he could to get them the hell out of there. Seeing two grown men being swallowed by a gargantuan maw was not something you want to dispute as being survivable. As far as he was concerned, his whole boat was just as vulnerable.

When he hit his max speed of nineteen knots he kept it up for as long as he could. In the far distance he could see land. When he tried to contact the Coast Guard, he could hear only static and threw the mike down in frustration after multiple failed attempts.

The engine started to sputter. "Aw shit. No, no, no. C'mon baby. Don't give up on me now." His mind started *wishing* it to not stop.

But moments later it did. One of the men on deck, asked, "Hey bud, what's going on? Why'd you stop?"

After lifting up his eyes from the gas gauge, he looked down in dread. There was only one last glimmer of hope.

"Fuel, my friend. Seems we may be out of it." Leaving the wheelhouse, he went down to the engine compartment to check the compartment fuel gauge for the inboard engines. It, too, showed the needle on empty.

Heading back up to the wheelhouse, he let the other three men know they were stranded, but he would call for help. He wasn't ready to tell them that comms were down also.

Tony was glad he hadn't smashed the mike in anger. This left him some hope that maybe he could get it working. Meanwhile, the men below were pacing and continuously looking out over the water. There was no doubt as to why. The seas were fairly calm, and it was eerily quiet. No gulls or birds were seen anywhere, and the sun was beating down on them.

As the boat gently rocked and pitched, he did his best not to show his fright to the men. Whatever creature had taken Harry and Louis was still out there. He didn't know what it was and couldn't imagine any known creature like that, let alone doing what it did. It made even the shark in *Jaws* seem like a walk in the park.

"Fishing vessel Sea Angel to Coast Guard," he called out repeating it 3 times. "Come in Coast Guard on emergency channel 13. This is a Mayday. Come in Coast Guard, or anyone."

He released the mike button and was met with only static. Not ready to give up, he made numerous attempts to contact anyone, any vessel who might hear him.

The men below were complaining and kept yelling up to the skipper to find out if he contacted anyone. Clearly and justifiably they were at the extreme end of nervousness now and about to enter the beginning territory of fright.

In the far distance an unnoticeable ripple appeared on the surface of the water, followed by a small wave. It slowly increased in size. It seemed to be heading in the direction of the boat. Even if one looked directly at it, it would not be easy to spot due to the sun and reflections bearing down on the sea surface, the natural waves, and the rolling of the boat.

Tony was resistant to calling it quits on the radio. It must have been damaged by what happened earlier, but he didn't recall being hit that hard. However, what happened likely distracted his attention away from the radio being damaged. Whatever the case, his radio was not working, and he had to find something else to call for help.

As the smaller wave became larger and closer, the skipper scrambled down to the emergency kit to look for his flares. Coming across the life jackets, he swore at himself for not making his clients wear them. After finding the flares, he grabbed four life jackets and ran back topside. He made them put them on, then quickly donned his before lighting off a flare.

Without warning, the sound like a huge explosion filled the air. The boat was hit from behind with a violence that shook the entire craft. The stern and propellers were instantly gone. Immediately the boat started sinking at its aft end. All the men on board were knocked to their feet. While Tony grabbed onto the helm for dear life, the men on deck started sliding toward the huge open maw filled with sharp, foot-long teeth. The head was huge and reptilian-like with black saucer-sized eyes that could only be described as looking dead. Tony looked in terror as he helplessly witnessed those guys sliding down closer to that hole of death. He could see them struggling fiercely but knew it was hopeless. He screamed to them.

"No, no. Oh for the love of God, please don't," he yelled. He held on to one of the aft stanchions with one arm as he bent over trying to reach one of them with his other outstretched arm. It was too late. He whimpered in emotional agony as he saw them sliding into the mouth of death. They were barely in before it closed, and one tooth easily pierced one of the men and tore it in half as if it was jello. Blood sprayed everywhere as it disappeared beneath.

He realized soon he would be next. Knowing his fate was inevitable, he wanted someone to find out that they had been there and that they had "existed". Finding a sign with the words Sea Angel on it hanging from the wheelhouse wall, he took it off and managed to throw it out into the gulf water. It would float and hopefully someone would eventually find it.

As the wheelhouse entered the gulf water, he did what he had not done since he was a kid. He prayed. His prayer ended with the Amen and then the water engulfing his head one minutes later.

14

Somewhere in the mid-Atlantic Ocean

Deep below the surface of the sea at six hundred feet, the USS Endeavor was slowly making its way through the silent waters. It was on a routine mission to a destination far away and was in no hurry to get there: The Mediterranean Sea. Along the way it conducted informal exercises and occasional drills to keep itself and its crew honed for unexpected emergencies.

It was skippered by Captain George Michaelson, an eighteen-year Navy veteran and decorated officer who had earned every bit of his way to the position he was in now. His second in command, or Executive Officer, was Commander James Woodson, a fourteen-year decorated veteran of the submarine corp. Together they ran a tight ship, which was necessary considering the conditions they worked under. Drills were mandated on a scheduled and nonscheduled basis. The crew had to be prepared for any and all possible emergency conditions.

Captain Michaelson was strict but fair. He ran his ship by the book and expected his crew to perform. Although he sometimes seemed harsh, he was still flexible enough to realize that some situations you just could not be fully prepared for because there was no formal training for some unexpected situations. Sometimes you had to think outside the box. But only when necessary and not to be flimsily used for the sake of getting off easy, especially when there was no real advantage for doing so. In many situations, the harder path was the better and most advantageous.

Currently things were quiet and uneventful. So the skipper decided to take a break and passed the con to his exec. As he started heading down to his cabin, the intercom broke through the silence.

'Bridge, sonar."

"Yes, go ahead sonar. This is the bridge."

"I have a sonar contact dead ahead bearing 067, range two thousand yards."

Commander Woodson grabbed the mike but remained calm. "Describe please."

"It appears to be large but how much is difficult to say. What I can say is that it seems to be closing in on us rapidly."

"Sonar, is it another sub?"

Silence for several moments.

"Negative. There is no indication of it having active or passive sonar. Our pings are coming off of it, but there is nothing originating from the bogey."

"Roger Sonar."

The commander turned his head to the helmsman as the captain monitored the situation.

"Helmsman, change course to starboard, heading 110 degrees. Increase speed to fifteen knots," he ordered.

The helmsman repeated the order. When the command was completed, the helmsman reported it out loud. The commander responded with "very well."

Michaelson then stepped in and said he was retaking the con. He heard and saw it all, so he now had something to worry about out there.

Speaking to his exec, he let him know about a tentative plan of action. Knowing that the exec was steering the ship as far from the approaching object as possible, he decided to continue that action and see if there was any type of response from the unknown bogey.

"Sonar, this is the captain. That wouldn't be a whale, would it?"

"No, sir. As I had said, there are no sounds or anything originating from it. Whales do emit sounds. This thing is dead silent and it's no submarine. There are no screw sounds coming from it."

"We are now on course heading 112, Captain." informed the helmsman.

"Very well. Sonar, what's that thing doing right now?" Michaelson asked

"Standby, sir." The sonarman looked intensely and manipulated some control.

"Captain, that thing seems to be turning in our direction. It looks like it's coming toward us again."

The captain and crew on the bridge remained silent. The tension in the air started rising again as if they were about to go to battle with a real enemy and not just a drill.

He had a decision to make and he had to make it fast. He didn't know what that thing was that seemed to be following them.

"Sonar, could it be a giant octopus or squid?"

The sonarman continued to study it and its movements.

"Negative, Captain. The giant octopuses wouldn't be that big, and it's not showing anything on the screen to suggest that it is. Giant squids don't behave like that. This is showing behavior that is like stalking."

Eyebrows were raised when he said that. What the hell? The skipper looked at his exec. Both officers seemed to silently communicate their concerns. The rest of the bridge crew seemed to remain calm, but the tension was felt among most of them.

The sonar operator was a second-class petty officer who had some academic training in marine biology before he joined the Navy and he was considered one of the best sonarmen on board. He had never said anything like that before. When he *did* say that the crew had little option but to take him seriously. That alarmed them even more because stalking behavior usually meant danger, even underwater.

"Exec, all hands to general quarters," ordered Michelson.

"All hands to general quarters," said Woodson.

The first-class Boatswains Mate, as part of his duties as Master-at-Arms on the bridge, got on the PA, blew his pipe, and verbally repeated the order.

"Now hear this. All hands to general quarters, all hands to general quarters. This is not a drill. This is not a drill. All hands man your battle stations now. This was an announcement that the crew was prepared to respond to but hoped they'd never have to.

"Want to change course again, Captain? asked Commander Woodson.

Michaelson thought for a minute. If he changed course, it's likely the thing would continue to follow them. He needed to try something a little different this time and told his exec his idea.

"Helm, change course to 270, increase to twenty knots. Let's see if that thing continues to follow us. Comms, see if you can contact that thing by radio. Just to confirm it's not a man-made object. Fire control, prepare to arm torpedo tubes one and two. Standby for arming until I get you the word."

"Aye aye, sir," replied the radio operator who immediately set his controls and started transmitting to the thing out there.

"Aye sir," same the bridge intercom speaker voice from down below. While the ship was maneuvering to the new course change and picking up speed, crew down below were quickly scrambling toward the torpedo area. They included a couple of gunner's mates and torpedo men.

No one could know at this point if the unknown was a threat to them. After ruling out anything manmade, like a submarine or even underwater robot vehicle such as from research ships, or any kind of large mammal or normal ocean creature very few, if any, possibilities were left. It was certainly leaving a completely mysterious sonar signature, the likes of which had never been seen before.

"No response from the thing, sir."

"Very well. Carry on monitoring it and report any changes."

No surprise. He commanded the radioman to transmit one more statement, then ordered another course change, this time in a drastically different direction and an increase in speed. He heard the muffled sound of the engines rev up a bit. If the thing didn't respond to the transmission and the warning to back off and it continued to stalk them, he would consider it a threat and take action to blow it out of the water.

They waited. No response. Sonar reported it to continue to follow them. Even with the course change and increased speed, it stuck to the ship's tail and seemed to be even gaining on them. There was now no question. Michaelson had to move fast and now make the fateful decision.

He looked at his exec. His exec nodded slightly, knowing what the skipper's next decision would be. He too felt there was not much choice.

The skipper went over to the ship wide PA and picked up the mike.

"Attention all hands. This is the captain."

As he spoke, everyone on the ship from bow to stern stopped what they were doing to listen. It was well known that whenever he got on the PA, there was a damn good reason for it.

"As you may or may not know, we have something of significant size following us. It has been determined that it is neither another sub nor any kind of underwater vehicle. It is also not a whale or any other form of ocean life. We don't know what it is. Despite continued communications, it has not responded. It continues to follow us and is, in fact, gaining on us. Therefore, battle stations will be activated as of now. Preparations are being made to arm the torpedoes and tubes. Prepare to maneuver. That's all."

He got on the intraship transmitter.

"Torpedo room, arm the torpedoes all tubes. Advise when ready. Fire control, standby at your stations in case we have to quickly surface."

After all stations acknowledged they were manned and his orders received and understood, he put the mike down. The exec asked sonar for the latest on his screen.

"Sir, the bogey seems to be getting closer." The commander came over and looked at it. "What... the... hell...is that? Captain!"

"Helm, starboard to 125, increase to twenty-five knots." Michaelson needed to shake this thing fast.

As the sonar screen was watched by several crew members including Commander Woodson, they saw the large blip become larger. It looked to be right up against the ship. It was likely more like a hundred yards astern of them and closing in.

"Bogey is closing, Captain. Staying right with us," said Woodson. Even with the turning of the sub and increased speed, it seemed to do no good. Not only that, but it was so close to them they had no turning room to maneuver for the forward torpedoes.

'Alright,' thought the skipper. *'If you want to play hardball, you son of a bitch, we will play harder.'*

Several minutes later, the torpedo crew advised him that all tubes were armed and ready. For the first time, they armed them for the real thing. They might really have to fire them at something that was an actual threat to them. Tubes one and two were the forward ones in which they were shot from near the bow. The other two shot toward targets astern of them.

The exec thought of something. Chances are Michaelson also already thought of that. Although the two men had their differences, in certain situations they often thought alike.

"Skipper, you don't think going topside would do any good?"

Michaelson looked at him and shook his head. "I knew you would ask that, Jim. If that thing could mimic our moves everywhere we went no matter what we did…well, I don't see much chance of it being any different by wasting our time with ballast emptying and heading up. We need to take it out before it gets *us*."

"Yea, I think so too. Ok. I can handle the fish men while you handle the maneuvering, if you want. Let's get this thing taken care of."

Michaelson nodded. He could see the tension in the bridge crew, yet they were fully prepared for what had to be done. They were especially picked for this ship and he had confidence in them. He always needed to ensure the feeling was returned.

"Torpedoes and tubes are armed and ready, sir" came the announcement from one of the bridge crew. He had heard through his headphones from the torpedo room. It was the second announcement from the fire control because they hadn't heard his acknowledgement yet.

"Very well," he replied this time. Sonar, range and bearing on the target."

"Bearing 180, range seven five yards."

Michaelson wanted to get a little more distance between them before he released the torpedoes.

"Helm, increase speed to maximum. Sonar, let me know the minute we are at least a hundred yards from it."

Ayes and repeat of the orders came from both crewmen to prevent any errors or misunderstanding. Everyone could hear the engines rev up. The vessel started gaining a little headway from the target.

"Captain, we are now one-oh-five yards from target."

"Very well, sonar. Fire control, prepare to launch torpedoes. On my mark. Sonar, slow down to fifteen knots."

Ayes came from both crews. While the sonar operator continuously watched the target's movement, the torpedomen were ready at their controls. All stations were ready to pounce like a tiger about to strike.

The captain wanted to get this right the first time. Even though the torpedoes had their own sonar to home in on a target, the skipper still wanted to ensure no miss by having the ship in the best position to fire.

"Fire torpedo number three."

The crew felt a slight jolt on the deck as the first one was let loose.

"Fire torpedo number four".

Both were now on their way to the target. The men back in the torpedo announced the firing completed of both weapons.

The captain went over to the sonar. Was he on the mark with this? Everyone watched and waited. It was only a matter of seconds now.

"Helm, flank speed ahead. Sonar, advise of any changes on the scope."

The entire crew waited anxiously for the sound of an explosion. If they missed the target, the torpedoes could come back at them until they ran out of steam. Michaelson didn't want to think about that anymore. He ordered increased speed to twenty-five knots once again.

15

Japanese Whaling Ship Suzaki

Now cruising along the northern edge of the Southern Ocean, the whaling fleet's processing ship cruised slowly, with no particular destination. With the knowledge that the Sakuru had gone down for unknown reasons, the captain found it difficult to believe that the same thing could've happened to the other two harpoon ships. The odds of just two of them going down were astronomical, let alone three.

Having heard no word from the other two harpoon ships for two days now, the captain decided to contact his government. Being the only ship in the huge Southern Ocean, finding two ships in the thousands of square miles would be a near impossibility and like looking for a needle in ten haystacks. An aircraft would have been of tremendous help, but unfortunately there was none that could help.

As for what to do now, he waited for the response from the government. It took a couple of hours to receive it. After talking with an official on the satellite phone and explaining the situation, he was advised to return home. There was nothing more he could do down there.

Reluctantly he agreed. He ordered the course change back to Yokosuka and soon the Southern Ocean was devoid of all ships.

Southern Ocean, the Arga

The ship was finally nearing its destination, the northwest corner of the ice continent. They didn't expect to find anything, yet it seemed different here than they'd seen along the way. The feeling of not seeing any life, especially with the absence of birds in the sky, was eerily disturbing. Gut feelings among many of the crew were correct. Something was environmentally wrong. It was almost like a ghost sea.

Beth and Tom had gone onto the bridge, just to get out of their offices for a bit, since each had spent some hours researching and trying to figure out what was going on in the environment. Right now they had nothing but questions and no answers to anything yet.

Suddenly, "Bridge, this is sonar, I believe we have a contact here, if you can believe it."

Everyone on the bridge nearly jumped when they heard that. A contact?

Paul picked up the mike immediately. "Bearing and range?"

"Bearing 035 relative. Range, likely about two thousand yards, give or take. It's relatively small."

"Could it be fish or a small whale?"

The sonar worker looked at it. "Don't think it's a fish. Small whale maybe, But aren't whales supposed to make sonar sounds? I'm not hearing anything from this one if it is a whale."

Paul looked at Beth. "That right, Beth?"

"Well, not exactly. Whales make those sounds when they choose to. They don't necessarily make them all the time constantly. Usually they sound for location purposes or communications with their young or other whales. Best not to assume it's not. This is their territory. Maybe we found one that's still around."

Paul nodded and got back on the mike. "Ok, Todd. Probably a whale or seal. We'll look for it. Thanks." He put the mike down and was about to change course for the area of the suspected seal when Todd came back on the intercom.

"Paul, saw another contact on the screen. Looks like it's behind the small one but is much larger. Can't tell yet if it's a whale. But it's awful big. I mean really big."

"I'll be right there", said Paul quickly. "Frank, you got the con," he told his first mate. He quickly left the bridge and seconds later was in sonar.

"Let's see." He bent over to take a look.

On the left of the screen there was, indeed a very large blip. With each sweep of the cursor line around the scope, it looked like it was closing in on the small blip.

"Orca, you think?" Paul asked Todd.

"Don't think so. Orcas travel in schools or packs. This is just one. Besides, it looks a little too big for an orca. Matter of fact, I've never seen anything so big on a sonar. Whatever it is, it's scary as shit."

The two men continued to look at the scope and saw what was happening. It sent chills down Paul's spine. Whatever the big thing was, it was closing fast on the small blip. It, in fact, dwarfed it. Like a predator and prey. What the hell would eat a seal and be too big to be a whale, let alone a Great White shark? He couldn't imagine.

Paul didn't want to see what was about to happen, yet it was if his eyes were drawn to the imminent horror. The next sweep brought the large blip to the back edge of the small blip. The sweep after that, only half of the small blip showed as the large blip was merging with it. It looked like the small blip, maybe a seal, was being consumed by the big thing. The next sweep showed only the large blip. The small one was gone.

"Oh for the love of God!" Paul said in a shaky voice. "Holy shit. What did we just see, Todd? "

He felt his heart sink and his stomach fill with knots. He stood up straight, looking ahead with eyes wide open and his mouth clenched shut.

Todd was equally shocked. "I think I'm going to be sick," he muttered.

Paul saw what occurred yet neither he nor anyone else could know what had merged with what on the screen. He had to find out because whatever happened or caused it to happen could be a serious threat to the Arga.

"Ok, listen. We don't know what we were looking at. I'm going to call an all-crew meeting for fifteen minutes from now. Fifteen minutes. Mess deck."Then he turned around and left. When he returned to the bridge, he had the first mate make the announcement.

Fifteen minutes later, everyone was gathered. Captain Paul cut right to the chase and told what was just witnessed. The scientists and other crew members were shocked.

George was the first to speak up in response. "Paul, we don't know that the little blip was a seal. It could have been anything. And maybe the large thing merely crossed over it and not actually consumed it. They might have intersected at different depths, just at the exact same area of water."

Paul looked at George. He knew the answer to that, just moments before the meeting. "Todd, you want to answer that, seeing you're the expert on the sonar."

Todd cleared his throat. "To answer your question, George—which is a particularly good one at that—normally I would say that's likely. In this case, though, I don't think so."

"Why not?" asked Tom.

Because after the merging of the two blips, the large thing turned and went in a different direction. After it completely left the area of the merging the small blip was completely gone. No sign of it. There's nothing that swims so fast that it would be gone from the sonar area in the blink of an eye. That's not possible. There's no question in my mind that the small thing was consumed."

"By what?" the group asked nearly at the same time.

"Well, that's what we will need to find out," Paul replied. "I strongly suggest that we find out what that mystery creature is. Maybe *it's* the reason the penguins won't go in the water and why we're not finding normal signs of life around here. I would almost stake my life on that."

Neither the scientists nor anyone else could disagree with that. Identifying the creature could be their answer, yet it would be only the beginning. How they would deal with it would depend on what it is. The first thing they had to do was find and identify it.

"Paul." It was Beth.

"If this thing obliterated all the life around here, I have a strong suspicion it would be dangerous to us as well. I think we all agree we need to identify it. But at the same time, we have to think of our safety as well. What's going to happen when we find it?"

"Good point Beth. Any ideas anyone as to how to safely approach this thing if we find it?"

Questions, good ones, suddenly erupted from among the group.

"Well we don't know the how of that because we don't know anything about it, let alone what it is."

"But suppose it's attracted to sound. Like our engines or sonar pings."

"Or movement," suggested Tom.

"Let's just go after it and try to kill it. We should have stuff on board that can do the job."

Paul raised his hands. "Whoa! Whoa, folks. Let's think this out. We need to plan this rationally and logically without endangering ourselves any more than we might already be. We have to know what we are dealing with first before we can plan anything. And we *will not* take any action before that."

Beth jumped in. "That's right. What do we know about this thing? Not much. We know it's very big and dangerous. That's a no-brainer. We suspect it has either chased away or devastated the marine life around here, probably including penguins. We need to be able to locate and identify it.We can find it with the sonar. But how to find its identity? That's the key problem here."

Another voice stated what all believed, at least for the moment. "It seems to be no known modern-day creature that could cause this."

"That's seems to be the case, Jim," Beth replied.

A crew member from the deck offered a suggestion. "What about a giant jellyfish? Can't they consume something like what happened here?"

A number of voices suddenly filled the room at the same time.

"Hey people, listen!. Listen!. Jellyfish don't inhabit these waters. Even though some large species can easily thrive in cold water, just not around here. And based on what I've learned about sonar, the blip was too large and solid to be a jellyfish. I think we can pretty much rule that out."

"What about underwater cameras? We've got them on board," said Tom.

Paul interjected. "Good. If it can be done safely, then let's do that. However, I suggest that we use them only when we believe we have located it. I will make that determination and let you know."

After some discussion, the group broke up and went back to their work stations. For now, those assigned would prepare the cameras, while others prepared their sounding equipment for possible imminent use.

Todd returned to the sonar because now the crew relied on him to relocate the beast. It might be a daunting task and it was possible they wouldn't be able to find it again. But they had to try for the sake of the environment, the marine life here, and themselves as well. Paul joined Todd at the sonar to see if the creature still showed.

***

In her bedroom, Beth sat at her room computer to do some research. As she typed, uneasy thoughts entered her mind. Her fingers brought her to the google engine. Even though her mind wasn't entirely focused on what her fingers were typing, what showed on the screen seemed to be a reflection of what her thoughts were focused on. *Megalodon.*

Being prehistoric and a great ancestor to the present-day great white shark, the idea of the creature being one of these was pretty far-fetched to say the least. It had been extinct for millions of years. Yet, if all known ocean creatures had been ruled out, which included giant octopus, giant squid and whales, the thought of this being the mysterious creature could not be ruled out. Even today, man knows more about Mars and other planets than about our own oceans. So who's to say, she thought.

But she didn't want to focus on only one possibility. There was more she could check on.

16

USS Endeavor, mid-Atlantic

Torpedo three had missed, which was confirmed. Michaelson then ordered number three tube to be rearmed. They waited for an explosion from torpedo four. There was nothing.

"Radioman, contact CINCATLANTIC to report the following: Current situation: we are under attack by unknown bogey and are forced to defend ourselves. Attempting to take evasive action. Believed negative for Russians or anyone else we're aware of. Negative submarine. Request help to these coordinates. STOP STOP.

"Get the coordinates and transmit immediately."

"Aye aye, sir."

"Fire control, arm tubes one and two. Sonar, what's the bearing and range on the bogey?"

The sonarman manipulated his controls and cursor on the screen and calculated according to what he was seeing.

"Captain, target's bearing is one-three-niner degrees. Range one-thousand yards."

"Very well." The skipper did some quick calculating of his own, then ordered the ship to come about. It was turning to face in the direction of the bogey. He decided he had just about enough of being followed and wanted the forward tubes to be ready to fire. He ordered the torpedomen to rearm the aft tubes.

"Tubes one and two armed and ready. Tubes three and four are ready as well, sir."

Suddenly, they felt the sub slow down. Then the shaking began and loud clanging noises and scrapings. What the hell was going on?

Michaelson immediately asked the helm what's happening.

"Sir, I don't know. I'm haven't difficulty maintaining our course."

They were already going at their max speed.

"Are you able to get full right rudder?"

"I don't know. I'll try."

Despite their attempts to maneuver, something was preventing them from turning. In fact, they seemed to be hardly moving at all, despite their screws turning at the maximum speed.

"Sonar, what do you see?"

"Captain, it looks like the bogey has caught up with us. It looks like it's merged with us."

"What!?" Michaelson ran over to the screen and was stunned.

It appeared something had the sub in its grip. In all of his nearly twenty years in the Navy and twelve of those working on subs, he'd never experienced or seen anything like this. They were in trouble. By what they didn't know. Right now the only thing that mattered was to get out of the situation.

He went to the periscope. "Up scope," he ordered.

As it was going up he grabbed the handles and turned to look astern. He could feel himself go pale as he took in the horrific sight. Something, some giant *creature,* had the sub's stern in its huge mouth. The screws were turning but in its mouth. He had to do something and now. There was little or no time to thing.

He closed the handles and sent the scope back down. Grabbing the PA mike, he made an announcement.

"Attention all hands. This is the captain. It seems we are in the grip of something that is preventing our movements. We don't know what it is, except that it's something hostile and big enough to hold this ship hostage. If this continues, we will lose all capability to maneuver the ship or even survive. Currently we are unable to break free from it. And it's starting to affect the integrity of our hull.

On the other hand, the only solution to this may be just as deadly. There is no way to defend ourselves except with the torpedo that's ready to go. By releasing it, it will fire into the thing's mouth and explode inside of it. But it will likely kill us as well. Everyone brace yourselves right now. Pray, and God bless us all."

Kermit, Texas

Compared to what happening in other parts of the world, Rita's home seemed to be the only sane area, quiet and non-chaotic. It was her day off from work and she was taking advantage of the sometimes-stressful days she had with classes and research. She loved her work and often she spent too much time trying to solve the mysteries of fossil origins and other things which she found too fascinating to put down. Translation: she often had a difficult time putting down her work to give herself a break.

Today she would concentrate on cleaning and straightening out things in the house because John certainly had no time for that except when he was off. That didn't happen as often with her because even with days off from surgeries or the hospital, he had to take his turn being on call, or sometimes to fill in for another doctor who was going away.

It was close to noontime. She just finished cleaning the kitchen and made herself a sandwich for lunch, which would be followed by an apple.

She had a habit of sitting in front of the TV to eat her meals when she was alone. The news was just coming on, so she relaxed as she watched the news anchor.

"This just in. Reports are continuing to come in about the disappearance of several Japanese whaling ships. Although the Japanese government was reluctant to make this public, sources have reported the mysterious vanishing of two ships down in the Southern Ocean not far from Antarctica. No one seems to know why or how this happened. It seems to almost be in conjunction with mysterious changes that have also occurred off the coast of Antarctica. Rebecca Mandin has the story." The screen then switched to her.

"Good afternoon, Tom. I'm here in New Zealand to try and make sense of what's going on off the ice continent about four hundred miles from here. It certainly is a mystery. That mystery is…"

The story caught Rita's attention because of its unusual, bizarre nature.

As the reporter continued, she was shocked to hear about the seemingly absent ecosystem down there. She wasn't a biologist but even she knew that animal life in an area always teeming with it just doesn't disappear like that.

Then when it went to the story about the Japanese whaling fleet, its lack of sightings of any whales and the disappearance of their ships, the reports became intriguing. Coincidence of the disappearances? No way to tell at this point. Little did she know that she would eventually play a part in this mystery.

Governments and investigators were on it. Hopefully, someone would find an answer to what happened. Finishing her lunch, she was soon at her computer for some off-duty research of her own.

On the Arga

Once the equipment was ready, Beth and a couple of assistants, lab technicians, brought them all up on deck to ready them for putting the live feed video camera into the water.

Beth decided on the best spot for lowering the camera into the water. It would be from the port side slightly forward of amidships.

"Make sure the line is completely secure on the camera, Mitch," she told her assistant.

He checked the attachment well and saw that there was no way it would come apart.

"Ok, Beth. Looks like it's pretty tight. Can't get any better than this. Want me to attach the other end now?"

The loose end had to be attached to the ship on a secure locking hook so it would not easily come off of it. The line itself was about two hundred feet long and was in a tight neat wind with the end in a position where, when pulled, the rest of the line wouldn't snag.

She looked at it. "Great. Ok, stay with the camera. No, don't attach it yet. We may have a way to go before we get to the site area, wherever that is. Going to check with Paul now."

"Roger dodger."

Beth went up to the bridge to discuss the next move. Tom was gathering his still camera in his little office cubbyhole. In case of anything that was observed on or out of the water, he wanted to be ready to photo-document that.

"Todd, what do you have on sonar?" Paul asked over the intercom.

"Nothing so far. Not even a small fish."

"Ok." It would not be easy finding the thing. Despite its large size, the Southern Ocean was still a mighty big area of water. But they had try and find it no matter how long it took.

Keeping in mind the amount of fuel they had on board, Paul had to monitor the amount. When it got down to a certain level, they'd have to turn and head for the nearest fuel stop which would be New Zealand. But for now, they had enough for at least another five or six days sailing at this fairly slow cruising speed. Now that they were in the general area of where they wanted to be, they needed to take their time in their search.

The next two days would be uneventful and monotonous. But it was the third day…

17

USS Endeavor

Things started dropping as the sub was forced to face downward. The creature still held it in its tight grip. The captain was afraid it could close its mouth at any moment and crush the ship. Then it would be game over. Everyone inside the sub on the bridge held on for dear life. Those in the aft sections of the sub did the same, except for a few who were literally caught off guard, some with their pants down as they fell off the toilets. It was a chaotic, terrifying scene.

" Fire one!" yelled the captain. "Fire two."

There was no time to think or contemplate as to whether or not the torpedoes would fire in this downward angled position. But seeing there wasn't much choice, all they could do was wait and hope it worked. Whether or not it worked, death was certainly on the table.

The blast was heard by all of the crew. They expected and were prepared for sudden death. What they got instead was a sudden and explosively violent propulsion forward as the huge maw suddenly released its grip. The torpedoes had met their mark and blew the creature to smithereens. Large chunks of flesh flew throughout the area, with some sinking and others rising toward the ocean surface.

When the forward motion of the submarine had stopped, the crew on the bridge looked around and briefly wondered if they were dead or alive. Soon the reality sank in and they yelled and cheered their joy at what they accomplished. Having been on the very brink of death and in a split second finding the danger completely gone was more than words could describe. They were alive!

They all turned toward the captain and applauded him for the fateful decision he was forced to make and its incredible success. But this was no time to celebrate right now.

He grabbed the mike. "All sections, report any damages."

The engine room reported some pipe leaks but no bulkhead breaches. The same for the aft torpedo room. The leaks were limited and there was no danger of flooding. Their saving grace was the lack of bulkhead breaches. If there had been a hole in any part of the ship's outer hull, it and the entire crew would have been swallowed by the sea.

The captain thought, *"By the grace of God, we will still live."*

"Damage control crews report to affected areas and then advise when repairs are completed. That is all for now. Good work to everyone."

He was not looking for praise. As far as he was concerned, it was the entire crew that had to be credited for their bravery in the face of certain death. He would speak to them later.

For now, he manned the periscope and took a look out there. Watching the absence of the creature as well as its remnants still floating around offered him the same sense of victory as if he had sunk an enemy warship. It had been a very real enemy and every bit as bad as a warship could get. His thoughts were created by what had occurred. '*I hope there's no more of those things out there! Whatever the hell it was'*

If only that were so. He soon ordered a course change to continue on their original mission.

On the Arga

After a few days it seemed like they were never going to find anything. The blank sonar screen echoed the underwater blankness. It was eerie and depressing at the same time. Todd could only stare at the screen for so long before sleepiness hit his eyes. As a result, he kept nodding off. He didn't want to, but he couldn't help it. It was almost like staring at someone sleeping. Everything had its limits.

Until something occurred, it needed to be business as usual. There were things that each of the scientists could be doing in the meantime because their work was never truly done. There was still lots of research to undergo and mysteries of the area to solve.

All was quiet on the bridge as the ship slowly trolled its way off the northwestern and northern Antarctica coast. The radar showed no contacts in the air. Rarely did planes ever fly over this area. When they did, it was for either an emergency evac, or delivering another team member or supplies. Even for those reasons, it had to be when the weather allowed. Here, the weather could turn on a dime. It could be a kitten one minute and a roaring lion the next. Antarctica is not known for having predictable weather.

Beth was in her workspace checking on data but her thoughts were not entirely on the data. She was concerned about those penguins and knew that the others were also. Going to the intercom she was about to contact Paul on the bridge but changed her mind and turned to go up there. It was only a few feet away. For now, she had to put that megalodon search on hold.

On the bridge, all was quiet. The helmsman steered and looked ahead. The ship was moving slowly ahead at only seven knots. The radar was showing nothing. The first mate, John Billingsley, had the con. Paul was likely down below in his cabin.

"John, do you know how far we are from where we know the penguins dive into the water?" asked Beth.

He looked at her and shook his head. "Not really, Beth. Do you know the coordinates?"

"Not offhand. But if you had the coordinates, would you be able to get us there?"

"Sure. Better check with Paul on that. I don't think there'll be a problem with that. With his blessing and the coordinates, I can get us there. Assuming, of course, we don't run into something in the meantime."

As she turned to head down to the cabin, she said, "If we find something in the meantime, we won't need to go to the penguin area. Be back."

Soon, with the coordinates in hand, she went to Paul's cabin and entered after he responded. They reviewed the plan briefly and he agreed it was a good one.

On the bridge, she handed John the coordinates on paper. The captain had let John know he was ok with that and to set course for those coordinates, still maintaining the same speed.

After the command from the first mate, the ship was now on course in a northeasterly direction, which would take it to the northern coast. The skies had turned cloudy and the wind had picked up.

Barbara Cornwall, the team's meteorologist had informed the bridge that she had picked up an oncoming storm coming in from the northwest. Her weather radar showed it as an average sized but significantly intense storm. Their ETA to where they were going was twelve hours from now. The first mate notified the captain. Orders were to first batten down any hatches with little to no traffic through them and tie down anything loose.

Winds were expected to be nearly hurricane force strength with possible gusts up to eighty mph. The first mate announced over the PA system, per captain's orders, this news. This was the last thing they needed considering what they were already dealing with below the surface.

Todd's voice suddenly broke out on the intercom.

"Sonar to bridge, sonar to bridge."

John picked up. "Go ahead Todd. What've you got?"

"Picked up a large size blip on the screen. Looks to be to our port stern and heading toward us."

"Range?" "

"I'd say about three thousand yards.

The first mate became alarmed but did his best to hide it.

"Do you hear any active pings coming from it?"

A few moments silence. "Negative. No sounds other than the returning echoes from our transponder."

This was both good and bad news, but he'd sort it out later. He got on the PA and requested the captain to the bridge.

Paul soon appeared looking serious. "Ok, let's get ready for our unknown. We can worry about the weather later." He turned to his first mate.

"John, make sure the scientists and their cameras prepare. Let them know what's going on."

He got on the intercom. "Todd, what's the range and bearing of the bogey?"

"Range, twenty-six hundred yards. Bearing 265. Still heading towards us."

"Roger, Ok, keep us posted. Let me know when it gets to two thousand."

Todd acknowledged it. Beth and Tom were notified and were in the midst of preparing their cameras and lines. Soon they were on their way up to the port deck to set them to the connections.

They could feel the seas kicking up a bit. The waves were about three to five feet with winds blowing at fifteen knots. The helmsman was doing his best to keep the ship on course despite the rolling and pitching.

Out on deck, Beth and Tom were connecting the cameras and special lines. As Tom looked up, he thought he saw something in the distance. He stood and looked. His eyes squinted as he tried to get a clearer view. His jaw dropped. It looked like it could have been a large whale because of its size but saw that it looked vastly different.

"Beth, look out there. Stop what you're doing and look out there," he told her while pointing in the direction of the sighting. As her eyes gazed out toward the horizon, they lit on something in the water which made them open up a bit.

"My God, what is that? Looks like...a... whale. Yet it doesn't. What the hell is that?"

She turned to him quickly and suggested they put the cameras in the water now. After making sure their small TV-type screens were on, Beth watched them as Tom visualized the creature at the water's surface. He was looking for the head where it might be identified.

They needed to let the bridge know. Looking up, he saw a bridge crew member outside on the bridge wing and got his attention.

"Target ahead of us to our ten o'clock position," he yelled up to the bridge wing. Let everyone know. We've got the cameras in the water!."

He yelled loud enough for the crewman to acknowledge who then ran in to inform the skipper.

While the bridge maneuvered for a better look at the unknown creature, Beth and Tom looked intensely at the screens, trying to discern anything about it that they could identify with regarding large marine life, other than whales and orcas.

As they searched the screens, they saw something that made them rethink their notion that is was just a marine animal that had stumbled into their area.

While the inside crew stared at the sonar screens, crew members on the outside decks saw to their port side something huge sticking out of the water. It was very long and curved and moving forward toward the direction of their heading. After spotting the USO, or unidentified swimming object as he called it, Tom let the bridge know about it.

Up on the bridge, Paul grabbed the binocs and scanned the water. He immediately stopped scanning, seeing something he'd never seen before. It was longer than any whale he'd ever seen. For twenty years he'd be skippering this and previous ships all over the world, with the Arga being his latest for the past five years. His eye catches of whales included the rarely seen Blue, the largest mammal in the world. But even that seemed to be small compared to this.

He knew sonar would show it as a large blip. He saw that it was swimming forward, but its head was yet to appear. It seemed to be heading to cross across the ship's course until it got to their starboard side. But what the hell was it?

"John, get a hold of Beth. Now!" he shouted as he continued to glare at the thing.

Moments later, John came back in. "She's holding the camera in the water and can't leave it."

"Tell her to look ahead of her and she'll see with her own eyes."

"I did already. She sees it on the camera."

Down below outside, Beth continued to hold the camera, slowly moving forward as the creature continued to head in the direction of their starboard side. Tom took his camera and headed to that side, knowing he could continue to record it as it came into the camera's view.

What Beth saw on her screen stunned her. The thing looked more paleolithic, more prehistoric than anything she'd ever seen. She was familiar with it as a marine biological scientist, although not as an expert in paleo-biology.

"Tom, you see it? Can you see the head?" She had to yell loudly for him to hear her. Fortunately, he did.

"I'm getting something here. Could be the front of the head or snout, whatever. I'm not sure."

He continued to stare at his screen. "Yes, I see something. I believe it is a head. A very, very large one. I think I detect an eye, but I'm not sure. Hard to say cause of the distance through the water. Good Lord, Beth, what have we got here? Some kind of underwater behemoth?"

Beth mumbled under her breath as she stared at the creature now disappearing from her screen. She pulled up her camera. Unknown to anyone else, her expression showed a slight grimace and worry. After the camera was back on deck, she put it down and ran toward the starboard bow to catch a visual glimpse with her own eyes. Amazingly it was still swimming in the same direction, seeming unaware that the ship was there.

She noticed now that the ship was barely moving.

Although marine biology was her specialty, still she was no dummy when it came to some information on other creatures. She had a hunch, but couldn't say anything to the others, not even Tom because that's all it was a hunch. But even so, she knew it was no megalodon. She hoped that hunch was wrong. If it wasn't, then they were in big trouble. She knew who she could turn to, which would be the first time in a long time.

The subtle turn of the thing was not missed by anyone. It was turning to its right. As captain, Paul couldn't afford to panic even as the thing turned toward the ship. Although there were times when nervousness and tension took hold of some of the crew in certain precarious situations, this *was* the ocean off of Antarctica where falling in would mean certain death within minutes. For most people, nervousness or tension under these circumstances came with the territory. That's what everyone signed up for here. But in this particular situation…

Something projected above the water just enough for evil looking eyes to be seen by anyone able to see them. That anyone was Paul and his first mate with their binocs. "No way" muttered Paul. "That looks like the devil himself." It was coming closer and the Arga was now directly in its path.

18

For now, Beth had to put off calling her professional contact. She had more things to worry about right now. In fact, the entire ship did. However, the big disadvantage they had was not knowing anything about it or what it is. They had no weapons on board because they were a research and science ship. This presented two major strikes against them: one, they had no way to defend themselves and two, they didn't know what this thing is fully capable of.

She ran up to the bridge while Tom stayed below monitoring the screen. He didn't seem to care that the thing was heading their way. He seemed to be entranced by the sight of something terrible unknown.

"Paul, you saw it? We have to get out of here!" she blurted out entering the bridge.

He turned to look at her and agreed. "Beth, what the heck is that thing?"

She brushed back her hair quickly and shook her head. "I don't know. I'm not sure. What I do know is that it's not in any of my marine mammal books and I believe it's a major threat to us."

He looked out at the thing now appearing a little larger. It was about a thousand yards out and still closing. He found it hard to believe.

He looked at her.

"You think this thing could bring us down if it collided with us?"

"Always think on the side of caution, Paul. That's what I do. And I know you do, too," she replied as she continued to stare intently at the creature which defied explanation, still heading toward them.

With her strong binoculars, she saw the large eyes and part of what seemed like a long snout as it swam steadily, not in any particular hurry. Perhaps it was just curious, she briefly thought. Then she caught herself. *No way. I'm not going to get caught in that kind of complacent thinking.*

"Tim, left full rudder to heading one-seven-five. Increase speed to fifteen knots," ordered Paul.

Tim repeated the orders out loud and then followed through. The ship then made a hard left toward the direction they'd been coming from. He wasn't about to let some creature from the unknown mess with *his* ship and possibly bring it down. If this was the thing that chased away, or ate, all the life in this area, who knows what else it was capable of?

As soon as the ship was at its heading, everyone on the bridge saw the creature suddenly disappear under the surface. Beth no doubt felt the same as everyone else. Fear and tension. Was this thing going to attack them?

"Increase speed to twenty knots." Paul ordered.

The engines revved up as the vessel picked up speed. The waters had become choppy which was echoed by the ship's pitching and rolling.

"Sonar, what do you see?" the first mate asked.

Todd replied right away. "The thing is following us and closing in. Bearing zero-zero-five, range twelve-hundred yards."

It was a fast swimmer, which was no surprise to anyone. By this time, the crew knew they could be in trouble. It was also the time when Beth had a serious clue as to what it could be. It was not something neither she nor anyone else in any scientific field could rationally come up with regarding its identity. Because if by some remote longshot she was right, it was not supposed to exist. Not anymore.

Not being a paleo-marine biologist, she could not identify the species. But she did have a clue that suggested it was prehistoric in origin. She didn't want to broadcast this out loud within earshot of anybody because they would likely think she'd gone off the edge a little too far. However, the only person she *could* tell that she knew could keep it secret was George. Being more of a stay-in-the-lab type of researcher, she trusted him to keep his mouth shut, at least for now until she investigated this further. Provided they shook this thing. If not, they might be visiting Davey Jones soon.

A sudden violent jarring of the ship forward caused some to nearly lose their balance while other crew members weren't so fortunate and ended up on the deck. The bang was coming from the starboard stern.

Up on the bridge, Paul was trying to give commands for whatever evasive maneuvers they could do. As he tried to order another course change on the mike, another stronger collision from behind shook the ship. This cause Paul to drop the mike and he grabbed it in time before it hit the floor.

There was no doubt in anyone's mind now that the creature was after them and it seemed to be relentless. Did it smell the food on board? Or did it consider those on board as food? A yes answer to either one would not be in their favor.

John, the first mate, had an idea. "Paul, we have a large chunk of some kind of meat in the freezer?"

"Yes, we do." He was thinking the same thing.

They had to do something fast before the thing breached the hull with its collisions. The way it was going, that wouldn't be too long from now.

Although he was cautiously skeptical that it would work, they had nothing to lose by trying. Being unarmed, they had to do whatever they could to stay alive.

He then called down to the cooks and ordered what would be needed and bring it to the stern outside, carefully holding on as this thing continued to bang against them. The deck crew were ordered to standby to assist. The meat and other food items that could be palatable to a carnivore would be quickly mixed with various poisons and then thrown overboard. There had to be enough of both to do the job. There could never be too much, but an insufficient supply of the poison could spell fail to do the job.

Another bang. The engineer down in the engine room announced over the intercom that there was a breach in one of the pipes down there. Some seawater was coming in. Paul then ordered all other available mechanics and maintenance crewman to help out for damage control.

At the same time, Paul had his first mate put out on a Mayday call on the radio. Although there were other research stations on the ice shelf, none would be able to help in this situation because this was the only research vessel down here that they knew of. The only chance of hearing from anyone was from a navy base in New Zealand. Sometimes the signals went through and sometimes they didn't. Down here, nothing was predictable.

Beth had to find out what this thing could possibly be. There was nothing she could do here but stand and watch. While she had the chance, she ran down below to her computer, hoping it would still work and logged back on again.

Googling quickly, she browed the search engine, found the many listings and picked one. She couldn't be sure what she saw because she only saw the back area, the eyes and part of a snout. That wasn't much to go on, but it was all she had.

She checked the pictures and information of as many large extinct sea creatures she could see. Many were quite bizarre-looking, and she quickly ruled them out. Others were possibilities and she wrote them their names. By the time she finished, she had five possibilities that could fit the description of the creature that was currently threatening them.

Her dilemma hit her without warning. What to do with this information? It wouldn't help her here. If this major problem goes away, she thought, then I'll pursue this further. For now, it was life saving time.

South Atlantic Ocean

Off the coast of Brazil, a fishing boat with two divers in the water spearfishing was lazily riding the gentle waves in place. The sun was filling the blue cloudless skies with its brightness while it added its heat to the humid air. There was no breeze. The reflection off the ocean's surface of the sun seemed to make the air even hotter.

The man on the boat sat lazily in his captain's chair reading a magazine, sunglasses and all. There were no noises except for gentle lapping of water against the boat hull.

He would occasionally look up and see the bubbles from the scuba tanks which, to him, was assurance that the men were alright. The subtle rocking of the boat was almost sedating to him; actually, relaxing was the better word and he enjoyed his occasional rented bouts out here with his boat. He'd never get rich doing this, but it helped pay the bills and keep food on his table. Who knows, he thought; maybe he'd do this forever. Until he was too old to handle the boat lines and responsibilities of operating and maintaining a rental fishing boat.

One of the area of bubbles stopped.

The man thought of his ex-wife and his young son, Paolo who his wife had custody of. Fortunately, the divorce had been amicable. In light of that, he was able to visit his son whenever he wanted. He couldn't keep him overnight without her permission and it was restricted to two nights per week.

When he did have him, he'd take him out for some fishing which Paolo loved. *My boy takes after his old man,* he thought to himself and smiled at that. One of these days he'd take him out for maybe some marlin fishing, but he'd have to build him up for that because that was heavyweight class in fishing. You had to be full grown, strong, and skillful at ocean fishing before tackling such a catch. There would be plenty of time, he told himself. After all, Paolo had his whole life ahead of him. He was still only twelve-years old.

The second area of bubbles stopped.

He decided to turn on the radio. Maybe a little music would enliven the monotonous boring silence. Finding a station with some nice calypso music, he started getting into it, moving around as if dancing in his chair.

Finally, he found his chair too restrictive. He jumped out of it and started moving and gyrating with the invigorating beat and sounds of excitement and adventure. Time was furthest from his mind. At least for the moment. As he danced, his mood seemed to change, and he smiled and laughed. Frequently he almost lost his balance with the movement of the boat and the dancing, but he managed to stay on his feet.

He stopped and went to grab a beer out of the small refrigerator down below. Figured while he was down there, he'd take a whiz and bring his drink back out.

Time finally caught up with him. Taking a look at the clock back up near the helm, he saw it was well after noontime. The men had been down in the water for longer than he had realized.

It didn't dawn on him that there were no birds in the air. Even though he was out in deep waters, he was not beyond the reach of seabirds who liked to stay near land. The air was empty of them. There was only the buzz of an occasional fly, out of place in a marine environment. It seemed to have lost its way, as if flies could do that.

When his mind finally did allow him to notice that something was wrong, his expression became one of concern. The strangeness of it then hit home. He looked down at the water in the area of where the men were known to have last dived. Gasping softly almost in a slight panic, he looked out at the water, thinking that maybe they might have swam off distant to the boat. There were no bubbles which likely meant they were somewhere else a short distance away.

He wasn't sure what to do. Should he wait here and hope they'll return soon? Or should he run the boat slowly around to see if he could pick up their bubble trail? He chose the latter and slowly circled around the area where he estimated they might be.

Despite his intensive search, he could not find their air bubbles anywhere. He couldn't help wondering if something had happened to them. For three hours he continued to search until his desperation was finally overcome by the reality of the situation. They would have run out of air long before this. There was no visible blood in the water so the possibility of both of them being taken by sharks was not that great. In fact, he hadn't seen signs of *them* either. Not that he would have normally. Right now he couldn't be sure of anything.

The sun was lowering in the sky and he waited as long as he dared, just before the sun sank below the horizon. It was time to leave. He didn't want to but there was no choice. Turning the boat, he headed back to the port where he kept his boat docked. It would take him about thirty minutes to get there.

As it got darker, he focused intently on the water ahead of him and the bearings he needed to maintain to stay on course. There was no way he could have seen the long blue-grayness following behind him. The only noise was that of the engines and his voice talking over the radio to the port police about the missing men and his ETA to the port.

The man had been out in these waters dozens of times over the years. But he had never experienced this: the appearance of deadness everywhere. No fish. Not even a bird. If something specific had caused this, could that something had anything to do with the disappearance of the men?

As he revved up the engine for a little more speed, he heard sputters from the engines. The fuel gauge showed just above empty. Shit! He spent so much time looking for the men, he forgot about the fuel. Now he would have to stop the boat to refill. Despite the quickly approaching darkness, he didn't have much choice.

Stopping the boat, he grabbed both gas containers and headed back to the stern. That's when he saw something that sent chills up and down his spine and made his hair stand on end.

The pitch blackness of whatever he was looking at blocked out the remaining light and was darker than the night. It engulfed the back of his boat. There appeared to be what looked like rows of foot long teeth, but he couldn't be sure. He took this all in within seconds. And in those seconds, he was swallowed into eternal oblivion.

19

Kermit, Texas

It had been a long day. Sometimes the hours seemed to drag on, while other times they seemed to race past her. Her classes went well and most of the assignments her students had to complete were handed in. Now all she had to do was look them over and grade them.

But it would be quite time consuming. There was no deadline to complete her task, but she would do well to grade them before the semester ended.

In the kitchen, she'd been preparing the evening meal. The kids were upstairs, and John would probably be coming home soon. But that was only a maybe. She never knew for sure because of the nature of his work.

The phone suddenly rang.

"Hello?"

"Rita, hi. This is Max Caldwell. I'm sorry to bother you right now."

Max was one of her part time assistants who helped in the lab.

"No, that's alright Max. How are you?"

"I'm good. I won't keep you long. I'm calling because I thought you might be interested in what I just heard on the news."

"Oh?"

"There's a ship down off the coast of Antarctica, I think it's British. Anyway, it's being reported that it has been attacked by a gigantic-is what they call it-marine creature."

"What! No sir." Her surprise was no surprise to him.

"Uh huh. And I know what you're going to ask next. No, it could not be identified. According to the scientists there, even though they didn't know what it is, they knew for certain it was no whale. Not even a blue whale. And it seemed to them to be at least as long as the ship, although they can't be sure."

She was stunned. An unidentified giant marine creature in attack mode. Today. In modern times. How can this be possible, she wondered? How and why would whatever it is show up now? And where in God's name did it come from? Most importantly, what is it?

"When did this happen Max? Did they say?"

"Oh, sometime yesterday, I think. Word just came in today."

"Injuries? Damage?"

"They didn't say, Rita. That's all I know. Thought you wouldwant to also."

"Thank you, Max., I appreciate the update."

After they hung up, Rita knew this was not news she could just sit on. That's just the way she was. She had to do something to find out more.

After finding out about the Japanese ships that disappeared mysteriously for unknown reasons, now this was happening. Coincidence? It's possible, she contemplated. But she had a gut feeling something very unnatural was happening in the world. She couldn't put her finger on it.

She was no investigator, except in her own field. Yet there could be a connection to that from what was seen out there. In her mind, it was never good to jump to any conclusions, so better to find out what she can first, no matter what it took. And that's what she started to do: by picking up the phone and starting from there.

On the Arga, 4PM

Down in these latitudes, daylight stuck around for a while. Fortunately for the ship, they were able to see the thing following them as long as it stayed at the surface. But there was no guarantee it would stay that way. If or when it dived, they could be in further serious trouble. There was no way of knowing what the creature's intentions were.

At this time, all non-scientist hands remained outside on deck around the ship's perimeter. A voice from the bridge suddenly blasted out from the ship's loudspeakers.

"Beth, please come to the bridge. Beth come to the bridge. You have a phone call."

From the main deck where she had been observing the creature with her binoculars, she quickly walked to the ladder-stairs on a ship-and climbed up one flight. She couldn't imagine who'd be calling her here, unless it was a family emergency back home in England.

The first mate handed the phone to her." Hello, this is Beth."

"Hi, Dr. Trenton. My name is Dr. Rita Bloomsworth. I am a paleo-herpetologist from Bradwell University in Texas. The US. I felt I needed to call you as a matter of possible urgency."

"Really?" replied Beth in a very surprised voice. This was a call she never could have expected. "How do you know I was here? On this ship down here?"

Rita had fully anticipated that question because she would have done the same.

She explained to Beth that she had to do some digging and telephone searching to find that out. Very many calls, some with heavily frustrating results. It was important enough, she felt, to make the seemingly insurmountable effort to locate the scientist.

Now that she had, maybe she could contribute something to help them out down there. That's what she told Beth.

"You say you're a…paleo-herpetologist?"

"That's right."

"I assume you've heard all over the news what's happening with us down here."

"Yes, I have," replied Rita. "And based on my latest research and a couple of discoveries, plus what happened to the Japanese whaling fleet, I believe there was enough justification for me to contact you as soon as possible."

Beth was now stunned. "Japanese whaling fleet? We didn't hear anything about that. You mean they were down here in the Southern Ocean?"

Rita, knowing the Arga was having issues of its own and was unable to hear the news, explained it all to her. In addition, she had mentioned about the downed oil rig in the Gulf of Mexico from something unexplained and no reasons to believe a fault in the structure itself.

"Oh my goodness. That's awful." Beth felt chills running up and down her spine. She realized they could be in far more danger than they had thought.

Without wasting any time, Rita started asking her questions about the creature. Beth responded with the best description she was able to give. It couldn't be a full one because all she could describe were the parts of it they could see.

"Dr. Trenton…"

"Beth," she corrected her.

"Ok Beth. Listen, I believe you're in very great danger. More than you know. Is that thing still following you?"

"Hold on a sec, Rita." She then asked the bridge crew for an update on the creature's position.

It was the first mate who checked and found out, and it wasn't very good news.

"We don't see it now. It's dived."

Beth told Rita that. Rita inhaled deeply and as softly as she could, hoping the scientist on the other end didn't hear her. She believed she knew several possibilities of the creature's species. Any one of them would be dangerous to all current sea life and humans.

But proof would be needed to convince the scientific world, the governments, and the rest of the world that what she believed was true. It could be a nearly impossible sell unless she had hard evidence. But how would she get that? For the moment she had to concentrate on helping the Arga if she could.

"Ok, Beth. You've got to get out of there. Get out of there as best and as quickly as you can."

"I agree. That's what we are trying to do. What do you think this is?"

"I can tell you what I believe it is and what I only think the species might be. But you've got to keep this quiet. Do not, under any circumstances, tell the crew."

Now Beth was getting a little frightened. She hadn't been so bad on that count. Until now.

"What about the captain, my colleagues?"

"The captain, ok. He should know because of his position. But in confidence only. Your colleagues: only the most trustworthy who can keep their mouths shut. This has to be kept under wraps for now."

"Rita, why this cloak and dagger? What is it that requires that?"

Rita then told her what she believed about its prehistoric origin and extinction some millions of years ago among many other creatures of that period of time. She told her what she thought its identity was.

"A Mosasaur? Oh dear Lord. Help us now. How can that be?"

"I don't know for sure without pictures or some other evidence. It was one of a number of giant marine predators that roamed the seas long ago. Maybe climate change brought them back to life. Who the hell knows? But I've got to get evidence that whatever it truly is, exists. Mosasaur or other giant. Otherwise, they will never believe me."

Beth understood who *they* likely were. Governments and other powers that be were always the greatest skeptics of everything that was not in a normal path of things.

Beth was in a semi state of shock. "So that could explain why all the sea life disappeared down here."

"Yes," replied Rita. "They had ravenous appetites and would virtually eat up anything and everything. Likely is the reason they went extinct. Ate up all their food supply. Would have eaten sharks and even whales with no problem."

Static suddenly came over the phone. Beth said she would have to end the call but thanked her very much for the information. There was nothing more that Rita could do but got a promise from Beth that she would keep the Texas professor posted after a quick exchange of numbers.

Taking Rita's advice, she went to Paul's cabin and informed him of what she had found out. She would take her time on telling her colleagues. There was no question of the necessity of keeping a very small loop of informed in this matter for obvious reasons.

She decided on the man who was the best with the camera. Although she didn't know how good he was a keeping a secret, she would make him an offer of scientific value he would be hard-pressed to refuse, if he agreed to and kept the secret until it was no longer necessary.

Paul returned to the bridge and ordered full speed back toward Tellmore. He would take no questions but did volunteer the reason being to escape the creature many of them had seen. Although some of the crew heard bits and pieces of the phone conversation when Beth was there, it was like putting a jigsaw puzzle together with more missing pieces than available ones. It was not nearly enough for them to connect the dots. So no one asked.

20

US Naval Atlantic Fleet Headquarters, CINCATLANTIC.

"Where is the Endeavor now?" Admiral Swenson was a little beyond concerned when it came to the ships in is fleet. The damage was determined to be minimal, according to the sub's captain, but it could easily have been much worse.

After he was told by his assistants where the sub was, he then ordered the sub to return to base. He considered a debriefing an absolute necessity.

"Please inform Captain Michaelson that I would like to speak to him as soon as possible after he completes docking."

"Yes sir," said his assistant, who was a captain in rank himself. On that command, communications to the sub was made.

Whatever happened out there was a mystery. George Swenson didn't like mysteries, especially out in the open ocean. And even more, especially with his ships. It because of such mysteries that ships in the past had disappeared for reasons which were unable to be determined.

He was told that ETA of the Endeavor to the Norfolk Naval base was 1400 hours tomorrow. Until then and his meeting with Captain Michaelson, it was business as usual.

On the Arga

With the creature having dived and the ship sailing full speed ahead back to Tellmore, it was imperative that they rely on the sonar to keep them informed of the creature's location. Not seeing the thing, Paul found it was significantly more unnerving than seeing it.

Todd had re-manned the sonar after a short break and now he was being depended on for finding the thing. Although he wouldn't be able to determine the depth of the creature, he could tell where it was in relation to the ship.

He did see the blip. With minor adjustments on a couple of knobs and setting the cursor, he relayed that information to Paul. Apparently, it was still behind them but a bit further off. Any further distancing of it from the ship was good news. They didn't know what it was capable of, but they preferred not to find out.

Meanwhile, on the stern Beth and George were setting up underwater video cameras. They had to set them all the way off to the port and starboard sides because of the prop's wake. Hoping to get a glimpse of the creature that was good enough for some kind of identification before it dived or swam away, they worked fervishly to get both cameras up and running.

After giving them a final check, they set the cameras in the water down to a depth of about fifteen feet. Having the small TV type screens set in transparent waterproof bags to protect them from the seawater, they watched the screens in real time.

There were a lot of bubbles. The water was unfortunately not crystal clear but still had up to ten to fifteen feet visibility. They thought they saw something in the distance but weren't sure. As with most of the others, they didn't know why it was following them. But they needed to get a better look at the thing. It didn't seem to be coming any closer on its own.

Using her satellite phone, she called up to the bridge. She had the number to the bridge's phone and decided it was too risky to leave the camera unattended, so the phone was sometimes a necessity.

"Paul, can you slow down a bit. We're in the process of getting videos of the thing but it's too far to see a clear image."

"That's pretty dangerous, Beth. If that thing catches up to us…"

"I know, I know. But just enough for us to at least see the head. Once we get that, we'll take a split second still shot of it and then I'll tell you to speed up. That's the signal that we got it. Just keep the line open here and have someone man it. We'll let you know the moment we get it. It won't take long."

"Ok, then. Here we go."

Beth could hear him give the command to slow to fifteen knots. She felt the engines lower in sound and the ship to begin to slow down a bit.

"George, here we go. Let's catch this SOB on the screen. Take your shot when you can."

"You got it."

Looking intensely at their screens, the two scientists strained to see what they could. The almost invisible dark blur began to darken and enlarge. It seemed to be catching up.

"Beth, you see this?" asked George loudly over the decreased but still noisy engines.

"Yea, and I don't like it."

They got a brief glimpse of the head as it revealed itself off and on through the cold, wake filled water. It was enough of a glimpse for them to realize the extreme peril they were in. This was reminiscent to Beth of the scene in Jurassic Park when the T-rex was chasing the vehicle trying to get away from it. Although she knew it was only a movie and not real, she had enjoyed it. Now, this was reality and she felt they were in basically the same position that those people were in. Only this was much worse. This was real. And so was the danger.

Now that they had gotten the videos and recordings, it was time to get out of Dodge as fast as their engines would allow. Beth called up to the bridge and told them they should now do that. Without question the engines revved up and soon they were pulling slowly ahead of the creature.

"Let's get these videos downstairs and get them set up. I think Paul should look at these, and Tom. Someone also needs to contact the marine authorities in the countries that have scientist stations down here."

"Yea. I can do that," volunteered George. "Why don't you let the bridge know and I'll bring these down to the lab. We'll check them out before I contact anybody and if I can get some stills on them, maybe we can send them the photos via satellite."

"Good idea. Let's go. Will meet you down there in a bit."

The two scientists separated. Soon the scientific world would know about this new discovery. What these ice world scientists didn't know is that other creatures of this kind were already making their mark in other parts of the world, to the detriment of all the creatures who lived in the sea. And man.

Kermit, Texas

"What has come to be considered a number of mysterious disappearances of marine life throughout the world-and people-is now believed to be connected to a mysterious marine life form that may be a new discovery. Many scientists are cautiously excited about it, but hope this possible new creature is not connected to the disappearances of sea life from the Gulf coast here down to Antarctica. Here's John Kimball, reporting from the Miami."

The screen then switched from Barry Kendall the anchor to the field reporter.

Rita was fixated on the news story. As she was hearing about the Japanese fleet, the US NAVY confrontation with a mysterious beast, and the Antarctica situation, she thought she heard it all. Then the screen showed the picture of something terrifying underwater. It was a still taken by the British Antarctica expedition. Her jaw dropped. She recognized what it was, and she couldn't believe her eyes.

What she couldn't have known was that the British Science Maritime Corporation had emphatically told the Antarctica scientists *not* to release that picture to the public. The last thing they wanted was to have a worldwide panic created and have every Tom, Dick, and Harry go out haphazardly and recklessly looking to kill it or them like those fishermen did in the movie *Jaws*.

Contrary to what they were told, Beth chose to release it anyway. People needed to know about the creature for their own safety and she didn't believe keeping it under wraps would be of benefit to anyone. Except maybe the scientists themselves. But she wanted no part of that.

21

Nationwide and internationally, the news spread with viral speed. Even in landlocked countries, the news caught everybody's interest. Though the trouble seemed to be purely marine in nature, still there was the shocking interest most people would have. This was not something that one could just brush off no matter where you lived.

Along the coasts of the United States and across the world, tensions and fears quickly increased as more word spread regarding the Japanese and American tragedies.

Navies, Coast Guards in various countries and scientific marine expeditions started combing the waters for the creature or creatures that were nicknamed the "Loch Ness monsters of the sea" by those who remained skeptical. The marine services neither admitted nor acknowledged their beliefs of the existence of these creatures. What they believed in, of course, was hard evidence. The scientists were not so quick to dismiss the nickname. But they, too, demanded evidence, which was required of their jobs. To their credit, at least in part, those scientists down in Antarctica, were providing that.

Scientists such as Rita Bloomsworth and her colleagues always knew and believed that dinosaurs went extinct millions of years ago with the last great meteor impact. Although Jurassic Park, in typical Hollywood style, gave birth to the possibility of cloning or bringing back to life ancient creatures that were known to be extinct, it was not an idea that was taken seriously. At least to the known scientific world.

It's not hard to realize that mammals and gigantic reptiles would be hard pressed, if possible, to co-exist. This includes within earth's oceans as well.

When megalodon existed, the ancient ancestor to today's great white sharks, it was so large and such a voracious eater, like today's sharks, that it ate itself out of existence. Yet, it did not rule the oceans. It was at the top, but not at the peak. That spot was reserved for larger, equally or more dangerous creatures than even the world's greatest and largest fish. It was actually a reptile that ruled the oceans for a time. For them, the time eventually came when they had to go. The oceans could not maintain a sufficient and efficient ecosystem for marine life and even for land animals with all the marine life being eaten up by gargantuan creatures. Food for them was just not sustainable.

For mammals, both on land and in the water, it was a remarkable and necessary change that needed to happen for the health of the planet. At some point in earth's prehistory, something happened to prevent true extinction of some creatures.

Although the crocodilians which include all species of crocodiles, alligators, caimans and other types, are actually dinosaurs which survived because they are the truest of survivalists and the toughest as well, they needed no magic wand or special consideration by nature. They didn't change much over millions of years except in size and habitats.

Nearly all other reptile species on the planet had perished. Those which were not meant to survive within nature's natural selection process had perished. But unknown to the world, something *had* survived which nature's natural selection process had chosen for extinction. There was a good reason why mother nature had selected this species for elimination from the natural world. Just as it had the same reason for extinguishing the existence of the Tyrannosaurus Rex.

Yet this creature had somehow "slipped through the cracks." Only the most foolish of scientists would welcome its comeback. For most, it would become an abomination of the modern world. For all marine travelers globally, sailing on the oceans would become a potential hell on the high seas.

Only now one scientist, after gathering all the evidence through research, current events, scientific investigations, and interviews with involved scientists, came to a horrific conclusion that defied all logic initially. As her investigation reached its conclusive end regarding the identity of the creatures and why they suddenly came back to life, she clenched her jaw and shook her head. "It figures. Son of a bitch." Luckily, she was alone when she said it out loud.

Kermit, Texas

Mosasaur. It took a lot of research and comparison studies to gradually and eventually come to that conclusion. It was just one of numerous marine giants that lived in a period of time during the age of the dinosaurs. It was from what is known, mostly among paleo-scientists, as the Maastrichtian age, which was during the late Cretaceous period—about seventy to sixty-five million years ago.

Although it may not have been the most dangerous of the giant marine carnivores, it's enough to worry all sea-going vessels everywhere because of its huge size, voracious appetite, and aggressiveness.

It was not possible, of course, to study a live one up close. What information of any details she could obtain were from the Antarctic British scientists who had used video cameras to capture whatever images they could of the creature which had been following them.

In finding out the various tragedies that occurred from mysterious circumstances in various ocean locations, Rita wasn't sure if there was one or more of these creatures. That's something she would definitely need to find out asap.

She needed some help on this and decided to start with first Samantha, then Roger. Sam was immediately and totally on board with her, in her determination to get answers to this and rid of the creatures if at all possible. She then called Roger.

"No kidding. Are you *serious*? How is this possible that they exist?"

Rita then explained. "Man caused this."

Roger shook his head in disbelief. "Man? What do you mean man caused this? You think some Jurassic Park guy got it into his head to make it the real thing?"

"No, no, no! That's not it. I'm talking about global warming."

She needn't say anything more. Roger got it and knew right off the bat where she was going with this. His momentary silence told her he understood.

"You think they may have come from the ice down there?" Roger asked her.

Rita inhaled as deeply as her thoughts. "Maybe. Possibly even the ocean bed. Considering the significant geographical global differences between tens of millions of years ago and now, they could have come from virtually anywhere, buried for all that time. Somehow preserved in the tremendous cold rather than dying out like all the other creatures. Yet, even if that's true, why *them* and no other creatures? That's what's got me baffled."

Roger cleared his throat. "Well, seems to me that something needs to be done and fast. I don't know the why or how, but considering that a lot of people have been killed on the seas, including those Japanese sailors and that there were no submarines around there at the time, we can only conclude that other than an explosion or fuel leak, something external caused those tragedies. And it wasn't human."

"Right. I'm going to contact the Navy and the national maritime sciences. Good grief. I'm thinking about all this and listen to what I'm saying. I feel like I'm in a freaking science fiction movie or something. I think the next line would be 'This can't be happening right now'.

Roger chuckled. "I hear ya, Rita. I wish that was all it is.. But wishing isn't gonna solve the problem. I will contact the Navy and whoever else I can think that should know and would be of help in this. This will have to go international."

With quick sign-outs, the two scientists began their announcements to all the appropriate powers-that-be. It would take a little time, but the way things were going, they didn't have a lot of that on their plates before something else happened. And it soon did.

The Southern Ocean, on the Arga

The ship's captain had decided to head west for a brief time in order to evade whatever creature had been around them. Until proven otherwise, he had to consider it dangerous to the ship and everything around it. His ultimate goal was to head on back home to Tellmore. Unfortunately, just being out at sea was now perilous because of what was beneath them. So far there hadn't been any attacks on the ship, but that didn't mean it wouldn't happen.

Over the radio and from news broadcasts, he had heard about what happened with the Japs. Although he was pleased that they weren't around now to hunt whales, still it was very disturbing to hear the tragic news related to two of their ships. It wasn't something any mariner would want to hear, no matter how intense any rivalry was. Deaths were never something to celebrate.

"Todd, anything on your screen?" Paul asked the sonarman over the intercom.

"Negative, cap. So far so good."

"Roger. Keep a close eye. We'll be turning about soon."

Todd acknowledged and soon silence reclaimed the bridge.

The day was cloudy and a little on the windy side. The swells in the water were three to four feet. Above them the silence also claimed the air, with no sea birds in sight anywhere around them. It was eerie to say the least. The crew had accepted the situation they were in for the time being. But it was clear that everyone was unsettled, including Paul. Everyone knew things were far from right, but they didn't know why. This feeling of unsettlement in everyone never went away.

"In three minutes, turn to starboard to bearing one-four-five."

The helmsman repeated the order verbatim. In three minutes, the order was made to turn, and the ship was soon on its new bearing."

"Increase speed to twenty-five knots."

Paul's command was made and followed through with. The engine noise increased in volume and they were now heading to where they needed to be right now.

Paul picked up the ship wide intercom.

"Attention everyone, this is the captain. I've turned the ship around, and we are heading now back to home port. ETA expected to be in 6 hours. I ask that everyone be vigilant at all times because there is something unknown somewhere beneath us. Everyone needs to batten down anything that's loose. Beth, please come to the bridge."

He had a gut feeling about something, but he didn't want to say anything out loud here because that's *all* it was right now. Anything he would say about it would be done in a more private area. Last thing he wanted was a panic situation.

Two minutes later, Beth arrived on the bridge. "Hey, what's up Paul?"

"Beth, our mission is over as of now. We cannot continue what you wanted to do originally because of the new clear and present danger. Have any new thoughts about it?"

"Matter of fact I do."

"Let's go down to my cabin. Can you get Tom and George and have them meet us there?"

"I'm on it. See you shortly."

"Ted you have the bridge," he told his second mate. "I'll be in my cabin."

"Got it, cap."

Ten minutes later, the four of them were in Paul's cabin.

"Folks, I don't have a clue what's out there. But what I DO know is that we are certainly in perilous waters, no pun intended. We are heading full speed back to port. I heard on the news about the Jap ships, plus other marine casualties. Then I heard about some guy being attacked on a fishing boat off the coast of Brazil by something that wasn't a shark. Then on top of that all, an oil rig gets attacked by something and is destroyed. What I'd like to know is what the hell is going on? Beth, what can you tell me from what you believe so far?"

Fishing pier Number Three, New Orleans, La.

"Hurry up, will ya? We're supposed to get underway in forty-five minutes. Stan, get those lines on deck prepared, especially at the bow. While you're up there, double check the stability of the mount. I want to know that it's as tight as it could get."

"You got it, cap." The deckhand worked fast, while others were preparing the rest of the one hundred sixty-foot fishing vessel *Sea Warrior.*

Reginald van Horten, or Reggie as he preferred to be called by his friends, had been seagoing for nearly thirty years. That's all he really knew, ever since he was a boy. His father had been a merchant marine officer when Reggie was only thirteen. After retiring from that service, his dad continued his seagoing ways by buying a fishing boat and bringing his son on board, hoping that Reggie would follow in his footsteps, not necessarily by joining the merchant marines. He hoped to one-day train him toward captaining a fishing boat: *this* boat and handing it over to him when it was time to hand over the reins. That did happen and since then he never regretted it. He didn't need any college to make good money. He did alright doing what he loved more than anything. Although it had its risks and disappointments now and then, still it was worth it. The payoffs, when they occurred, were huge. Although he never married, he considered the sea life his bride and

he wouldn't have it any other way. His fiftyish, rough looks gave him the stereotypical appearance of what a fisherman-more likely a fishing captain-should look like. At least to some people. Some people had even commented that he reminded them of Quint, the fishing captain in the movie, *Jaws.*

Like Quint, he was a stern captain and tolerated neither insubordination nor freeloading when they were underway. Ocean fishing, despite its seemingly benign job type, was considered one of the most dangerous jobs in the world. A lot depended on the weather, sea conditions, what kind of fishing you were doing, and what kind of crew you had. Reggie wanted the best crew he could get. He paid very well, but he demanded top notch experienced fishermen for that. That means every crew member was required to know all there was to know regarding everything from boat handling and seamanship and fire safety to how to catch, hold onto, and process the kind of fish he normally was after, which was swordfish. And they had to *work.* That's what they were getting paid for and that's what he expected.

This particular trip would be as different from the hundreds of others he had made over the years. As he looked out to the other boats and saw several other crews scrambling to prepare for getting underway, it seemed to make him more aware of the increased danger of what they were going to do. In his mind, it was a necessity rather than foolhardiness. There would be no catch involved here and no money reward. He wasn't sure exactly why he felt the need to do this. All he knew was that he *had* to. He believed in letting his crew in on it and gave them the opportunity to back out without any repercussions if they chose to do so. None of them did. Each one of them had enough respect and admiration for their captain to cover for the others.

Unlike a few other captains, he didn't see his job or catching fish as being competitive with others. He wasn't out here to beat the other guy. His job was to catch the fish and make money, for his crew and himself. They all had families to support and depended so much on this job-and him for that matter. When it came right down to it, he really *was* more concerned for his crew than for himself. Although he did his best not to advertise that to the others, the fact is they knew anyway. That's why they loved him and always worked their hardest to accommodate him as he did for them.

This trip was different, and it was enough to unnerve him. He didn't unnerve easily. Unlike most other fishing expeditions when he was quite confident they would return to the docks as usual once they filled the tanks, he was as unsure as unsure could get this time. He saw the men coming down to the last preparations and realized he better not show what he was feeling right now. For them.

"All set up here, Reg." The deckhand, Sid, let him know that the newly purchased harpoon gun set on the starboard bow was set firmly in place and that the two hundred-foot line attached to the harpoon was attached with all the expertise that a boatswain could muster, making it highly unlikely it would become detached.

"Very good, Sid," Reggie responded. Check aft for me to see where everyone is on this, will ya?"

"Sure."

He looked at his watch. Departure time in thirty minutes. Time to grab a coffee and head on up to the wheelhouse. He needed to set the navigation and make sure the charts were all in order. Once he received the final word that all preps were completed, the final countdown would begin. He turned around and left.

The Ross Sea, on the Arga

Having a close encounter with an unknown sea creature was not the ideal way of having a proper expedition. The fact that they had to divert from their normal research ops to one of unprecedented strangeness and uncertainty could make one feel as if they had been transported into the twilight zone. But this was reality and they had *seen,* albeit briefly, part of the unknown creature. It did exist but its identity still remained an unknown certainty.

As they neared the land, Beth wondered what would be next. What *could* they do? They could continue normal operations and research- business- as usual, so to speak. But she would have a difficult time with that. If what was happening here would place any boat or ship in jeopardy, there could be no business as usual. What if what was happening here was happening elsewhere in the world? She had to find out. That meant going to her office and getting on the computer.

Up on the bridge, Paul was making preparations to dock. He slowed the ship down as they neared the docks as the crew readied to throw the lines. Thirty minutes later they were nudging the ship gently against the dock with all the fenders out and the lines connected to the stanchions.

Beth felt the ship stop and the engines slow down. Soon all was quiet as they were turned off. They were home. But she was in the middle of finding out something about what was going on in the world outside of Antarctica.

Some of the news on the internet revealed mysterious beast sightings around the world, most of which were off the coast of the southern US. She saw news about the destroyed oil rig in the Gulf of Mexico and eventual findings of remnants of what was believed to be a fishing vessel called the

Sea Angel. Reports of a gargantuan sea creature, still not identified, came through, although they were skimpy. Yet, a number of people seeing what seemed to be the same thing. She already knew about the tragedy of the Japanese whaling fleet. More reports of missing people with unfound bodies were mentioned.

22

Galapagos Island region, South America

Known to no one in the general public at the present time, much of the area's wildlife was disappearing at a significant rate. Where there was once a healthy population of turtles, now the animals were few and far between in number. Fish known to inhabit the waters year-round were almost nonexistent. With the sea life dwindling down to almost nothing, now even the sharks who preyed upon the fish for food were forced to look elsewhere. From a visual standpoint, if one were to gaze upon it, the Galapagos Islands and their waters appeared the same as usual.

But there were always scientists studying the region, including those from National Geographic. These were the first to realize that something had changed, and it was not necessarily for the better. Two of these scientists/journalists were from NG, Rick and Carolyn Johnston. A married couple who just happened to also be marine biologists. They had been sent down by the Society to study the effects of global climate change on the region's marine wildlife. Their concern radiated back and forth from each other as they gathered more information about what was going on.

The two scientists were scuba diving in the waters off one of the islands, noticing the absence of most of the smaller fish that normally lived there. Their microphones within their masks were essential for communicating each's other findings.

"Carol, let's see what's on the other side of that mound over there," he said, pointing toward it.

"Ok," she replied. Here the waters were crystal clear and pristine. No contamination by the hands of mankind marred these waters.

The coral reefs, with their rainbow colors, were sights of exquisite beauty which dazzled even the most experienced scientist divers. The quiet serenity of the back and forth waving motions of the small seabed plants did not challenge the peaceful tranquility of their surroundings. Rather, they hid what would soon be revealed to the scientists.

Although the couple loved to explore, even off the job, this was no curiosity fun trip. They were looking for clues, which could be anywhere behind or beyond any mound or ridge. As they swam toward it, Rick thought he saw something sticking out from the other side of it. He wasn't sure if it was anything or not, but he beckoned Carolyn with his hand to move forward.

Just beyond the mound, the scientists saw what the most disturbing sight they'd ever come across. It was a huge, Galapagos turtle—actually a part of it—lying on the sea floor. It had been bitten in half, almost with surgical-like precision.

Coming to it for further, closer examination, they tried to figure out what could have done this. Although there had always been large numbers of sharks in the area, today there had been none that they could see. The area of the huge bite was no doubt big enough to make them think that something very large and predatory had killed this animal. They knew that sea turtles were a favorite meal of tiger sharks. But there were none of those that inhabited these waters. Something didn't seem right about this killing. This was not a known way a shark would've killed it. Even a great white could have done this; yet they had seen neither of the species anywhere nor any other shark species.

As they examined the half turtle, something caught Carol's eye in the distance, and she looked out toward it. It looked like something large, much larger than this. She wasn't sure if it was just an underwater boulder or something else.

"Rick, I see something over there," she pointed out. "Let's go check it out."

He nodded and the two started swimming toward it. As they got closer, the object became larger and larger. It didn't take them long to see what it was. It took a few moments for the shock to hit them. Then the processing in their minds took over before they could react. What presented itself to their visual discovery would be something no scientist would ever want to see.

It was about forty feet long. Just beyond the huge six-foot-plus rounded gash in its side lay the large tail fins of a marine mammal. They knew from its head and body configuration that is was, or had been, a humpback whale. The gash itself was almost as deep as it was wide. It wouldn't have taken much more of a bite for it to be sliced in half. Entrails, fat, and other material floated out of it.

"Good God, what the hell could've have done this?" Rick couldn't remember the last time he had seen such a horrific sight.

"I don't know, hon," Carolyn replied. "But I think when we are finished here, we need to get back and report it. But what bothers me just as much as seeing this is what we are *not* seeing."

They looked at each other. Their eyes communicated and each knew. It was time to get out of here and they wasted no time in heading back to the boat.

***

The world was changing but not for the better. Where it started out with Rita Bloomsworth in Texas in discovering on a hunch, word in the scientific community had spread like wildfire and soon the entire world knew what was going on. There was plenty of evidence pointing toward identification of the marine beast that prowled the earth's oceans.

Because of the multiple locations worldwide of attacks on marine vessels, coupled with the sudden disappearance of much of the world's marine wildlife, governments along with the scientific community had to come up with a plan to hunt down and destroy what was beginning to destroy the ocean's ecosystems. The problem was that no one knew how many of the creatures were lurking in the oceans. It was impossible to know for sure. Studies were being made by some of the world's foremost marine scientists, along with marine paleontologists and oceanographers. Along with these scientists was Rita Bloomsworth.

In Odessa, she worked nonstop to find out how they managed to "come back to life" after a known extinction of millions of years. Her conclusion should have been surprising, but it was not to her. She had surely hoped it would not have been true. For the scientific mind, it would have been the find of the "millennium", a discovery of something besides crocodilians that was truly from the prehistoric world. Yet, from the viewpoint of human logic and practicality, it could be a death sentence for mankind and animal life as we know it today.

These Mosasaurs, like all other giant dinosaurs, are not compatible with life on earth with the creatures that exist today. One or the other would be wiped out. It didn't matter if they were terrestrial or marine. Rita knew that if the world's oceans and all normal life on earth were to be saved, all of these creatures would have to be destroyed. In the short time they've been "re-existing" already a large percentage of the ocean sea life has disappeared. She believed that currently the world's oceanic ecosystems are out of balance because of these creatures. The survival of the planet, no doubt, is in serious trouble.

At her desk one Tuesday morning, the phone rang.

"Professor Bloomsworth."

As she listened to Sue Williams, her friend who worked at the oceanographic institute in LaJolla, her mind started racing. It was confirmation from one professional to another that she had positively identified the creature at one of the locations where a sailboat had been attacked. This time it was in the Pacific.

"Were any photographs taken of it?" she asked.

"Yes," said Sue. "It was pure luck. There just happened to be another boat in the area of the sailboat and someone on *that* boat was taking pictures when the creature suddenly appeared out of the water. It actually dwarfed the thirty-foot sailboat.

“How did you find out about it?”

“It was on the news on TV. Special report, just a few minutes ago. I was off from work today and saw it at home. Thought you’d want to know.”

Rita was astounded. She couldn’t believe it. This was one of those times when she wasn’t able to watch TV.

“Sue, by the brief picture you saw, how can you be sure it was a mosasaur?”

When Sue told her about seeing the long pointy jaw, the sharp spines along its back and tail, and the gargantuan size of it, that sealed the deal for identification. The world certainly had a new problem on its hands, along with the thousands of others. One would be bad enough. More than that would be too terrible to think about. How do you stop a bunch of gigantic creatures in the oceans that aren’t supposed to exist anymore? Most of the world had likely never heard of them, let alone know what they are.

After thanking her friend, she sat quietly for a few moments processing this new information in her mind. Because this was publicly broadcast on the air, she knew that the government would very quickly find out about this. Maybe they could figure out how to combat this. But she didn’t believe the US alone could handle something this global. This was undoubtedly international, and that required international efforts to eradicate the problems. She picked up the phone and made the call to someone who she had once been connected to. With luck, that person was still around to reconnect to. Because *that* person could hold the key to solving the problem.

Tellmore Station, Antarctica

Inside the station, there was tense activity. The normal research of the scientists was put on hold because of the new world crisis. Unlike most global crisis’, this one extended its effect all the way down to them. The fact that they had been pursued and chased by something huge, narrowly escaping destruction, made it all the more real.

Many of the scientists were trying to keep up with what was going on with this in the outside world. Computers and the internet were being used, as well as well as what they could find out on their limited TVs. They could receive CNN occasionally and today was one of those occasions. What was happening seemed to be spreading everywhere on the globe. Governments were expressing huge concerns, the fishing industries were hollering for help because their livelihoods and food catches were being killed off, and even the tourism industries everywhere were seeing record lows like never before.

Beth was focused on what she was reading on the news internet when a voice on the loudspeaker asked for everyone's attention.

"Attention everyone. Will everyone please go to the dining hall for an important meeting. Everyone is requested there in fifteen minutes."

She was thinking about discussing about the situation anyway. Maybe someone read her mind. "Good," she mumbled to herself. She wanted to get a coffee anyway. No time like the present.

Getting up, she made her way out into the hallway and ran into George.

"Heading over there now?" he asked.

"Yes. Going to get coffee now anyway." They started heading out, leaving the dorm and office building. As always, it was bitterly cold, but at least it wasn't snowing. The skies were cloudy, and those flakes could come down at any time without warning. So could the winds. It was a part of Antarctic life that they all knew and got used to. They walked across the campus to the larger blue building about fifty yards away.

"Yea, I could use a cup myself," he replied. "I guess we need to find out where we go from here."

They reached the door and entered the dining hall. "You got that right, George".

There were already some people in there, having grabbed their hot drinks and sitting at a couple of tables. More started coming in after Beth and George. In five minutes, the place had nearly everyone in there, all seventy-five people, including maintenance and first responders.

Beth and George took a seat and a table with two other scientists, a firefighter, medical technician, and dispatcher. There were fifteen long tables in the dining hall. Most of them were filled with others from throughout the station.

Beth saw Paul and waved when their eyes met. He took a seat at another table. Soon the chief scientist of the station, Ben Gilmore-a marine ecologist-stood at the microphone and called attention from everyone. It was 9pm and the skies were lit up as usual as if it were twelve noon.

"Thank you all for coming," he started out. "We have to talk about what is going to, or needs to, happen because of this crisis situation."

Everyone's eyes were on him and all ears were ready to receive his output.

"If anyone has any information, new or otherwise as I'm talking up here, please lift a hand and I'll stop to listen. I only ask that you save your *questions* for after I'm done. I may have an answer to your question before you ask it. If I don't, then save it for when I finish talking. Any recommendations afterwards will be considered. Sound ok?"

A few agreeing mumblings and many nods of heads told him he could begin.

"Feel free to grab a coffee anytime. Ok, here's the deal."

Ben started a brief verbal synopsis of the world and station situation, including the event recently experienced by the *Arga* and its crew. After making some comments and giving some of his opinions how this situation would affect the operations and purposes of the station, he made it clear that it should not affect the reasons they were there.

"We cannot ignore whatever scientific reasons explain our being here. Yet, at the same time, we can't ignore what's going around us either. Everybody agree?"

Heads nodded followed by a number of yesses.

"Ok, good. Has, um, anyone come up with any ideas of what we are dealing with here, specifically the species of marine animal?"

Beth remembered talking to Rita on the phone. Here was the time she should say something. And she pushed forward with it, telling out loud what she had been told by her expert scientific colleague.

She heard some gasps and saw shocked looks on faces that never saw this coming, including Ben's. Except from the *Arga* crew who already knew.

"But no one on your ship saw the head, just a body, like reports made around the world in lakes. How could that professor know that for sure? I understand there were a number of various types of marine dinosaur species. These could be any one or number of them. That is, if that's what these things are."

Rita looked around at everyone looking at her and took a deep breath. The truth was not hard to tell. But yet it was not easy to have to tell it.

"Based on what Professor Bloomsworth saw and studied, along with another colleague of hers, they made great efforts to identify the species. Not just with pictures, but also from multiple reports from witnesses who had seen various parts of the animals. Combined together, they were able to eventually conclude that the creature, or creatures, could only be from a Mosasaur. And, in my opinion if they started appearing down here, where there's one, there are probably more.

She paused for a moment to let that sink in.

"Now, I've been doing some research on it, while trying to fit in what I normally do. What I did find, along with the disappearance of the sea life and the abnormal penguin behavior we saw is that we initially concluded here that these disappearances were caused by a marine creature at least as big as a humpback, if not larger and far more dangerous than any Orca. When you consider that, along with all the tragic incidents that have occurred in the different oceans by eyewitness reports, it can only validate what we have concluded and those of the experts up in the US.

What we are dealing with is a creature from seventy to about sixty-six million years ago that went extinct. A few facts about it that I found out:

it lives mostly near the surface of the oceans, killing and feeding on literally anything it could sink its teeth into. And it has large conical teeth which dwarf those of today's great white sharks. It has four flippers: rear and front, with the front larger. The long heavy body and a couple of the flippers have been eye witnessed for real. Whoever saw them of course had no idea what they were looking at. Also, when the dorsal part of the body was seen above water, spines were notices along the entire length. The length of the creature, from a combination of all reports, was concluded to be about fifty to sixty feet. That's all I was able to find out right now."

Everyone in the room was stunned as they processed this shocking revelation and a brief silence filled the air. Until one of the scientists posed a question that was the proverbial, but brief, elephant in the room.

"Beth if this is the case, how could these extinct animals have come back to life? Or were they *really* extinct and were just now discovered still existing?"

From Charlie Goodman, an ornithologist, it was the perfect question.

"It seems that it has to do with global warming. At least right now that's the general consensus."

Ben suddenly interjected. "And you think that these things came back to life with the warming of the waters? That they were in a sort of, well, suspended animation for millions of years?"

Beth continued to feel all eyes on here. The silence was deafening.

"Well what else, what other explanation could there be? I mean, there's no proof of that of course."

"So…. if that's the case, the next thing is what to do about it. At least, what can *we* do about it?"

Ben seemed to believe what she was saying. Whether anyone else actually believed her or not didn't really matter except figuring out in the long run how to get rid of the creatures.

"What about capturing one of them?" asked someone in the room.

Beth was surprised at that one. "I won't ask who asked that. Normally with creatures we are familiar with in modern times, that would be a possibility. But in this case, if that was tried, the persons trying that would almost certainly be killed. That's like trying to capture a huge grizzly bear charging at you at full speed with a butterfly net. Not possible I'm afraid."

Ben took the floor again.

"Well, we have to collaborate and figure out what we can do down here. The waters here, as everywhere else in the world, are treacherous. Too much to take any unnecessary chances. For now, we need to suspend any marine expeditions that are absolutely unnecessary with what's going on now. Beth, will you be talking with your American colleague or friend anytime soon again?"

"I can," she nodded. "What about looking for the thing with the Arga?"

Ben raised his eyebrows a bit. "You really want to do that? Considering what almost happened to you and the ship? And what would you hope to accomplish? You already saw it on sonar and part of it visually. The ship is not armed and can't destroy it. But it can destroy *you* and everyone else, not to mention the ship. No, I'm afraid I can't really allow that."

As far as the danger, no one could dispute that. "Anyone else have a question?" asked Ben.

There was none. For the moment.

"Alright. Let's carry on normal ops for now. Any promising ideas, my door is always open. Office, that is. Beth, let me know when you've talked with your friend. See if she or any of her marine experts have any ideas. Meanwhile, I will contact London and see what ideas the powers that be might have. We have to stay in the loop and be a part of whatever international plan someone comes up with, without completely ignoring our original purpose here."

"Ok boss. Will do." Beth got up with George and soon everyone was heading out the door.

"George, this is sure going to be a major undertaking. How can we possibly concentrate on our normal research with this crap going on?"

He shook his head with a sheepish smile. "If you ask me, unless everyone else in the world cooperates and does this at about the same time, I don't know how the hell we can kill these things unless we bomb them. And we don't even know how *many* of them there are. And what are *we* supposed to do? We have no weapons down here, let alone cannons or other things, especially on the ship."

Something George said stopped her in her tracks, leaving George five feet ahead of her before he stopped and looked back at her.

"What?" he asked.

Beth was deep in thought. George saw it and knew when she looked like that she was coming up with a brainstorm. He hadn't worked with her for so many years without knowing at least *that* about her.

Her eyes then lifted up to meet his.

"What?" he asked again.

"Come on. Let's get to the office, and I'll tell you."

23

US Naval Station, Atlantic Fleet Headquarters, Norfolk, Va.

The Rear Admiral's assistant, Captain Sidney Pelton, approached his boss, Admiral Robert Downsworthy in his office with photographs in his hand.

"Sir, these just came in," he said quickly handing them to the man behind the desk.

"Oh good, I've been waiting for these."

The voice was quiet and calm which often hid his true emotions or what he was really thinking. It was part of Admiral Downsworthy's character to ensure that any anger or frustrations he might feel would not transfer to others. In the past, he often saw others become immediately incensed with the same emotions. It was part of his job to maintain control and order. Becoming unhinged could negatively affect any decisions he might make. That would not be good.

In his twenty-five plus years in the Navy, he only had one-what one could call-true meltdown. And that was all it took to ensure it never happened again. Although the incident which put him on the edge was relatively minor, he prided himself on maintaining control over things, especially his own behavior.

The middle-aged boyish looking man with the slightly gray hair looked down at the pictures and flexed one eyebrow upward slightly. What he was looking at in one of the pics could have been an elongated neck.

"Sid, this looks like part of the Loch Ness monster. You sure this is for real?"

"Look at the next ones, sir."

This time his second eyebrow went up. "Well I'll be damned."

"These just came in a few minutes ago from NOAA."

He almost couldn't take his eyes off of them. "They sure have good satellites to take these. Looks like this thing just popped out of the water. This is the first head shot, isn't it?"

"That's right sir. First time anyone has actually seen it. And the photos didn't actually originate with NOAA."

The admiral looked up at the captain in surprise. "Really? Who got them then?"

According to reports from NOAA, a marine archeologist or anthropologist in Texas received photos from another scientist who'd actually taken the photos. The person who took the pictures is stationed in Antarctica. At one of the stations down there called Tellmore."

"Antarctica?" The admiral was stunned. "Are you saying that this creature has also been sited down there as well? This better not be an elaborate hoax or someone's head is going to roll."

"No, it's definitely not a hoax. Can't be when you think about it."

"No, captain. I'm afraid you're right. There's no way. In a sense, I kind of wished that it was. As I see it, this could turn out to be far more problematic that we think."

'Seems so, sir. Anyway, apparently, he-or she-had been in contact with the scientist in Texas. What their connection is uncertain. What we *are* certain of is that this creature is prehistoric, is NOT extinct-at least not anymore-and has been seen by a number of people in different areas."

"Sid, get me Admiral Brenner on the phone. I want to know if he has seen similar reports or has received similar photos like this. If this is just local then maybe our fleet alone can deal with this. If this has gone global, heaven help us. I want confirmation on this before I do anything."

"Right away sir."

The two-star admiral picked up the phone to contact his secretary. He had heard of someone on the news who might be an expert on this beast.

"Amanda, see you can find out the name of that professor down in, uh I think Texas. I'm not sure which university she's associated with. I thought I heard the name Odessa mentioned on the news. Anyway, she is either a marine biologist or maybe archaeologist, I don't know. Something like that. You may have to do some digging. But see if you can find out for me and if you do, let me know what university she's with."

She acknowledged. Continuing on with his work now was a way he could maintain staying on top of everything he was responsible for. The nature of his rank and duties left him little spare time. He had a conference to go to in a couple of hours and had no time to waste wondering about monsters and all other such crap.

Odessa, Texas

Rita was surprised to hear from Antarctica. She certainly remembered Beth.

"Aha, I see," Rita said after the initial welcoming small talk. "Well listen Beth, I can't recommend any seagoing adventures based on what's happening. If you do get underway, realize that it's at your own peril."

She listened as Beth told her what her plans were. She needed Rita's opinion as to whether it could work based on what she knew about the creature. Her jaw dropped when Beth laid out the groundwork and what would be used in those plans. Her expression quickly changed to concern.

"I don't know, hon. Not only would that be expensive to obtain and install, but I don't even know if harpoons are even made anymore. Even if they are and you get one with its firing mount, going after one of these things would, in my opinion, place the endeavor at the very top of the danger scale. It's one thing to 'poon a whale. It's an entirely different ballgame when you're talking about a leviathan life-killing predator from the Cretaceous period. You'd be asking for some serious trouble, girl."

There was a sudden knock on her office door.

"Come in. The door opened and it was Mandy, her assistant. Rita put up a finger as she finished her conversation with Beth.

"Ok, listen. I gotta go but call me if or when it's been decided that it's a go. I don't want you guys getting slammed. I think you know what I mean by that. That could mean a one-way trip for you and I don't want to see that happen. Please think very carefully before deciding. Get back to me, ok?"

As soon as she put the phone down, Mandy spoke.

"Rita, someone from the Navy is asking for you."

"From the *navy?"* Although she was surprised and instantly wondered why they would be calling her, she just as quickly realized this could be an opportunity to get the navy on board, so to speak, toward resolving the elimination of these creatures. The key words were *could be.* The question was, *would they?* There was only one way to find out.

"Patch them to my phone, Mandy."

As soon as the transfer call ring sounded, she picked it up and listened to the caller.

"Ok, I'll hang on." she said into the phone. Now why would a navy admiral be calling her? Maybe he saw her reports that were aired on tv. That had to be it.

A minute later he was on the phone, quickly introducing himself and where he was calling from. She was surprised that she was talking to the top brass, the head of the entire US Navy Atlantic fleet. It was almost surreal.

His revelation of the reason for the call was not entirely unanticipated. When he was told that the Pacific was infested as well, there was no longer any doubt that the problem had indeed become global. He was reaching out to anyone and all who could provide information about the creature. The more information he could obtain, the greater the chance they could eliminate the problem. Except for a very few die-hard scientists who were against killing off what they considered the discoveries of a lifetime, no one else wanted another Jurassic Park out of control on the planet, especially on the high seas. Rita was one of those few who had serious expertise on paleolithic marine predators. Right now she was needed, and he minced no words to let her know that.

They talked for several minutes before the admiral had to go. He left her his number and extension. They would be talking again. With the initial information she provided to him, he could now start a plan of action and begin working up the logistics to activate that plan when it was ready.

Unfortunately, with each day that passed, more lives could be lost at sea. So time was not on their side. At the same time, he had to make sure that the plan would work. It had to. The survival of the planet and its inhabitants depended on it.

Tellmore Station, Antarctica

"Are you out of your mind, Beth?" It was the way that Ben asked it that almost made her feel like she had told him she would jump into a volcano so she could make it stop erupting.

"Ben, just hear me out for a second."

"No, Beth, listen to me first." His tone had quickly settled down because of his deep respect for her and her work.

"First of all, the cost. Very expensive. I don't think the British government would provide the expenses for that. Second, it's very difficult, if not impossible, to obtain what you would need to arm a ship with a harpoon. The Arga is not built for that."

"But it could very well work!" Beth quickly interrupted.

Ben shook his head and waved his hand back and forth. "No no. Now wait a minute Beth. What you are asking is to change a fully functional research vessel into a whaling type ship. I know it's not whales we would be going after. Rather, something more infinitely dangerous. *Think* about it, please. I know you want to do this, but think of the lives you'd be risking unnecessarily, not to mention the ship. Chances are, you would get only one shot at it. In fact, it would likely be a one-way trip for you and the rest of the crew."

Beth started realizing that he was probably right. He had basically said the same thing as Rita had. Ben could see she was thinking about what he'd said and hoped that she'd come to her senses. This was far too dangerous for them to activate such a plan. With the huge cost and the greater danger, the chances that it would work were far from guaranteed. And when it didn't, what would they have to show for it? A sunken ship and more lives lost.

"Have you been in touch with your friend in America?"

Beth nodded. "Yea, just spoke with her earlier today."

"And what did she say?"

Beth looked at him in silence with a slightly sheepish grin. Her head nodded.

"Just as I might have thought. Same thing as I said."

Ben looked at her with understanding. “Look. Let the military services handle this. It’s obviously a large enough problem which is far too much for a small operation like ours. They have the equipment, munitions, and armament to be able to take these things out. Besides, what would a harpoon do in comparison to a 5-inch cannon?”

Beth shrugged her shoulders in surrender. “Guess you’re right. I don’t, well, particularly like the odds anyway, now that I think about it. And” she sighed, “I don’t want to be the cause of others’ deaths because of something I pushed for.”

She looked back at him. “Ok.” She turned around and walked out of his office.

***

It wasn’t a feeling of defeat. Not at all. It was the frustration of coming to a new realization and finding out that if there was going to be any solution to this world crisis, it would have to be dealt with by others. In the end, it really didn’t matter *who* would be the source of the solution. It was more important to the world, as well as mankind, that unless these creatures stopped their path of death and destruction—which was more than just unlikely—they would unquestionably have to be destroyed. Even her conservationist scientific mind had to make room for reasoning and logic.

24

Atlantic Coast, United States

Twenty miles off the coast of North Carolina, two vessels were making their way southward. Their destination was Florida. Both were sailing together, having departed Delaware two days earlier, with intentions to arrive in Ft. Lauderdale roughly three or four days later. They had no deadline. It was early June and the weather was forecast to be sunny to tolerable. No storms were predicted during their several days journey.

One of the vessels was a forty-five-foot sailboat called the *Anna Marie.* She had a crew of four with a skipper named Bob, who owned the boat. He was well experienced with sailboats and could sail it blindfolded if he had to. The other boat was a smaller skiff, about twenty-five- feet in length, with two inboard engines and a crew of three. The skipper was a woman named Rachel. Her boat was the *Winifred B.* She wasn't as experienced a sailor as Bob. Nevertheless, she drove her boat enough times, without incident, to be able to sail it all the way down the coast.

They sailed close enough to each other to be able to see the persons on the other boat and wave; yet they were apart far enough to minimize even the slightest chance of a collision. Occasionally they communicated with their radios.

Each skipper ensured that their boats were fully equipped with all that was required by law and then some. Although most were not wearing life preservers, there was enough on each boat for all the persons aboard. If weather conditions or the currently calm seas became worse, the skippers made sure that each member would know to put on his or her preserver and that they would be easily and readily accessible if the need arose. When they arrived in Ft. Lauderdale, they had to put them on before they arrived at the docks.

Today the skies were partly cloudy, the winds were mild, with the anemometers spinning enough to indicate on the meter wind speed of nine knots. Seas were approximately one to two feet. Out here there were a few gulls that flew overhead now and then.

While some of the crews were manning the deck and enjoying the gentle movements of the boats, others were getting drinks or food below. Everyone was having a great time and enjoying the trip.

On the Anna Marie, static output erupted from the communication radio, with a voice coming through in the background. It was unreadable so the skipper had no clue as to what was being said. There was no indication of any emergency from anywhere. But then if there had been, he wouldn't have been able to tell anyway from the static.

Bob picked up the mike and decided to test it for output and readability. He called the other boat to make sure they could still be read.

"This is the Winifred B. We read you loud and clear, Anna Marie."

"This is Anna Marie. Roger, we also read you five by five. Thank you."

He breathed a sigh of relief. The static was from something else.

There it was again. This time the voice sounded like it was from someone in distress. Not a good thing to hear out at sea. There was no way to tell where it was coming from or who was sending it. Unlike previously when it was one time, now it was continuous. He was compelled to answer it to at least try to find out who it was and if help was needed. Maritime law had its requirements for providing assistance whenever possible.

Bob sent out his radio message inquiry. He couldn't know if the sender was receiving his call. For all he knew, they could be hundreds of miles away. Unless he could hear actual coordinates, he couldn't know the location.

He transmitted again, identifying himself and requesting coordinates. Seconds ticked by which seemed like hours to him. Then the blast of static once again. The voice was louder and higher pitched this time. There was no doubt in Bob's mind that this was a call for help, and it was needed quickly.

With great difficulty, he was able to decipher what he believed he heard for coordinates. Putting down his mike, he contacted the Winifred B and relayed to Rachael what he was going to do, asking her to decrease their speed to two knots along with his speed decrease. He didn't want them to become separated.

After she acknowledged, the boats slowly moved forward. Bob pulled out the navigation chart to find the coordinates he was able to decipher of the distress caller he had written down quickly. Finding them and then determining where *they were* currently, he was shocked to learn the caller was only about seven miles away, southeast of them and ahead. That put the caller in deeper water.

"Winifred B, this is the Anna Marie, over."

The reply came quickly.

"Rachel be advised there's a boat in distress southeast of us and ahead. About seven miles. I don't want us to separate. We need to respond asap and assist."

"Copy that, Bob. We're with you. Go ahead and we will follow."

After calculating the bearing on the chart, he turned slightly to port. He advised the crew and ordered the sails lowered all the way. He revved up the engines to maximum safe speed.

Twenty minutes later they could see part of what looked like a yacht. As they got closer, they saw the tremendous damage on it. The stern wall was gone, it was halfway sunk into the water, and there was no one on board.

"Oh my God," muttered Bob. He looked around the boat for survivors in the water but didn't see anyone. He called out in case anyone could hear him. Only silence was the reply.

Picking up his mike, he transmitted his findings. Her boat was just now coming up on them. The entire crew stood out on deck at the disturbing discovery. All wondered the same thing.

Yea, what the hell happened here? And where is everyone?

There was no one from the boat in the water. The crews checked for bodies, but none were seen. Ever so slowly the destroyed yacht was sinking and soon would be completely consumed by the sea. Whatever did this make quick work of it.

They all talked rapidly trying to come up with the answers. The possibility of an explosion was considered but gradually ruled out. No one had seen neither boat parts nor body parts floating around, not near or far. This was a mystery that somehow defied explanation.

***

Fifty feet below, it swam lazily as if it had all the time in the world. Ironically, it did. It sensed vibrations and sounds coming from above. Once again, it decided to explore before doing what it was best at.

Coming around in a circular pattern, it maneuvered its body with its flippers and looked upward. This time the strange looking objects were not moving. It decided to choose one. Slowly it started inching its way up.

***

It was skipper Bob who called the Coast Guard on the radio. Citing their coordinates, he agreed to stick around in order for the helicopter crew to easier spot them and the area for boat parts or bodies.

"I'm going to circle the area nearby to see if we missed anything," Rachel informed Bob.

"Ok," he replied. "Don't go too far."

It was like a huge explosion, except it was different. The suddenness would have scared even the most experience, hardened ghost hunter. Except this was no ghost and no dream.

Water flew everywhere in a blink of an eye. In the middle of all that water was a gargantuan head, the likes of which no one had ever seen before. It was larger than either of their boats. Although it lasted less than three seconds, it was long enough for the brain to process the even-more horrific sight of Rachel's boat in the middle of what looked like a bus-sized mouth. In the split second that it took for this to happen, it just as quickly disappeared back down into the depths. The *Winifred B.* was no more.

The shock of what Bob and his fellow crew had seen was the only thing that kept the boat from responding instantly. Before the crew could say anything or yell, Bob was the first to recover. He didn't waste any time and soon they were heading at full speed back to shore. He called the Coast Guard and relayed the emergency of their situation, deciding not to mention about the sea monster until his mind could settle and speak to them convincingly enough so they wouldn't believe he was a 'crazy man'. At the same time, he hoped and prayed they would *make* it to shore alive.

***

Once docked at a pier somewhere in the southern part of North Carolina, Bob thanked God having made it. His crew were still numb from the shock of what they had witnessed and struggled to find rationality and logic from what happened. Although they could not find those, tears and slowly coming to terms were the only ways they could grieve and recover.

Once the police were contacted, the Coast Guard was quickly brought into the investigation, and it wasn't long before the local and federal authorities and others from the government showed up where the fledgling boat crew was.

An endless amount of questions was asked of them, after it was fully determined that no one there was injured or hurt. The creature, albeit for just a second or less, was graphically described by the crew as best they could.

Until confirmation could be obtained about the creature they claimed to have seen, all the authorities could advise Bob with was that he continue to sail to his destination but closer to shore. They reserved the right, however, to strongly suggest that they find another mode of transportation out of the water. This was a dilemma that the experienced captain had to make a decision from. It would be one of the hardest he'd ever had to make.

US Navy CincAtlanticFleet, Norfolk, Va.

Two days later, Admiral Hugh Downsworthy was on the phone with the captain of the USS Bickford, which was currently docked. It was a destroyer that had come in four days ago from deployment from the Mediterranean Sea. Although he really didn't want to use them and send them out so quickly again, he didn't have many other options. The others were out at sea further away.

Captain John Meager was a well experienced and well-decorated officer of nearing retirement age. He'd been captain of the Bickford for five years. Downsworthy knew him as well as anyone could. They'd been friends for most of their naval careers. Trust between them was never an issue; nor would it ever likely be.

"John, you know I hate to send you back out. Damn it, I know it doesn't seem fair, but you see where I am with this?"

His calm willingness and understanding almost made Downsworthy feel guilty. In a sense he did. However, friendship aside, he had to make the decision not leave it up to his friend. He had to by virtue of his position. Meger well understood that, which is why he agreed to undertake this special mission. They agreed to meet that evening at 1900 hours at the officer's club. It was a Tuesday, so the club would have quiet spots where they could sit and talk without competing with a lot of noise.

1900 hours, Norfolk Naval Base

"That's quite a plan, Bob."

Downsworthy sipped his drink. "You know me. I'm not one to pull out all the stops if they need to be pulled out. Right now, we—the world—are in a crisis situation which could, no doubt, threaten our very existence. That's why I'd like you to be one of the participants in this extermination project."

"Who else?" asked Meger.

"I'm sending out ten ships out to sea here in the Atlantic. I've been in touch with the other commanders of several other fleets including Asia. This is an all-out war, so to speak, and that has been clarified with them. Fortunately, they are all on board with this. They've had their problems with these things as well and have no qualms about taking them out. Still…"

The admiral sipped his drink. Meger looked at him. There was more.

"The problem involves numbers. We know how many missiles we have, how many torpedoes and other underwater explosives we have. But we don't know how many of these creatures are out there."

Logistics, when it came to battle conditions, was an ever-present, all important issue. These general quarters type of issues would require pre-planning and more than enough supplies to confront whatever was out there. Although the creatures were similar to submarines only in the sense that they stayed underwater most of the time, that's where it ended. They attacked without warning from underneath.

"Well, the sonar and other equipment will have to be used 24/7. And the crews would have to be on standby for GQ, ready to activate at a moment's notice."

The admiral nodded. "That's correct. And from what I've been told by the experts, the…" They were suddenly interrupted by a club officer who quickly approached to the admiral.

"Sir, I'm sorry to bother you. But I thought you should know. We just got a request to look for you here by your office. They are requesting that you call them immediately."

Downsworthy looked at him and then quickly whipped out his cell phone and made the call. Although he wasn't one to advertise his emotions or what he was thinking, the silent mouthing of the words, "Oh my God" was evident to Meger and he knew it was bad. Looks like the timetable for getting underway might have just sped up.

25

When the news hit the airwaves that a humpback whale was found dead with a huge gash in its side that was larger than the largest great white and even orca could make, it seemed to validate many of the reports that something monstrous beyond modern imagination was lurking beneath the ocean surfaces. Scientists were no longer shocked at most of what they were learning. However, the more reports that came in and the more they learned, the more urgent resolution of the global crisis became. From one local "hot spot", which ironically happened to be in the coldest waters on the planet, it spread like wildfire. For the world's oceans and sea life, as well as mankind, this was very bad news.

Tellmore Research Station, Antarctica

The personnel, including those of the Arga, realized and had conceded to the fact that their original idea of using a harpoon would not be just expensive: it would be impractical and equally likely, ineffective. They would be dealing with something far beyond what they could handle. Their recent past experience proved that. For the time being, they could only continue on with their normal research. Traveling now would have to be only by air or ground.

USNavalCincAtlantic Fleet Headquarters, Norfolk Va. 1100 hours, EST.

Admiral Downsworthy got off the phone. Plans were now set in place and several ships were prepared to get underway. All crews who were on liberty were contacted to report back to their ships asap. Deck crews were preparing the lines. All logistical supplies and food were being loaded onboard all the vessels for a possible lengthy mission. Departure of the fleet would be in three hours.

USNavyCincPacFleet, SanDiego,Ca

*0900 hours, PST.*Rear Admiral Harvey Johnson, commander of the Pacific fleet had been in regular touch with Norfolk. On agreement with Admiral Downsworthy, he was also preparing some of his fleet. Having had been in contact with the commanding Admiral of the US Navy, Admiral Wilburn of the joint chiefs in Washington DC, the respective fleet commands were now authorized to use whatever necessary in their fleets to combat and eradicate the global threat throughout the world's oceans, providing they did not cross any international ocean boundaries with other countries.

As on the eastern seaboard, a number of ships were preparing to get underway. Both fleets would include in their arsenal one aircraft carrier, two Los Angeles Attack submarines fully loaded with wired guided self-homing torpedoes and capable of firing them both fore and aft on the vessel, three destroyers, three Littoral Combat ships—also known as fast frigates-- and one helicopter carrier.

Several special antisubmarine helicopters would be used, fitted with torpedoes of their own. The MH-60R Seahawk was one of the best and most appropriate for the mission at hand. These choppers could also carry missiles and would be fitted with four AGM-114 Hellfire air-to-surface types, all non-nuclear. These aircraft could detect, track and attack anything on the surface or below. They were fast and accurate.

Both fleets would be widespread throughout the entire northern Atlantic Ocean. Because the US frequently had ships sailing in the Mediterranean, those were already given orders for their new mission. Of the several that were there, one was docked in Italy for ship repairs. All were fully armed. When the one that was being repaired was ready for sea, it was ordered to get underway to join the others in the new global battle. Additional ships would be ordered out if necessary.

The Pentagon, Washington, DC

Admiral Henry Johnson was a tough, no-nonsense naval officer. He didn't get to his position by mere chance. He could've accepted a post at any of the fleet commands or continued on as a at sea fleet admiral.

But once he got his second star, he had the option to choosing another position. The choice he made is why he's here now.

Once plans were in place, in coordination with all fleet commands, and everything was nearly in place, it was just a matter of waiting for the departure time to arrive. All Fleets were ready to go, including the 9th fleet in southeast Asia.

In all there would be dozens of ships, from several submarines to two aircraft carriers, a helicopter carrier and the rest destroyers and their escorts. These were just the Americans and it looked more like a World War sea mission than anything else. In a very real sense, it was.

Washington had not been sitting on its fantail. The United States was collaborating with its allies from Europe to South America. Unlike trying to get multi-country cooperation with dealing with a controversial diplomatic problem between nations, this was an entirely different ballgame. This was not the world against itself but in effect one determining to save itself. Everyone knew it. There would be no problem getting everyone on board-except for one country who never got on board with anything going on in the world.

The Pentagon conducted a press release regarding the worldwide plans for annihilation of the sea creatures which seemed to have taken over the seas. The press released was authorized by POTUS which soon was heard by every home in America.

One hour after the news was broadcast, the Atlantic Fleet got underway. Its mission was called *Operation Seakill.* From Norfolk, a number of other ships were added to the fleet when reports of a number of other killings and destruction of boats were reported from the seas just south of Greenland down to the Caribbean.

From Europe, the UK sent out a fleet out into the Atlantic and the North Sea. Russia sent out a force into the Black Sea and the Pacific Ocean. Other countries there which contributed to the fleets included France, Italy (to assist the US ships in the Mediterranean), Germany, Sweden and Norway.

Below the equator, South Africa, Bolivia, Chile and Argentina contributed several of their destroyer ships and one submarine from Argentina.

In the Pacific, the entire international fleet included various kinds of ships from China, Japan, Australia, and even the Philippines. In essence, nearly every part of the world's oceans was covered in the monumental task of destroying what was trying to destroy them.

***

Odessa, Texas

Word had gotten to her from the university that her advice and data she had provided to the Navy had set off a worldwide mission, the likes of which she had never heard of or seen before. Her eyes were glued to the TV as she saw pictures of huge numbers of ships which seemed to be everywhere. If this was what World War II looked like out at sea, she was glad she had missed it. 1969 was a good year to be born in.

John came in and sat down. "Hey, what's happening here?" he asked with his eyes riveted on the screen. "Holy shit, what is happening out there?"

Rita explained. "This may very well be the beginning of the end for them," she said.

"Damn, I hope so." Then the screen changed, and it showed a huge sea creature that had never been seen in modern times.

"What the hell is that?" he asked pointing at it.

"That, my darling, is our current nemesis and just one of many. A sea dinosaur, thought to be extinct for millions of years. Until now. I'll explain it to you sometime."

While John continued to watch the live news about the situation, Rita left the room to do whatever she had to do. He seemed to be both fascinated and drawn like an addict to what he was seeing, and it was mixed with live as well as past video clips.

As the ANN broadcaster voice narrated a live picture of several naval ships out in the Pacific, he saw a sudden sideways type movement of one of the ships. For a moment, he thought it was just a glitch of the camera. That thought instantly dissipated when the fleet started maneuvering suddenly to the left side. "What the hell…?" he muttered under his breath.

"Something's going on here. Not sure yet what it is." The broadcaster remained calm but clearly was as startled as anyone else. "Take a look at the ship up near the left of the camera screen.", he said. A yellow circle suddenly appeared as the ship again appeared to be shoved violently to its starboard side.

"Rita, quick. C'mere. Look at this Hurry up!" Rita ran back to the living room and saw again what appeared to be the ship again being hit from the side by something under the water. The fact that the ship was moving while it happened made her jaw drop almost to the floor. Her hand quickly covered her mouth as the broadcaster and camera zoomed in again closer to the stricken ship.

Neither one of them said anything as they watched the shocking event unfold before their eyes. The ship was turning with the others. John was trying to figure out what kind of ship it was. Having been in the Navy many years ago, he was able not to determine the type and he knew the types pretty well back in the day. It must have been a fairly new type because he'd never seen anything like that before.

The broadcaster's voice became more urgent sounding. The vessel turned more. As it did, something below it hit much more violently. Because of the angle of the turn, it nearly capsized onto its starboard side. Just as it was hit again even harder, it looked like it rolled completely over on its side when the camera suddenly cut out.

The anchorman returned to the screen.

"We apologize for that. The signal was lost but while we are trying to get it back, we've all seen what happened there but are at a loss right now as to the source of that event. In the meantime, reports are coming in that that fleet is searching for the cause of it. Reportedly they are fully armed and ready to counter whatever it was and if was one of those creatures. We'll bring you the latest when we receive more information. Meanwhile, over in Europe…"

John turned the volume down and looked at his wife.

"Well, what do you think Professor? Could these sons of bitches you said they are do something like that?" He sometimes called her that as a tease. She knew it but didn't mind.

Rita looked down, thinking but unsure. Certainly, they were massively big, larger than any biological thing in the sea today. Because these dinosaurs went extinct long before man showed up, the untrained could easily say yes. Despite all the extensive research and studies that have gone into and still go into paleolithic life, only the most educated guesses and theories based on all the discovered evidence can make any conclusions acceptable to the scientific community. A few things have been proved beyond a doubt that they were true. This, however, was not one of them. There was no way to tell if these things were strong and powerful enough to sink a ship; especially a moving one.

With a shake of her head, she could only reply with, "I don't know, sweetheart. I wish I did."

***

The vessel being attacked had to get away from its close neighbors if there was to be any chance of the fleet detecting what it was and blowing it out of the water. Inside its command center and on the bridge, communications were continuous, and the ship started maneuvering to port to distance itself from the others.

In the sonar operations center on one of the destroyers, the sonarman detected something huge in the water that seemed to be targeting the new combat ship. On his screen, he could see the large blip with each sound emission from the ship as it bounced off the object. As the ship veered off to their left away from the group, surprisingly the thing didn't follow it. It didn't act like the typical land predator, or any other kind known to man. He reported this to the bridge.

A question came from the bridge. "What's the range and depth of it now petty officer?"

The operator looked and calculated its range and approximate depth from the visual and equipment readings.

"Range is six-hundred yards. Depth is…" he looked at the various readings and location of the blip on the screen… "one-fifty feet currently."

"Very well, sonar. Keep on it." Then the click.

On the bridge, the captain ordered the OOD, or officer of the deck, to contact the USS Peligrin. It was one of their fast attack submarines.

Contact was made and the orders began.

"Pelegrin, this is Ingersoll. Bogey is six hundred yards from us, depth one-five-oh. One-five-oh. Can you position to take it out, over?"

The XO, or executive officer of the sub, provided the response.

"That's affirmative, Pelegrin. We are presently at..." and he provided their geographical coordinates. We are positioning. We will not release the fish until all friendlies are in the clear. Please advise of the group position when at least two thousand yards from the bogy, over."

"Roger, we copy Pelegrin. Out."

The fleet commander, a rear admiral, was advised of the plan. Only his authorization to engage would set it into motion. His orders for the fleet to increase speed and turn to bearing 049 began this motion.

As the strategic maneuvering was occurring, all the ships kept their eyes via sonar on the bogey. Whatever it was, it was no submarine. Subs could be easily distinguished from living creatures via sonar. Whales had also been ruled out because this thing never surfaced. And it was much bigger than them anyway.

On the Pelegrin, the captain was maneuvering his ship for weapon engagement. On the mike, he started preliminary orders for this.

"Forward torpedo room, this is the captain. Prepare tubes and torpedoes number one and three. Prepare torpedoes numbers two and four. Do not fire until I order. Standby."

"Aye, Captain."

"Aft torpedo room, prepare tubes and torpedoes numbers five and seven Prepare tubes and torpedoes numbers six and eight. Do not fire until I order. Standby."

"Aye, Captain."

The captain put down the mike and walked forward. His orders came fast.

"Helm, periscope depth to sixty. Hold your course."

The helmsman repeated his orders word for word as required. As he did so, the skipper grabbed the handles of the periscope as it raised to his eye level and he peered through the oculars. Although he hoped to get a surface glance at the bogey, he didn't count on that kind of good luck. Instead, he needed to check the position of the fleet. He saw that they had quickly pulled away. He could fire only if the fleet was not in the direct line of the torpedo's path. If it missed, he didn't want for it to home in on any of the ships. The bogey had to be well to the left of the fleet's relative position to his.

He grabbed the mike. "Sonar, what do you have?"

Moments later, "Sir, I see a large bogey, three hundred yards ahead, bearing 005. Depth, seventy-five feet." That said it all. The fleet was clear of this thing.

"Very well. Movement?"

"Yes captain. It appears to be moving toward us. It's now two-five-oh yards ahead."

Damn it, it was heading right toward them! He didn't have much time.

"Very well. Helm prepare to dive on my word to one-five-oh feet. And then increase speed to twelve knots. XO, announce all hands to general quarters."

"Aye sir. Prepared to dive to one-five-oh feet and increase to twelve knots"

The XO quickly made the announcement.

"Dive. Dive!"

With the descent, the skipper took the mike.

"Attention, all hands. This is the captain. We are about to engage in what we had come here for. The creature is out there and heading right toward us. We don't have much time. Let's get this thing and do what we need to do for this planet. Torpedo rooms, fore and aft, standby for firing, on my command."

As soon as replies came from both respective areas of the ship, the skipper checked the sonar screen next to where he was standing. He saw the thing. It appeared to be following them."

"Crap, we have to get a little better firing angle. Helm, steer to 015, then 005. Second bearing on my command."

"Aye sir. Setting course to 015 now."

"Very well." Grabbing the mike, he ordered to standby at the ready. The men were ready to push the button.

Now he was ready for the second bearing. The order went out and the sub changed course once again.

"Sonar, depth of bogy."

"One-five-oh feet sir."

"Forward torpedoes." After a few seconds, then "Fire, fire !"

Everyone on board felt the backward jolt of the ship as each torpedo shot out from their port and starboard tubes.

"Both fish are out, sir." Soon after they were released, the torpedo mates rearmed the tubes. As long as they were facing the thing, these fore tubes would be used. Only if they were in retreat would the aft ones be used.

The skipper looked through the periscope as the sonar operator watched each of the fast-moving smaller blips on his scream race toward the large blip at an incredible speed. Everyone was praying for a hit.

The waiting was tormenting for all on board. It was not much different from attorneys outside a courtroom waiting for a jury's verdict. You didn't know what the outcome would be, and it could be a matter of life and death for certain persons involved.

The explosion was felt by the crew as the blast waves hit the sub, followed shortly after by the sound waves. The captain did not think there would be any damage, but he had damage controlmen check the ship anyway as a precaution. Soon cheers and yelling followed. The skipper brought the ship up to periscope depth to check for any remnants of the creature on the surface. As soon as he spotted them, he smiled. It was a confirmed hit.

"Target taken out. Congratulations everyone." The word went out over the mike to the rest of the crew throughout the ship. The skipper had the communication officer radio the fleet commander and it wasn't long before word got back to San Diego. Still, he knew this was probably just the beginning. No one knew how many others were out there. Hopefully, none in this area.

He set a course to rejoin his fleet. The hunt would continue.

26

Never before had there been such a global undertaking with this much international cooperation and unity in this particular war. In both world wars, there were two sides which fought against each other. The goals included to conquer or avoid being conquered. That was the simplest way to put it, although there was, of course, much more to it than that. The world was truly divided then.

In this case, there could be only one winning side. It was now humans versus marine dinosaurs. This was no longer the age of dinosaurs and it was up to humans to make sure it stayed that way. It was crazy, absolutely nuts that this was happening. If she had told anyone this without any of the events happening, they would have recommended her for a strait jacket.

Rita was glued to the TV at home. Once the remnants had been found by one of the vessels there and examined before other sea creatures could consume them, they were confirmed to be from a reptilian creature that had never been seen in modern times. She knew as well that, although the killing of the first Mosasaur by humans had been accomplished and was good cause for congratulations of prehistorical proportions, this was no time to celebrate. Not yet. There was a whole world that had to be scoured for more of these things.

Having kept in regular touch with Sam, even her friend was happy but cautiously so. And in remembering her short communications with her new scientific colleague down in Antarctica, because she knew how to make the call to there, she decided to get in touch and let her and her fellow Antarcticians learn of the good news along with the continued hunts. She would ask them to keep an eye out for any more down in their waters. Without delay she picked up the phone and made the call. She mumbled stupid to herself for not thinking of that sooner.

The Black Sea

The Russian ship *Lenin* which was the size of the old US destroyer escorts from WWII, had been patrolling the entire region for about a week. Their sonar detected nothing, and they had radioed their lack of findings. Nearly the entire sea had been searched by them and one other ship. Its captain was no dummy and had realized from the beginning that it would be futile because a creature from the ocean, especially that size, would not be able to travel to a virtually landlocked sea with only river tributaries that lead to it.

***

Meanwhile in the northern Atlantic, ships from other European nations had joined the hunt. Although all their sonars were in full operation, so far nothing out of the ordinary was detected.

Three hundred miles off the western coast of the UK, the HMS Wellington noted an anomaly in the water. It was a huge blip on the sonar which forced all eyes on its screen. The captain also continued to follow it, assessing whether it was a bogey or something else. They all waited to see what it was going to do.

"What is the range there?" he asked the sonarman.

"500 yards sir."

He was readying to order preparations for the torpedoes when suddenly it decreased in size and then seemed to disappear from the screen. They waited a minute or so for it to reappear. It did about two minutes later, this time a little further away.

"What the hell…?" The skipper wasn't sure what to make of it.

"Not to worry sir," said the operator. "That was just a whale."

"Really?"

It came up for air, which accounts for the size decrease. That's what it looks like on our sonar. The creature we are looking for likely won't do that."

"Ah, I see. Carry on then, lad."

***

Throughout the world, it seemed all nations with naval abilities were patrolling their waters. Except for WWII, it was virtually unprecedented.

About ten thousand miles away off the coasts of New Zealand, that country's navy was also at work, searching for something unlike anything else before. Although there were no reports of any attacks down there, it was not knowing where these creatures would pop up that unnerved everyone. Not finding any didn't mean they weren't around.

One crew member on board the New Zealander ship HMS Binghamton came up with an idea which, at first, sounded silly and out of the question. When nothing was seen on sonar anywhere, the idea was born soon after. But it would be a serious challenge and one that could or should not be acted on a whim because of its extreme danger.

Baiting is usually for fishermen or hunters on land. This kind of baiting to lure a sea monster was one for the books or a good sci-fi movie. After some thinking, officers eventually realized there was some merit to it. The problem of this idea, which eventually got to this ship's captain, was twofold, however.

One, there appeared no large enough sea life in the waters to catch and use as bait to lure in one of the creatures. There was no guarantee any were around anyway in their patrol search area. Two, was there anywhere they could obtain a large enough fish or mammal to use as bait?

"How about a dead cow or horse, sir?" asked one of the bridge crew-a quartermaster who seemed to hit the nail on the head. That peaked the captain's interest.

As farfetched as it was, it seemed to be one solution. But there were too many variables in it. The greatest enemy for its use was time. It would take a lot of time to search for and obtain something like that.

"No, I don't think so, Kevin," replied the skipper. "It could work under the right circumstances. But these are not." And he explained why.

It wasn't just time that was against them. They would also have to deal with the Naval Admiralty in posing such a request which would likely be their first roadblock. That in itself would also be their first and only delay.

The quartermaster understood and continued with his normal duties. Their search area expanded to further out. The skipper had made sure the ship's weapon systems were armed and ready, prepared for a battle which could occur at any time. For now, all they could do was search for something that wasn't supposed to exist.

Tellmore Research Station, Antarctica

There was never any boredom there because there was always something to do in each of the scientists research areas. Despite the current goings on in the world, they still needed to continue what they were there for.

When she got the call the day before, it was good to hear from her American friend up in Texas. Finding out more recent news before it reached them down there was a nice bennie, but nevertheless no less disturbing.

The call didn't last long because of a storm approaching from the west toward the ice continent's shelf, causing intermittent static. After they said their brief goodbyes, Beth started to wonder how they could manage keeping an eye out for the underwater creatures from on land. That would be impossible. They would need to go out on the Arga and *that* would certainly be a huge, dangerous risk for the entire ship and crew. They had no defense against the creature if it attacked, as they already had found out. They had been lucky then. That luck might not be with them the next time.

She knew about sonar transponders that could be lowered from helicopters. Down here that was their only way of keeping track in the surrounding seas. The only risk would be to those of the helicopter crew. Leaving her desk in her room, she headed up to the bridge to see what Paul thought of that.

When she got there, he wasn't on the bridge. When she found out he was down in the galley getting some coffee she went down there. At one of the tables in the small eating area, she saw him, grabbed a coffee and then joined him at the table.

"Hey Paul, got a thought."

"Yea Beth. What's up?"

"Well, I talked with my friend up in US. Told me about ships all over the world searching the oceans to kill these creatures. I thought that maybe, because of the extreme danger to the ship, we might keep an eye down here with the use of chopper transponders. Since we can't do that ourselves. Any thoughts you have on that?"

He sighed. "Already thought of that. Argentina is our closest neighbor and they have ships, as well as helicopters, scouting and searching. They told me, last I talked with them, that one of their ships would be coming closer to us to search for them. They've got plenty of sonar, as well as underwater robot vehicles."

Beth rubbed the back of her neck. "So. Looks like all bases are covered. There's nothing more we can do here, is there?"

"Sure there is," Paul replied. "Just continue our normal work here. Let those outside of here take care of what need to be done. Hopefully, we'll keep up with the news and pray they get rid of these things. I think we are pretty safe here."

Taking a sip of her coffee, she nodded her concession.

27

On a beautiful sunny day off the coast of southern California, a boat was pulling a skier across the relatively calm waters that made the Pacific Ocean so much more inviting. The five youths that were a part of this boating/skiing excursion had been drinking quite a bit, which included the ever-desirable beer on a warm sunny day such as this.

It was late morning and they had been on the water for only an hour. Although they noticed the distinctive absence of the usual large number of watercrafts that were a daily sighting, they weren't the slightest concerned about that. In their various levels of intoxicated states of mind, the only thing they cared about was their drinking and having fun.

Despite that, the three teenage boys and two girls were alternating their keeping an eye on their fellow skier who appeared to be enjoying the ride of his life. The sixteen-year-old already had two years of water-skiing experience under his belt and was now particularly good at it. Even when his skis ran into part of the wake from the boat, he had no problem staying on them.

In the distance, a boat from the California Department of Wildlife and Fish had noticed the boat with the skier and wondered why they were out there after all the warnings were broadcast to the public. They sped up and decided to check on them. The two officers were quite a distance from them. One of them tried to radio them after identifying themselves. They could not have known that the boat was full of relatively inexperienced youths who had not turned the boat radio on. They realized that when there were no replies to their several calls to them. The driver then sped up a little more to try and catch up to them.

The elongated swell of water behind the boat was not noticed by anyone. It followed the boat at every turn. If one were not looking at that exact area of water, it would not be noticed.

The skier did a complete turnaround on his skis, first one way and then the other. It was not a move a novel skier could do. The youth bounced up and down on the waves, managing to stay upright without much effort. As long as he held on to the rope handles, there was little chance he would fall.

The boat crew were too impaired to notice the water hump following their skier. But in the distance, on the California patrol boat, one of the officers holding binoculars was able to see the anomaly in the water, which made the hairs stand up on the back of his neck. Not knowing what it was, he could only discern that its stalking-type movement posed a serious danger to the boat and skier.

"Bill, I see something behind that skier. I don't know what the hell it is. Can you speed up to the max?"

"You got it," Then the engines revved up to their max as the speed increased. As they slowly neared the boat, the hump seemed to loom larger and closer to the skier and boat. Those on the boat remained oblivious to the potential danger.

"What the hell…?" The officer driving the boat was just as perplexed as his partner. Although they had no clue as to what was following the boat their police officer's gut feelings kicked in and the considered it a life-threatening threat to the skier and boat.

Without a second thought, the driver kicked the speed up to the max as the patrol boat gained ever closer to the other one. They couldn't fire their weapons at the hump because it was too close to the skier. But somehow, they had to warn the boat crew and get them to get to shore as fast as possible.

As they slowly pulled alongside the boat, close enough to use their megaphone but far enough away to avoid a side collision, Jason picked up the megaphone.

"Hello, driver of the boat." He could tell the crew was not in the clearest of mindset. *'Damn that alcohol'.* He could have stopped them and arrested the driver for driving a motor vessel while impaired. Right now, that priority had to take a back seat to the imminent danger behind them.

The crew all waved and laughed toward them, not yet understanding their situation.

Jason quickly yelled out for them to head toward shore immediately.

"There is something in the water which is posing an immediate threat to you. Get to shore, please." He vigorously pointed toward the shoreline.

"Hey officer, what the hell are you talking about? You going to arrest us?" This from one of the intoxicated crew members.

"Look behind you. Look behind the skier!"

A couple of the drunk knuckleheads looked back while the others downed another beer. At first, they didn't notice anything. Then the patrol officers saw their eyes bug out. Reality finally hit them.

Surprising the officers with their quick response, despite all that booze in them, they yelled at the driver to head toward shore as the patrol boat pulled back and maneuvered away from the endangered boat. The numerous water violations of the crew were quickly forgotten by this new threat. There was not much more the officers could do except hope they got to shore in time.

The boat started to turn and head toward the shore, which was at least a half mile away. The skier had seen the wildlife officers and knew the boat was heading in, although he wasn't sure why. But he could not have known the reason. Until…

He looked toward the crew who were now returning his stare. They kept flinging their arms, trying to get him to look behind him, pointing at the same time. That clued him to something, and he turned his head to look.

It was at that moment it happened. Something huge erupted out of the water. The last thing the skier saw was gigantic teeth and endless darkness.

When the boys got to shore, they headed to whoever they could find to report what happened. Unfortunately, they were a few miles south of where they had boarded the board and all their stuff, including cell phones, were there. The first people they came across they were able to get their message through to clearly and soon, the San Diego police were there to take their information and statements.

For the police, it was not easy to determine how credible they were because of their drinking. The smell of booze was on them. Yet even so, their frantic and terrified behavior seemed to be too genuine to be from alcohol. Whether or not it was true, they had to act fast in case it was.

As soon as they were told about the sudden vanishing of the skier, police patrol boats were dispatched to the scene as well as lifeguard boats to help in the search for the missing crew member. In addition, from what was described as a gargantuan creature that suddenly appeared and disappeared with the skier, the cops realized this was beyond what they were capable of and the Coast Guard was immediately contacted. It was a chain reaction of events which eventually led to the intense search in the waters for the skier by the Coast Guard and for the reported creature by the nearest naval vessels.

Odessa, Texas

Although Rita had started the ball rolling in bringing the news of these creature's existence to the world, for those millions of people who hadn't seen any of them it was still a hard sell. But for those who had, there was no question of what they were.

The US government had sent out scientists from the NOAA to capture images of them using remote and highly technical equipment which could be spared if attacked and destroyed. Rita was fortunate to have a friend connected to the NOAA and was able to obtain a copy of one of the images taken in the North Atlantic. Even though it wasn't exactly crystal clear, the picture revealed enough to identify them as Mosasaurs. The one in the picture was shown to be fifty feet long, with a long tooth-filled snout that was about the length of a man's height. It could swallow a man whole.

As thoughts of what was going on swirled in her head, the phone suddenly rang, almost making her jump out of her chair. "Hello?"

It was Samantha.

"Hey, girlfriend, I just called to say congrats to you for discovering this. Look what the world's doing now."

Rita's sheepish grin reflected her feelings about this.

"Well, Sam, let me tell you. I am glad something is being done about it, that's for sure. But the feeling is bittersweet. Look how many people have died from these things. And the boats and ships that sank."

"Yea. I hear ya," replied Sam on the other end. "They're saying on the news now that global warming of the waters caused them to come back to life. That is definitely hard to believe. Resurrection of dead dinosaurs? Sounds like a B-rated sci-fi movie. No. Make it Z-rated, for a movie that should have never been made. Hey, something's coming on the news, hold on."

Rita held the phone to her ear as she listened to Sam's TV. Sam had apparently turned up the volume. She could hear reports of more deaths of attacks, and some of the creatures being blown out of the water by naval weaponry. The reports mentioned that even the Russians and other countries were involved in a multi-national effort to eradicate them. It was something no one had ever thought would be seen in their lifetimes.

After Sam got back on the phone, they chatted for a bit about the news and then promised to keep in touch before hanging up. Rita sat quietly contemplating the situation. Maybe the world would now realize that anything was possible in it. Literally anything.

North Pacific Ocean

On the naval surface vessels *Winslow* of the US and *Tomeka* from Japan, both had been apparently surveilling the same creature. But it wasn't by accident. With appropriate translators on each ship, they had been able to coordinate an attack on the creature from different directions without putting each other in the line of fire. Whoever was lined up to fire the torpedoes, the other would get out of the way after being informed. If the torpedoes missed or the creature moved to a different area, whichever ship it was closer to would take it on. It was tricky because of the unpredictability of the creature's movements.

On the *Winslow*, all hands were at general quarters. Sonar had pinged a large target about five hundred yards ahead, bearing 025. While sonar notified the bridge where the captain currently was, the communications officer notified the Tomeka captain who then immediately set his ship to position them out of the fire line from the Americans. The Winslow was preparing to fire and it had to be done quickly.

The target remained on its steady course but constantly moving, so the US captain had to maintain a steady course and distance continuously. All firing systems were ready for the order, torpedoes were in their tubes on the aft decks. They were homing torpedoes which were guided by target movements rather than heat signatures from engines.

The *Tomeka* had to be prepared just as much in case the target slipped away or the American torpedoes missed. Then while the Americans were reloading their tubes, it would take its turn in attacking the creature. Neither captain would allow this thing to get away. There was no rivalry in this. This was the kind of team effort that both of them liked.

The *Winslow* was now in the appropriate position for firing. The captain gave the order to fire control. "Fire torpedo one. Fire torpedo two!" The slight lurch in the ship indicated their release. "

"Fish number one and fish number two in the water captain."

It was the Chief Torpedoman's job to let the skipper know the order was completed.

"Very well," he replied. Then, "Helm, change course to 275, increase speed to twenty. Engage."

Sonar looked at the two fast moving blips on his screen and counted out loud the decreasing distance between them and the target on the bridge mike. They were heading right toward it and continued to do so as the target gently changed its direction. The creature had no clue what was coming.

Both ships were well out of range of the impending explosions but stayed close enough to safely witness them. They waited tensely. On both ships, one could almost hear a pin drop.

The sonar operator noticed the large blip suddenly disappear from the screen. To the untrained eye, that would suggest the target was hit. But there was no untrained eye here. This operator saw big time trouble.

"Bridge, this is sonar. The bogey has disappeared, but there was no explosion. Contact not confirmed. I repeat, contact not confirmed."

On the bridge, the captain exchanged a stunned expression with his XO. Something had gone wrong. Either the torpedoes had missed, which was highly unlikely; or, they had malfunctioned. Occasionally, but not very often, a torpedo could malfunction and not explode when it was programmed to. But even a so-called dud could still explode and cause destruction or death if one let down their guard. These duds were still just as dangerous and more unpredictable.

The voice from the sonar room rang out. "Captain, I see two blips moving fast directly toward us, range one thousand yards."

"Son of a bitch. The damn things missed. Captain…!"

The skipper thought exactly the same thing as the XO and shouted out the order. He didn't know why they missed because their aim was right on the target. But he didn't have time to dwell on it.

"Helm, left course to two four zero. Hold your speed. On my command, change course to two six zero, then prepare to change again on my command."

"Aye aye, captain. Changing course to two four zero."

"Comms, notify *Tomeka* we have a problem. Let them know our target dodged our bullets. The fish are still active, and we are now fast-tracking to dodging *them.* Ask them to proceed after the target."

The comms officer responded immediately. The message was now sent to the Tomeka. Once they received, the Japanese captain wasted no time in taking over the changed situation.

While it started searching once again for the creature, the *Winslow* was undergoing its zigzag course. This is a tactic often used by surface warships to prevent, or at least make more difficult, enemy torpedoes to hit their target. Sometimes it works, but as most other things in life, it's not foolproof.

The skipper knew their chances of outrunning it were not in their favor. Unless the fish reached their maximum distance of run time, the ship could be hit. It would take only one of them to sink it if it hit in the right spot. He kept in constant contact with sonar.

"They are gaining slightly, captain," he said. They are now nine hundred yards.

"Very well. Helm, change course to 230."

As they felt the destroyer turn, he had another idea.

With mike still in hand, he ordered fire control to prepare for another firing, and the torpedomen to arm torpedo tubes three and five. This time they would have a very different target but one equally dangerous.

"Attention all hands. This is the captain. We are maneuvering to avoid our own torpedoes which have missed our target and have now placed us in their bullseye. We will be firing two more of our fish directly at them. Everyone remain at their stations. Fire control, standby for orders to engage. Helm, change course to 040 and remain steady on that course."

Another voice, the XO. "Bridge to damage control. Standby for possible infiltration or other damage. Everyone to ensure that all watertight doors are secured. All watertight doors and hatches are to be secured now. All stations report your status now."

As the acknowledgements all came in quickly one at a time, the bridge was soon assured that the watertight integrity of the ship was secure. Should they be hit, there would be possible serious damage and perhaps much less chance of a sinking. But again, nothing was ever guaranteed.

“Tubes three and five armed” yelled out the torpedomen on the bridge mike.

“Very well.”

“Captain, fish are now eight hundred yards away and still heading toward us.”

“Very well, sonar. Helm, let me know when we are at course. Fire control, stand by.”

The tension in the air was so palpable and thick that even a knife would have trouble cutting through it. It was either sail or sink or this time: live or die.

“We are now at 040, sir.”

“Very well. Fire control, on my command.”

For the lives of his crew and his ship, he had to make sure these didn’t miss. The timing was everything. So was the position and distance. Close enough to hit them, but far enough away to avoid serious damage from the explosions.

“Sonar, distance.”

“Seven hundred yards sir.”

“Very well. Fire control, on my mark. Fire!”

28

On the *Tomeka*, sonar operators kept their eyes glued to the screen looking for the slightest indication of the vanished bogey. No one knew if it had disappeared from the area or just swam too deep for the sonar to reach it. But they could not stop now. It seemed that son of a bitch pulled a fast one on the Americans and they weren't about to let it do that to them too.

They conducted a complete grid search of the area. Turning on their depth sounders, they searched as far below the water surface as they could for the elusive creature. All of the crew remained on standby and the torpedoes on both sides of the ship as well as gun mounts were fully armed and manned.

As they maneuvered about, something hit the ship with so much force that everyone on board felt it, from bow to stern. Throughout the ship, various items that weren't secured had fallen to the deck.

On the bridge there was a sudden flurry of activity.

"Sonar, report!" the captain belted out. At the same time the xo asked for reports from the bow and aft lookouts.

Sonar reported a large bogey underneath.

The captain had to make a quick decision. What would be his next move? He got a sudden idea, although it was risky and there was no guarantee it would work.

"Helm, increase speed to twenty knots and head toward the surface at a twenty-degree angle. Torpedo chambers, arm tubes number four and five. Advise me immediately when they are."

His second in command knew where he was going with this. It was a brilliant idea if it worked.

Torpedo tubes four and five were at the stern of the ship and would be fired in that direction. It was a very long shot and the chances of hitting the object were incredibly slim. But they had to try. At best, it would blow the thing out of the water. At worst, it would hopefully chase it away and buy them some time.

As the ship angled upward and increased speed, sonar spotted the bogy on his screen a bit further away from the ship, but still too close for comfort. The large blip seemed to be taking its time following them.

The announcement came over the loudspeaker that the tubes were armed.

"Good." The skipper took the mike in hand and ordered the command to fire."

The ship jolted forward as the torpedoes left their tubes.

"Increase speed to twenty-five knots and change course to 154. Decrease angle to surface to fifteen degrees."

The ship had to get enough distance between them and the explosion, if they were lucky enough for it to happen. It wasn't long before they were shaken by concussions in the water. By God, they had hit the thing!

The captain didn't want to celebrate just yet. He had to be sure.

"Sonar, report!"

"Sir, I think we got it. The large blip I saw earlier has vanished from the screen."

Putting down his mike quickly, he went across the bridge to the sonar and bent down to see for himself. The stern determined look on his face softened a bit as he looked at the blank screen before turning into a slight smile.

His twenty years in the navy and ten of those as a captain had paid off. His numerous successes even in the worst of times had earned him offers for the admiralty position, but he had turned it down. His love to captain a ship far overpowered the temptation for command from behind a desk.

"Otsukaresama", he mumbled under his breath. Then he stood up and grabbed the mike. Speaking loudly he announced, "Watashitachiha seiko shimashita. Otsukaresama!" *We have succeeded. Good work men!*

Cheers went up from the bridge crew and he knew throughout the ship as well. He then ordered for them to surface. He then ordered communications to contact the American ship to advise them the beast was dead.

***

After the *Winslow* received the message that the *Tomeka* got the bogey, a brief cheer went up, although greatly subdued. They themselves still had a problem on their hands. There was no time to waste.

Unseen as well as unheard on the sonar at a particular moment when the sonar operator glanced away briefly from the screen, a large unknown quickly passed the torpedoes heading toward the *Winslow*. The metal fish headed toward the object which had passed them, and their radar homed in on them.

As fast as the torpedoes were moving, the unknown's faster speed soon brought it up to the ship with the torpedoes not far behind. When it arrived at the ship's port side, it dove deep at the last second before it could hit it. The torpedoes did not have time to make such a sudden direction change.

The explosion shook the entire ship and blasted a huge hole in its side. More explosions followed as the fuel tanks and inflammable ammunition on board ignited. Water quickly filled the area inside. The large vessel started to list to port.

Despite all that the captain and crew could do, the ship was doomed. The damage was far too extensive for the ship to be saved. The *USS Winslow* would be a catastrophic loss for the Navy. There were only a few survivors lucky enough to have escaped after the abandon ship order. The captain was not one of them.

***

On the surface, the captain and his exec stood outside the topside bridge hatch. They were stunned at their witnessing the huge explosions of their American counterpart. Horrified, they couldn't seem to take their eyes off the sight as they put their binoculars up to their eyes and saw the ship already start to sink.

Immediately the skipper told the exec to order the ship on a heading toward the stricken one to look for survivors. In addition, he also ordered communications to the American's nearest command about what they witnessed.

The skipper was at a loss for words. Despite never having known or met his American counterpart, he still felt the loss of a fellow mariner deeply. It was a tragedy not only for the Americans, but for him as well. He had been helpless to prevent that from happening, despite his heroic attempts to do so.

He couldn't have imagined what could have caused such a disaster. He knew that *his* torpedoes did not cause that because they had struck something behind them far below. The explosions down there told him that.

The man was highly intelligent and smart enough to remember that the American ship had sent out two torpedoes of their own, with no hits. If they were the homing type, could they have somehow malfunctioned and set their new sights on their home ship-the ship that had sent them out in the first place? He knew that was possible, given the right circumstances. But those circumstances would be quite rare and more unlikely than not that they would come together to provide the ignition for such a disaster. Still, it would not be something he could immediately rule out.

What he didn't know was another problem. Was that the only beast out here, or was there another one? For now, his attention could only be to look for and pick up any survivors.

Minutes later, the exec came back up and told his skipper that four Americans were found in the water and picked up. One of them had a bad injury to his leg and was taken to the infirmary. The other three had only cuts and bruises for which they were also treated.

Although there was of course the language barrier, there was usually one of his crewmen that knew English. Soji Yakamoto, an engineer's mate petty officer, was called to the infirmary. There he was able to find out from the Americans their names and if they knew what happened to cause their ship to explode and sink.

Two of the crewmen knew that their own torpedoes had failed to hit the beast. One of them, a second-class petty officer, had been on the bridge, which was the command center of the ship. The other was a seaman who stood outside as a deck watch lookout. He happened to see the torpedoes coming back at them. While he yelled as loud as he could they were about to be hit, he ran to the other side as far from where they hit as possible.

He was lucky and managed to avoid the bulk of the blast, not to mention surviving the explosion and sinking at all. But at the first abandon ship command in which there was no time to activate the lifeboats because of the quickness of the sinking, he was able to be one of the first to jump into the water.

After notification of the sinking and the pickup of the survivors was made to the nearest US Naval Base, which was in Hawaii, the sub started making its way enroute toward the islands where the survivors would be transferred via highline to the destroyer that would meet them halfway. That ship would, in turn, take them to Pearl Harbor where naval investigators would discuss the tragic event as part of another new investigation.

CincPacFleet, Us Naval Base, San Diego, California

Inside the huge command center, there was the usual hustle and bustle of busy military personnel, either manning equipment, rushing back and forth with messages for this admiral or that captain, and communications taking place, with countless messages being passed back and forth.

It was the job of one of the areas of the center to keep tabs on fleet ships underway in the Pacific and Asiatic waters which were hunting huge targets that weren't supposed to exist. If these beasts had never been positively confirmed and identified, the navy would have brushed all of this off as some cockamamie delusion of a nutcase. But when at least two of their ships had been hammered and sunk by what was then called unidentifiable swimming objects or "USOs" as one called them in an untimely sense of humor. It didn't take long for the admiralty to move on it.

The global problem was the first to inherit international cooperation by most developed nations. Ships were combing the waters over every major ocean and sea throughout the world, including the Southern Ocean. The Antarctic stations no longer had to worry about having to go out and hunt for one of these things. In retrospect, their last attempt nearly cost the ship and crewmembers their lives. After that, they stayed on the ice to hunker down and pray that the problem would be solved soon.

Just as the west coast fleet command was doing their share, so was the east coast. Disregarding any differences between naval regions and countries was a necessity in order to come to a quick resolution.

In his office, Admiral Turner, a two-star fleet officer, was being briefed by his assistant, Captain Donald Wilkinson.

"Sir, the four survivors from the *Winslow* have been checked out at sick bay and are expected to make a full recovery. Physically, that is. Emotionally, they are a bit of a wreck."

"Well of course they would be, Don," Turner replied. "Look what they've been through. Good God, what an event! Now that I mention it, God had to have been there for these men to survive."

The captain agreed.

"Now I want to know what the status is of the Pacific hunt. Have any more of these things been found out there?

The captain looked down at the folder in his hands and opened it up, searching for the data that would answer that.

"Well, sir, so far five of the creatures have been eliminated. That is, what we believe to be the creatures. Sonar and other reports confirmed they were not natural sea creatures or mammals, such as whales, giant octopuses, or anything else large normally found in the sea today. They could only have been these, misa or mosasarues, whatever they call them. According to those science reports anyway. And they were definitely not submarines."

"Any recent sightings?"

"No sir. The last one was a week ago."

Admiral Turner nodded and looked down at a paper on his desk.

"Ok, Captain. Let's keep the fleet looking for at least three more days. If none sighted anywhere, including Asiatic waters, then I'll call them back in. We have to be sure that there are no more of them out there."

"Yes sir," replied Wilkinson. "I'll let you in that time. Course you know that there are no guarantees."

Turner looked up at him. “I’m well aware of that, Don. There never is in a lot of things. We can’t keep this up forever. I’ll keep a few ships out there for several days after this. But I want most of them to either come back in or assume their normal assigned missions. Carry on, Captain.”

The captain got up to leave then turned around.

“Sir, one more thing. Do you know how Atlantic is doing?”

The admiral leaned back in his seat. “Last I heard, they are nearly on par as we are. No new killings in the last several days. Not of the beasts and not of any innocent civilians. Thank God.”

29

Within the next few weeks, there were no further sightings of the prehistoric beasts. Hundreds and even thousands of ships, both naval and otherwise, had pounded the marine "beats" around the world to eliminate anything gargantuan that could be blown out of the water. Even civilian volunteers went out in their yachts and other type boats to assist in the searches Although the US and allied navies were careful to positively identify by way of sonar any such targets underwater in order to differentiate large marine mammals, such as blue whales from the mosasaurs, other less military or professional marine hunters weren't so careful. As a result, although tens or possibly hundreds of the prehistoric creatures were believed to be killed, a couple of dead blue whales were discovered among the casualties.

As less sightings were found over time, ships started returning back to their home bases. In both the Pacific and Atlantic, the US and other allied navies returned home. The *Tomeka* had been thanked by the US Naval Command for their role in helping the *Winslow* when it did and picking up their survivors. It was now back in its home port of Yokosuka.

The Russians, UK, and France had contributed to the global fleet hunt. France and Russia had downed two of the creatures, each within their respective waters. The UK found one off the coast of Ireland and quickly dispatched it to its end. In South America, the Bolivian and Argentinian navies hunted their waters. Only one creature was found, and it was quickly eliminated by the Argentinians. On the western side, The Peruvian and Chilean navies patrolled their waters but found none of the creatures.

The New Zealanders found none in their waters. They were gracious enough to sail down to the Antarctic coast and cover those waters for any more signs of the creatures. On their sonar screens, blips that were fish and a few large mammals showed up. Life seemed to be returning to normal. The ship contacted their ice station with the news. That news would be passed on to all the other stations. The cheers that erupted among the scientists would not be heard by the ship's crew members. But they knew.

A few days later, the ship was back in their homeport of Devonport.

***

Nassau, Bahamas

Weeks had passed and there were no more sightings or attacks reported. People all over the world became relaxed and slowly things and activities returned back to normal.

Tourism had slumped down to abysmal levels in the Bahamas, as well as everywhere else during the horrific Jurassic-like period. Now with the creatures gone, people began to feel safe again. Once again the beaches were crowded as if nothing had happened.

In their beach hotel suite, William and Patricia Johnson and their daughter were settled in and were changing into their swimming garb.

The Johnsons were visiting from North Carolina and had come here on vacation for a week. It was their first time visiting the Bahamas and so far they loved it. It was hot but not unbearable. Their view of the Atlantic from their fifth-floor balcony was spectacular, which was why they chose this hotel.

Bill was a textile manufacturing plant engineer and had worked for the company for fifteen years. In his early thirties, his tall muscular features and blondish good looks could make him an eye-catcher for some women. And he was. But his real strength was in his firm belief of humbleness, which made him completely oblivious to his looks, other than personal pride in his appearance. No one should look sloppy and disheveled in public. His other strength was in his belief of a marriage and family being permanent and loving. He believed strongly in both and relied on his Christian faith to keep him on the straight and narrow.

Patricia or Patty, as most of her friends called her, used to be a Mary Kay salesperson. Her youthful face made her look several years younger than she was. With her husband's six figure salary she didn't need to work anymore. Although she discussed finding a steadier part time job that didn't require so much traveling with Bill, they decided she should take a little time off to think about whether she wanted to be a permanent stay-at home wife or work part time. There was no rush and they were pretty much financially secure.

"Ok, Is everybody ready?" Bill asked as they gathered up their beach gear. Bill had the cooler in one hand filled with ice and cold soda, and towels in the other. Pat gathered up the towel for their daughter Tonya.

"Ok sweetie, ready?" she asked her daughter.

"Ready Mommy."

Ten minutes later they had settled onto a spot on the beach, roughly thirty feet from the waterline. Close enough to walk in quickly but far enough that even at high tide the water would not touch them.

"Daddy, please! Can I go in?"

A family of three, Jason and his wife Shirley and their two sons were about thirty feet from the Johnsons. The boys ran in the water as the Johnsons were still settling on their spot.

“Ok sweetie. Say close to the beach. Hear me?” Pat took no chances when it came to the ocean and her daughter.

“I will.” Then little Tonya turned around and headed into the water, staying close to the waterline as she promised. She sat down facing her parents with her little bucket and scoop and did what any child would do with the sand and the water. They smiled as she watched her enjoying herself. The day was very warm, sunny, and bright. There was just a slight breeze and the sea was calm. A perfect beach day.

Bill and Pat Johnson had never been here or any other part of the Bahamas before. They had been to other places before outside the US. Rather than repeat an excursion somewhere they had already visited, they decided that this was the perfect spot. Bill had two-weeks’ vacation he had to take during his plant’s yearly mandatory shutdown. It was a wonderful time for him to get away for a while from his manufacturing supervisor position and spend time with his family. Nothing like this, he thought, to relieve the daily stress on the job. Pat loved it, of course, being the stay and home mom that she was. Any extra time she could spend with her husband was always a huge plus for her and Tonya.

There were quite a few people in the water. The two beach neighbor boys were older than Tonya and were able to enjoy the deeper water. At the furthermost perimeter of the swimmers were three adults who seemed to be lazily lounging in the water, with one on his back and the other two with their hands flopping up and down as if they were trying to see who could intentionally sink the furthest down. Then they swam away from the back-lounging bather.

Back on the beach, while Bill was sitting on his beach chair with sunglasses and all reading his book, Pat sat on the blanket saturating her legs and thighs with the strongest sun protection lotion she could find. Because she was red haired, her pale fair skin was particularly vulnerable to the damaging rays of the sun, so she had to be extra careful and apply extra lotion. Her skin would burn in minutes without it. Even so she needed to limit her exposure to the sun.

One of the men furthest out that had been swimming parallel to the beach suddenly was no longer there. No one noticed. No one in the water was being monitored: except for little Tonya, who continued to play facing the beach, completely oblivious to anything else that was going on in the water behind her. One of the sons of Jason and Shirley noticed out of the corner of his eye a man suddenly going under. Other than that, everything seemed normal. He didn’t know what to make of it but figured the man was just going down for an underwater swim.

The two men at the swimmers’ outermost perimeter who had seemed to be “playing” the “who can sink the deepest” game were no longer there either. This time, someone on the beach happened to notice. But the potential witness was not sure what she saw. She just happened to look at their spot out there and saw them both disappear under the water at exactly the same precise moment. It looked like they were only a few feet apart. Just before they went under, she thought she saw a hump rise just above the surface and then quickly vanish back down.

Not sure if her eyes were playing tricks on her, she kept looking out there waiting for them to resurface. They never did. The alarm bells went off in her head and she turned to her beach neighbors to find out if they had seen that also. They had not, unfortunately.

The woman could not let this slide, so she got up quickly and ran to the nearest lifeguard to let him know what she had just witnessed. The guard stood up on the stand in front of his high seat and with his binoculars scanned the entire area of swimmers. The man took his time, searching each section carefully.

Some of the swimmers were moving in the direction of the beach, although it seemed they were still oblivious to what happened near them. The disappearances had been mysteriously silent and insidious.

Suddenly without warning a huge wave-like hump of water appeared followed nearly instantly by something monstrous breaching the water and diving headfirst back in, with terrifying huge jaws engulfing another two swimmers, swallowing them whole. There was no spouting of blood.Everyone on the beach screamed, jumped up and ran further from the water. Bill and Pat ran down and grabbed Tonya out of the water and turned back, running quickly toward the safety of the beach. The lifeguard continuously blew his whistle, alternating with screams to get out of the water.

Those left in the water moved as fast as they could to the beach until finally no one was left, and the water became eerily calm. The shock overtook everyone. Cries of terror filled the air. Tonya cried loudly, not understanding what had just happened. She could only sense that something bad happened, which frightened her even more.

It did not take long for law enforcement in the town to get involved, followed quickly by the government. Authorities there had notified the governments of the Bahamas, the UK, and the US of this latest tragedy. Although there had been no longer signs of the creatures anywhere in the world, the world had been shown that it was wrong. Like a cancer cell, it would only take one for another global catastrophe to emerge and spread. *If* the beast was female and pregnant.

No one could have possibly known.

It was.

30

After the investigation in Nassau of the deaths and reports of an unknown sea monster by a few witnesses who had caught just brief glances, the news spread quickly throughout the world.

In Texas, Rita was stunned. Not one report throughout the world was made of any more sightings or other detections of the creatures. It seemed all had been wiped out by international naval efforts with bombings, torpedoes, and other deep-water engagements with mass non-nuclear deadly weapons. Numerous surveillance vessels as well as battle engagement vessels marked the oceans throughout the world, determined to get each and every one of the beasts.

After a time of peace and quiet and no more attacks, people began to relax. This incident was certainly not something anyone needed or expected. Was this a loner who had escaped the worldwide attacks against its fellow creatures? If it was, they had to eliminate it fast. Despite her scientist-desires to preserve and study a live specimen of what was supposed to be an extinct species, the rationality and practicality of trying that on a huge and deadly species of animal that could not co-exist peacefully with mankind far outweighed any scientific urges.

Because it was the only one detected and seen, as far as she knew, there was the remote possibility, she realized that it could be female. This was the only time she had actually considered gender in these things. However, now that this was thought of, she had to act fast. Picking up the phone, she made a long-distance phone call which she hoped would alert and then get the proper authorities to expedite what needed to be done even more quickly.

***

Within hours, Bahamas authorities requested immediate assistance from the US and UK naval authorities after witnesses described the devastating attacks at one of their beaches. Those who had disappeared were never seen again and the families of the missing loved ones knew what had happened to them. Still, to say that they had an exceedingly difficult time processing that and accepting their tragic losses would at the very least be a huge understatement.

Both the Johnsons and the neighboring beach couple had surviving children. Tonya was right at the beach line, so Bill wasted no time in grabbing her out of the water when the incident occurred. Both sons of Jason and Shirley had fortunately seen the attack and had not been far out in the water. They pell-melled it back to the beach the moment they were aware of the attacks.

As with many of the beachgoers, they packed up their belongings and decided that they did not want to be there anymore. The desire to be on the beach and enjoying what was thought to be tranquil waters had suddenly deflated as quickly as a balloon poked with a pin.

***

After going through numerous channels, phone trees, attempted connections and even more patience, Rita finally got through to whoever was in charge. Despite her lack of navy or other military experience, still she had the expertise necessary to advise on the current situation that the navy was involved in. She seriously doubted the navy had its own paleo-herpetologists.

After identifying herself with credentials and her role in all of this, she explained why she was calling to a Lieutenant Brickmeyer of the Navy's Oceanographic section. He was in Washington DC and she hoped he would listen.

"Lieutenant, are you aware of the situation which has just developed down in the Bahamas, specifically the Nassau area?"

"Yes ma'am. We got word about an hour ago and ships are enroute there now if they are not already there. Why do you ask?"

"Well, based on my expertise in herpetology, what I know aboutthese creatures, and the fact that only one, that we know of right now, is still alive. And it's down there."

"We know Professor and we will take care of it. It will be destroyed as soon as we find it."

Rita sighed before continuing on. "Sir, I appreciate that. It is imperative that it be found and destroyed as quickly as possible. And it is not just because it kills people and all living swimming creatures in the ocean and throws off the entire marine ecosystem."

"Well that is certainly more than enough motivation to find and kill it I think, "he replied inarguably.

"Here's something else that you can add to the mix. *If* it is a female, it could be pregnant. If it gives birth, there will be another beast or more swimming somewhere in the world. And that would be like finding a needle in five haystacks considering how much ocean there is."

The officer did not see that coming. "Wait a minute. This thing would lay its eggs somewhere in the ocean. Are you serious?"

"Couldn't be more so Lieutenant. Unfortunately for us, this creature does not lay eggs."

"Not lay eggs?" he replied. "I thought all reptiles, and I assume that's what this is, lay eggs?"

"Most reptiles do. This one is believed to spawn live births."

The officer was surprised at this bit of information but then why should that make a difference?

"Shouldn't matter I think," he responded. "Whether they are eggs or live."

She then explained to him the increased urgency of the matter. If the creature were to be an egg layer, chances are the eggs would be deposited in relatively shallow waters in order to avoid the crushing pressures of deep ocean waters. Despite the near impossibility of locating them without high technological equipment and a well-calculated educational guess, it would still buy them some time to find and destroy them.

The matter that this creature spawns live births means that it must be found quickly before they are born. There was no way to tell now if that has already happened, if it's a female and is pregnant. The question of urgency leaves no question as to what must be done.

"Lieutenant, if it does give birth, both of them will swim away. Even if it spawns only one baby, that is one too many. The oceans will still suffer, and maybe more people too. And although we may be certain *right now* that there are no more creatures out there, we can't really be sure. Look how much we *don't* know about our oceans. Fact it, we know more about Mars than we do about our own oceans. Can you dispute that?"

The officer had to concede to that. "No, I guess I can't. Look, I will contact whoever I can get a hold of down there and see what I can do to speed up the process. I can't guarantee it will speed up the process any more than it is, but I will pass on this information. Maybe that will light a fire under their butts, pardon the expression."

"Tell them this information is from me and who I am. I appreciate your help on this. Thank you, Lieutenant. For the sake of all of us I hope they are successful."

"Me too. Thank you, Professor. Take care."

That is it, she thought. She did her best. Now it was in the Navy's hands to do something about it.

***

US naval vessels suddenly flooded the entire perimeter of the Bahama islands. No armada of naval vessels had been seen in such force and numbers around a relatively small area since WWII. The mission as in such a war was to find and destroy.

Upon arrival at the islands, on orders from the fleet admiral, the ships dispersed to search around the entire geographical area from north to south. All the equipment that could be utilized to locate the target or targets was utilized. The word came that the creature must be found and destroyed as quickly as possible or the global problem could return.

South of Nassau, something was spotted by a ship's sonar and focus by that vessel turned toward that target. The blip was large and seemed to move slowly in a southeastern direction. It was moving toward the open Atlantic. After some investigation, it was determined by sonar NOT to be a submarine or whale. The ship increased its speed in the direction of the bogey and the fire controlmen on their equipment were ordered by the captain to prepare the gun mounts and torpedo tubes.

This was going to be a one-shot deal and they had to make it good. Their communications to the rest of the fleet regarding this sighting seemed to energize the fleet's movements toward them. No other sightings by any other ships had been made. This could be what they were looking for.

In a strategic move, some of the fleet headed east and then would turn south. The rest would head west then turn south. The goal was to corner the target so it could not escape into open ocean where it might never be found.

The finding vessel continued to pursue the target. It was now about three miles away. The distance was gradually decreasing, but not fast enough for the skipper. He ordered an increase in speed until they were doing twenty-seven knots. It was almost full speed. Consequently, after about five minutes, the distance to the target was now two miles.

Unfortunately, it was still a little too far for torpedoes, so the captain had to wait to give the fire orders. He did not know how deep the target was. The sonar operator might, however, when they got close enough.

After about twenty minutes, sonar reported that they were two thousand yards from the target. The operator gave his best-estimated depth as about thirty feet below the surface.

"Fire control, torpedoes, recheck tubes for armament, tubes one and two. Gun mount, remain manned and recheck cannon for armament."

The captain wasted no time in assuring that all guns and torpedoes were ready to go on his orders.

The last time the five-inch cannon located on the forward deck had been used was over in the Persian Gulf during the Iraqi war, and at Guantanamo

Bay, Cuba, where the US Navy had its former Naval base for practice exercises and equipment calibration as well as certain other operations.

The announcement then came over the ship's PA system. The boatswain's pipe blew first.

"Now general quarters, this is not a drill. All hands to general quarters. This is not a drill. All sections report when manned and ready."

As many times as this announcement had been made during the countless numbers of drills over the years, none had close to the same impact as the actual thing. The fact that this was real made it all the more chilling. The urgency and scariness if it, in fact, seemed to make the crew man their emergency assignments even faster than the drills. One could easily become complacent after countless numbers of drills. When the real thing came up, however, there was not the slightest level of complacency exhibited.

As the ship drew closer to the target and all sections had reported in to the bridge, sonar reported the distance. The captain ordered the "fishmen" to standby for firing. After confirming the target was well within range and proper depth, he gave the order.

The ship's slight recoil indicated the firing. The skipper looked over the sonar operator's shoulder, both focusing their attention on the sonar screen. They saw the two small, elongated blips heading directly toward the huge, rounded target. The moments were tense and felt by everyone on the bridge. It would be a disaster if the shot missed and no one wanted to bring up that possibility out loud. The target could turn or dive at any moment. Although the torpedoes were homing according to movement, still there was never a guarantee.

As the blips merged with the target nothing happened, and it seemed they had a miss. Just as mouths opened to groan loudly, suddenly the large blip disappeared. The concussion was felt in the water, confirming a hit. The two men kept looking at it for possible reappearance of the blip, but it did not reappear. They had hit their target!

The news spread quickly throughout the ship. Knowing this was the last creature to be eliminated and they were the ones that did it made them all cheer the more. The captain, although he lifted his fist and exclaimed, "Yes", he dared not say it too loud. Choosing to remain cautious and not being overly optimistic, he ordered sonar to scan for any more possible creatures before returning back to the fleet. None had been seen and when checking with the rest of the fleet, no other creatures were sighted anywhere around any part of the islands.

The creatures were finally gone.

EPILOGUE

It took many months for the great elimination, as some people called it. The world was finally at rest, relatively speaking. For the first time in history, most nations who had capable navies cooperated with each other in one global effort to eradicate what could have been a potential cause of death of the oceans and, possibly, eventual death of mankind.

Life as before started returning to normal in the world's oceans. In the Antarctic, seals and penguins were beginning to repopulate the Southern Ocean and the waters around the ice continent. Predators, such as leopard seals, returned to once again be the menace to penguins that they always were. It seemed a small price to pay for elimination of the much greater menace that once was.

There were no more attacks from ocean creatures on people, except for occasional shark attacks. Everything was, for the most part, back to normal and the scientists returned to their normal research, include those Antarctica stations that were more than happy to get back to their normal routine.

Back in Texas, Rita Bloomsworth breathed sighs of relief knowing the problem was gone. She knew it would take quite a while and be quite complex because it was not only knowing how to find the creatures but finding out how many there actually were swimming around. That was the hard part.

Deciding not to dwell on it, she put it all out of her mind and set her mind to moving forward with her normal research. Out of sight, out of existence again, and out of mind. She began her focus on her next paleontological find, a small fossil of either a rare or unknown species of some small animal. Reptile or mammal? She would find out for sure.

Geologists, climatologists, and other scientists from NOAA gathered for a conference to discuss the repercussions once again of global warming and climate change. The latest global event was added to the ever-growing list of negative impacts on the world from the global climate changes that were ever ongoing. Perhaps if drastic changes were made in the world to significantly decrease the negative impacts of humans and industries around the world, then maybe the world could be saved: if not in this lifetime, maybe in the next generation.

While all this was being discussed, subtle changes around the world continued.

***

Deep at the bottom of the Bering Sea, the seabed stirred slightly. Subtle movements suggested something living stirring beneath the sand. Was it a crab that normally lived there? Or something else?

The End

CHECK OUT OTHER GREAT DEEP SEA THRILLERS

THE BREACH
by Edward J. McFadden III

A Category 4 hurricane punched a quarter mile hole in Fire Island, exposing the Great South Bay to the ferocity of the Atlantic Ocean, and the current pulled something terrible through the new breach. A monstrosity of the past mixed with the present has been disturbed and it's found its way into the sheltered waters of Long Island's southern sea.

Nate Tanner lives in Stones Throw, Long Island. A disgraced SCPD detective lieutenant put out to pasture in the marine division because of his Navy background and experience with aquatic crime scenes, Tanner is assigned to hunt the creeper in the bay. But he and his team soon discover they're the ones being hunted.

INFESTATION
by William Meikle

It was supposed to be a simple mission. A suspected Russian spy boat is in trouble in Canadian waters. Investigate and report are the orders.

But when Captain John Banks and his squad arrive, it is to find an empty vessel, and a scene of bloody mayhem.

Soon they are in a fight for their lives, for there are things in the icy seas off Baffin Island, scuttling, hungry things with a taste for human flesh.

They are swarming. And they are growing.

"Scotland's best Horror writer" - Ginger Nuts of Horror

"The premier storyteller of our time." - Famous Monsters of Filmland

CHECK OUT OTHER GREAT DEEP SEA THRILLERS

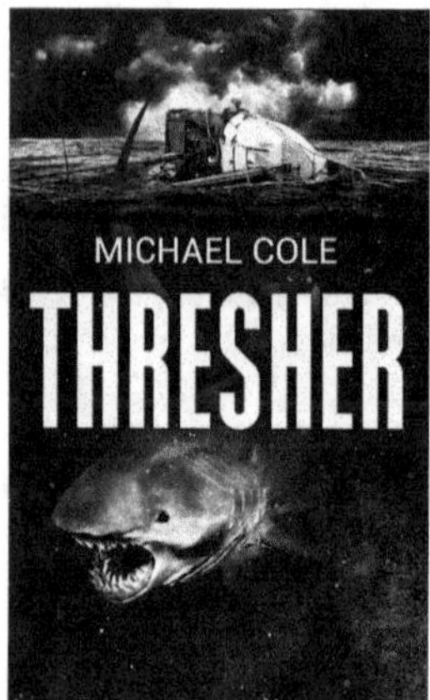

THRESHER
by Michael Cole

In the aftermath of a hurricane, a series of strange events plague the coastal waters off Florida. People go into the water and never return. Corpses of killer whales drift ashore, ravaged from enormous bite marks. A fishing trawler is found adrift, with a mysterious gash in its hull.

Transferred to the coastal town of Merit, police officer Leonard Riker uncovers the horrible reality of an enormous Thresher shark lurking off the coast. Forty feet in length, it has taken a territorial claim to the waters near the town harbor. Armed with three-inch teeth, a scythe-like caudal fin, and unmatched aggression, the beast seeks to kill anything sharing the waters.

THE GUILLOTINE
by Lucas Pederson

1,000 feet under the surface, Prehistoric Anthropologist, Ash Barrington, and his team are in the midst of a great archeological dig at the bottom of Lake Superior where they find a treasure trove of bones. Bones of dinosaurs that aren't supposed to be in this particular region. In their underwater facility, Infinity Moon, Ash and his team soon discover a series of underground tunnels. Upon exploring, they accidentally open an ice pocket, thawing the prehistoric creature trapped inside. Soon they are being attacked, the facility falling apart around them, by what Ash knows is a dunkleosteus and all those bones were from its prey. Now...Ash and his team are the prey and the creature will stop at nothing to get to them.

www.ingramcontent.com/pod-product-compliance
Lightning Source LLC
Chambersburg PA
CBHW071517170626
46811CB00007B/2886

* 9 7 8 1 9 2 2 3 2 3 8 7 3 *